A
REMEDY
FOR
DEATH

Michael McGaulley

Author, *THE GRAIL CONSPIRACIES*

Author's main blog and website at
www.MichaelMcGaulley.net

ALSO BY MICHAEL McGAULLEY

Science technothrillers

The Grail Conspiracies

Joining Miracles

You will find a sample of *The Grail Conspiracies* at the end
of this book

International mystery and crime

The Man Who Created Ghosts

Infinite Doublecross

Career Savvy People Skills Series

*How to Ask the Smart Questions
for Winning the Games of Career and Life*

*How to Use Mental Pickpocketing to Get to the Truth
Without Seeming to Ask Questions*

Table of Contents

"What a caterpillar calls death, we call a butterfly"

Unknown

"That is one of the privileges here at the clinic: We provide a remedy for death."

Hubert Langwein, M.D., Ph.D.

"You're opening very dangerous doorways! Once they're open, there's no stopping what may come through from the other side!"

Katherine Remington, Ph.D.

THE HAUENFELDER CLINIC

THE CHOSEN ONES

IT WAS THE FIRST TIME that either of them had been in the Clinic's formal dining area: a long room decorated like the baronial hall of a Bavarian hunting lodge.

Parsons Couldsen, in whose honor the dinner was being held, sat at the head table along with Dr. Rausch and the visitors who had flown in that afternoon with Couldsen. They were not introduced, but were easily recognized: two American Senators, and the British Opposition Leader.

At the end of the meal, Rausch tapped his fork on a water glass and called for attention. "We now come to a special moment. We are all very grateful to Mr. Couldsen for the tremendous encouragement and support he has given our work from the start. Without his contribution, the Hauenfelder Clinic would literally not exist."

COULDSEN PULLED HIMSELF to his feet and took the microphone. They had seen him when he arrived in his helicopter earlier in the afternoon, and he looked as he did in the news stories on him as the Billionaire Media Baron—tanned, seemingly fit, a commanding presence. Now he seemed shrunken, his color worse.

After a pause to command attention, he began: "Most of you know how I came to support the research here. I had my first bad heart attack a few years ago, when I was way too damned young to die."

He paused for a sip of water.

"What you may not know is just how damned close I came to not making it. I had what they call a Near-Death Experience, and found myself up at the Pearly Gates. There was an old guy with a beard there, smelling of week-old fish. 'I'm St. Peter,' he said. 'What's that in your briefcase?'

"'Some of my money,' I told him. 'I'm having the rest sent up later.'"

"'*Money*! Didn't anyone tell you that you can't take it with you when you come here?'"

"'*Can't take it with me? The hell with that!*'" I told him.

Couldsen paused a moment, then went on: "That's when I told that old bastard, 'If I can't take it with me, then I'll stay down there *with* it! *Hell no, I won't go!*'

He repeated "Hell no, I won't go!" and paused for the laugh, then went on. "I started doing some serious thinking, lying in that cardiac ward realizing what a damned close call I'd had. It struck home how final death really is. I made up my mind that I wasn't ready to go, and damned well never *would* be ready. That's when I decided to do something about it—especially when they told me I was not a good candidate for a heart transplant."

He sipped more water before going on. "So now we're gathered here at the Hauenfelder Clinic, this magnificent laboratory of the future, *because we are the chosen ones.* Self-chosen by our achievements in the course of this first lifetime."

He looked around the room. "We in this elite cohort are here because of our accomplishments, because we are the innovators, the leaders! We are the ones who *deserve* to live on! We are the ones who are making that happen!

"But there is only so much we can do in this one all-too-short lifetime we've been given, the proverbial 'three score and ten.' Three score and ten, even twice that, is not enough for the people who are bringing about the better reality."

Couldsen paused for another sip of water. His face was noticeably more pale; his voice was weakening.

"We are the ones who *need* to live on, who *deserve* the remedy for death that is being manifested here! We are the trailblazers, the ones with intelligence, intellect, and creativity, the ones who *can* and *are* creating the world of the future, and we *should*, we *must* live on, for decades upon decades, for lifetime after lifetime!"

ATTACK

DR. RAUSCH TOOK THE MICROPHONE as Couldsen sat, visibly drained.

"Mr. Couldsen," Rausch continued, "is unique in all the world. Rather, *was* unique. Until recently, there wasn't another like him, anywhere in the universe."

He paused, and the crowd clapped on cue.

"Then we began to think that if *one* Parsons Couldsen was such a good thing, why stop there? Why not *two* Parsons Couldsens? Better yet, why not *three*?"

Rausch's wooden delivery made it obvious that he was reciting lines prepared for him by someone else.

A door at the end of the room opened, and four young men rode bicycles into the dining room. Daulby recognized the lead rider, who wore medical whites: Hans-Georg, the medical technician who had set him up in the flotation tank yesterday.

The other three wore tuxedos, looking strangely out of place on bicycles. Their faces were expressionless, and they seemed to focus only on the back of the rider ahead of them. The chain of bicyclists circled the long dining table once, twice, three times.

Daulby wondered why this sideshow, until he looked more closely at the faces of the three in tuxedos: all were identical. Triplets? He asked himself. Then the reality struck.

"It's incredible! It's ghastly!" Kate exclaimed at that moment. "They're *all* Couldsen! *Three more Couldsens! Young versions of Couldsen!*"

The room erupted into applause, and Couldsen took back the mike. "Looks like them boys come from good stock. Great work, folks."

THE LIGHTS DIED abruptly, leaving the room lit only by the table candles. As they watched, bewildered, a gust of air moved up the table, blowing out most of the candles.

"Was it something I said?" Couldsen chortled.

"This is an old building," Von Schwalbenbach said. "Perhaps the wiring needs to be repaired."

"Goddam it, you already *had* it rewired! I saw the damned bills. For what it cost, seems you wired the place with gold."

If the power is off, Daulby wondered, then why is the public address system still working?

The room was pitch-black. A sudden metallic wail filled the darkness. Daulby covered his ears against it but the shriek cut through, now breaking into a sound that seemed like shrill metallic laughter.

A heavy thump by the front table, the sound of someone falling. A terrified scream, "*Hilfe! Hilfe*! Help me!" cut off by the sounds of gurgling, gasping.

The electricity flashed back on, as startling as lightning, revealing a clump of men struggling to pull one of the tuxedo-clad bicyclists away from a body on the floor by the head table.

The two others in tuxes stood by the wall watching, stationary, mute, faces impassive.

Hans-Georg, helped by Von Schwalbenbach and a couple of the other staff, yanked the attacker to his feet. His expression shifted from wild passion back to the expressionless mask he had worn earlier. His tuxedo was torn and rumpled. His bloodied hands gripped a leather belt. They used the belt to strap his hands behind his back, then frog-marched him to another room.

Others helped Dr. Rausch back to his face. Blood gushed from his nose, and red marks were forming around his neck where the belt had been strangling him.

Couldsen sat frozen at the head of the table, his eyes locked wide open, all color drained from his face. Daulby wondered if he was dead.

"What in hell possessed him—the Vehicle—to do that?" Daulby asked.

"Yes, exactly. *Possessed*—the perfect word."

ARTIFICIAL TEENAGERS

THE LIGHTS FLICKERED off again once, twice, then came on to stay. Some of the staff ran from the room; others sat, visibly stunned by what had happened.

Von Schwalbenbach came back and called out an invitation to a party in the swimming pool.

"Feel like a walk?" Daulby asked.

"I feel like getting as far away from here as possible," Kate replied.

They headed for the lake. It was a warm evening; the air was still, and the lake was smooth and clear as glass. The lights of the village across the lake shimmered across the water like colored party lights.

Doug Dalby had been a medical professor, specializing in neurosurgery and brain research. That was before the scandal broke, and before the murder of his wife and daughter. In the months since, he'd lost 30 pounds and his hair had gone fully white.

Kate Remington, tall, lean, dark-haired, was a psychologist specializing in Multiple Personality Disorder, also termed Dissociative Identity Disorder. It was a topic that made other researchers uneasy, and she had lost her grants. Coming to Hauenfelder Clinic in the Austrian Alps seemed her best choice . . . until she arrived to find she had been lied to: it was not in the Alps and not in Austria, but rather in a scenic but impoverished dictatorship forgotten since the collapse of the Soviet empire.

They settled at a small gazebo on the end of a dock. There was no moon, and they more sensed than saw the dark mountains that ringed the lake, great brooding presences in the night.

Daulby knelt on the dock and dipped his hand into the water. It was icy.

"Forget about swimming away from here," Kate said. "It's fed by glaciers, it never gets warm."

"How did you know I was thinking that?" he whispered, settling back on the bench.

"Because I've been looking for a way out of here, from my first days. Not that I'd swim away, even if it were possible. I couldn't leave Karen here with them."

"Even if we could, there's no safe place to swim to—we don't even know where in hell we are—not even what *country* we're in. is."

"'Where in hell'—you got it right first time. I think we *are* in hell, *trapped* in hell, with no way out."

NOW THE MOON emerged from behind a cloud, throwing an eerie blue light on the dark mountains that surrounded them. The lights of the village across the water seemed tinier and more insignificant than before. And even farther away.

They sat quietly for a while, each lost in thought. Then Kate turned to him and asked, "What do you think about that incident at the end—the Vehicle going berserk and attacking?"

He shook his head. "I don't know what to think. You tell me."

"There are a number of possible explanations. First, of course, was the possible coincidence with the lights going out, and so forth, leading to some kind of mass hysteria. It *could* be that, but I don't think so. You and I weren't the only ones who felt it. Everyone experienced something— that was obvious from the faces."

"People couldn't wait to get away—away from that whatever it was—*is.*"

"It seems that something tangible *did* happen, the question is just *what* it was. You comment then still seems totally on target. Remember what you said? 'What in hell possessed the Vehicle to do what he—it—did?' Underline the word 'possessed'"

"I'm not . . . what is it you're you suggesting? That he—the Vehicle—was possessed by some kind of . . . of malevolent spirit?"

"Isn't that what the work here is all about? Facilitating just that kind of move—so people like Couldsen can move over and come back into fresh young bodies complete with all of this lifetime's smarts already waiting there."

SHE WAS SILENT for a while, then said, "That first day, when I arrived at Hauenfelder, I was enchanted by the place. With the mountains, the lake, the clear air, it seemed like I was living in a postcard fantasy. But then," she shook her head and her voice dropped, "then I began to get very different feelings. As beautiful as it is here, I think there's also a dark side."

"Dark side?"

"The work being done at Hauenfelder is unnatural, and I think very dangerous. We saw that tonight. But even apart from that, I find there are strange, troubling . . . Let's just say I feel strange *energies* operating here. *Malevolent* energies. *Angry* energies. Haven't you felt things?"

"Neurosurgeons aren't trained to recognize ghostly energies." He didn't want to talk about the strange sounds he'd heard, the strange sense of intruders in the night.

"The electrical effects, the lights flicking on and off, the noises on the sound system—those resemble the hallmarks of classic poltergeist activity." She turned to him. "And certainly that bizarre episode of the Vehicle we all saw attacking Dr. Rausch. You *are* familiar with the term poltergeist?"

He shrugged. "I half-watched a TV show on that stuff when I was wandering around after . . . after I lost my family. It got into poltergeists— phenomena like knocking in the walls, things flying through the air, strange malfunctions with electrical and electronic equipment. I remember a case that occurred in a law office in Germany. Among other things, the office phone supposedly dialed numbers on its own doing, hundreds of calls in an hour to the phone company's automatic time clock. They were dialed much faster than any individual could punch in the numbers. Most of the time, the calls were made when no one was near the phone."

She nodded. "That was probably the Rosenheim case, back in the late 1960's. It's a classic poltergeist effect, carefully researched by a university team. Even the skeptics agree that something extraordinary happened. But nobody is sure what really was going on. I could talk your ear off with other cases like that, investigated by competent scientists, most of whom arrived as skeptics."

A cloud passed over the moon, and it suddenly seemed chilly. Kate continued: "In the majority of cases, poltergeist manifestations take place around early teen-agers."

"Why teenagers?"

"There are no definitive answers, only theories. According to one theory, the material force to achieve these effects is gained from tapping the frustrated sexual energies of adolescents."

He shook his head. "But there aren't any teenagers here."

"There *are* the Vehicles, which, in a sense, are *artificial* teenagers. They could be providing the energy. Or they might simply provide the *doorway* for other entities to come through."

Daulby felt a deeper chill in the still night as a ripple of wind moved across the lake. Another cloud moved across the moon, and it became very dark.

FOUR MONTHS EARLIER

CANNIBALS

University Hospital. Chicago. 6:10 P.M.

Take me to the cannibal, Daddy. Please!

Jenny's words echoed in Doug Daulby's mind. By now, Jenny and Jackie would be headed to the carnival. He wished he had gone with them to see the big smiles as Jenny swept past on the rides. She was already seven; how many more years would the carnival interest her?

He pushed the thought away to focus on the tiny creature on the operating table. Draped so that only the top of the head was exposed, it could almost pass for a human infant.

They were calling it Chimp Donnie.

He sliced across the shaved skull from ear to ear, then loosened the fascia, teasing the scalp to separate from the bone.

Daulby's prematurely white hair, his size — 210 pounds spread over six feet — and his booming voice, had earned him the nickname Doc Polar Bear.

But he still moved with the grace of the athlete he'd been, and his fingers, long and supple, had a sensitivity that amazed students. They seemed to function independently of his mind, allowing him to work fast in close tolerances without missing a beat in a conversation.

Tonight, he didn't feel like conversing. Tonight he just wanted to finish and get the hell out of there. He was wishing now that he'd never gotten into this, never even come up with the idea.

But now there was no going back.

When the incision was complete, he lifted the entire top of the chimp's skull free and put the skull section in a pan of Betadine solution to keep it sterile for replacement when the operation finished.

Take me to the cannibal, Daddy.

REPLICA

Evanston, Illinois. 6:15 P.M.
JENNY WAS Mrs. Benson's last student of the day, and when she saw her mother, she begged to stay "just another minute" to play the new piece she had learned.

Jackie blinked away tears as Jenny played. It was such a privilege to see a replica of herself as she'd been at seven, the same golden hair, the same angelic face she knew from her own old photos.

But Jenny, thank God, didn't have her tendency to chubbiness; that would make her life easier.

Jackie loved the elements of Doug she saw blended into their little creation. Definitely Doug's eyes, everybody said so. Maybe that meant she'd grow up to have Doug's intellect. But hopefully without his compulsive career drive. That would really be the ideal combination.

"She has remarkable talent for someone so young," Mrs. Benson whispered to Jackie. "She's such a wonderful little girl, such a wonderful personality, such a bright future ahead of her. You and Dr. Daulby must be very proud of her."

"We are," Jackie said, "she's the most wonderful thing that's ever happened."

"LET'S HAVE DINNER at Baskin-Robbins, then we can go to the cannibal," Jenny said as they left Mrs. Benson's. It was a quiet, tree-lined street of older, well-kept homes. There was little traffic here away from the main commuter routes.

"We need vegetables with our dinner," Jackie said, thinking how much she and Jenny would miss Doug tonight.

"We can have banana splits. The bananas and cherries will be our vegetables. Then we'll go to the cannibal."

Jackie dug out her car keys. What difference would it make if they lived it up on junk food for one night? Life is short. "Okay, sounds good to me. But it's just this one —"

She broke off when she saw two men materialize from behind a van. One held a gun.

This can't be happening! a voice inside her head screamed. It can't be! Not to us!

"Just give us your purse," one of the men said. He was thin, almost frail, with light blond hair and wire-framed glasses. We just want your money. Give us that and we won't hurt you or little Jenny."

Jackie fumbled for her wallet. Then it struck her: Jenny! Why did a mugger know Jenny's name?

She kicked, connecting with the man's leg, and he went down. She dove to swoop up Jenny. The second man grabbed her from behind and slapped a white cloth over her face. She sniffed the bite of ether. She tried to scream, but it was no use.

As her world went dark, she saw Jenny struggling against the grip of a third man, dressed in black. He pushed a white cloth against her face, and Jenny's movements slowed. Then her body went limp.

"Doug! Help us!" Jackie gasped as she blacked out.

CROSS-SPECIES CHIMERA

Take me to the cannibal, Daddy. please!

Jenny's voice still echoed in his head. That had never happened before, never broken through his concentration, and he wondered why tonight.

Cannibal — carnival. The last vestige of her baby-talk, a family joke now.

But he couldn't take her to a carnival tonight. Not tonight, of all nights.

Tonight's work had taken months to set up. It *had* to be tonight. Tonight, or maybe never. The window of opportunity was open, and he had to slip through that window before the politicians and bureaucrats slammed it shut again.

Take me to the cannibal. Please!

Cannibals! The word struck him. Is *that* what we are tonight, feeding on one for the sake of another?

"Dr. Martinson is extracting the donor tissue now," one of the surgical nurses said.

He glanced through the glass wall to the second operating room where Martinson was working on the other subject, a human fetus aborted minutes earlier.

Martinson's role in opening the tiny soft head of the fetus was as exacting as his own. The fetus was 18 weeks, and weighed about a half-pound, with a head smaller than an orange. It would provide the material to implant into Chimp Donnie's brain.

The operation itself — implanting the human fetal brain cells into the brain of a young chimp — was certain to succeed: the two little creatures were nearly 99% genetically identical, so the human tissues should quickly grow into and become part of Chimp Donnie's brain.

Cross-species implants, human to animal and the reverse, were becoming common in the scientific community. There was even a term for the living creatures that resulted: *chimeras*, creatures with living parts from multiple species.

As far back as the 1980's there was the "geep"—an animal created in the laboratory by combining the embryos of a sheep and a goat. It grew up to look like a goat, though covered in patches of sheep's wool.

In another lab, they successfully grafted part of a quail embryo into a chicken embryo, resulting in a chicken with a quail's brain and characteristic sounds.

Who could forget the picture that went around the world of the mouse with the human ear growing on its back?

More recent experiments with chimerical creatures included the lamb fetuses into which human stem cells had been infused, resulting in the possibility that in time human livers could be grown in sheep for transplantation to ill humans.

Other researchers had transplanted human stem cells into the brains of baby mice, and the human cells had grown to make up about one percent of the mouse brain.

A team had implanted human stem cells into the brains of monkey fetuses and allowed them to grow there for a month. Autopsies conducted after the monkey fetuses were aborted revealed that the human neural cells had spread and grown throughout the monkey brains.

Most of those experiments had involved creating the chimeras at an early, fetal stage. But that would mean finding a pregnant female chimp, opening her under anesthesia, and operating on her fetus while it was still in the womb. That added layers of complexity that Daulby was not prepare to deal with now.

Daulby resolved to vault several steps, and implant from a human newborn, just aborted, to a chimp newborn.

Since human and chimp were genetically so close, it was virtually certain that the human cells would grow within the chimp without rejection. Hence the real question was whether the *larger* experiment would succeed. Would Chimp Donnie grow up to prove Daulby's hypothesis?

And if the experiment *was* successful? What then? What doorways would that open?

He knew he was risking his career as a researcher. He had set this experiment up in secret, he had not followed the protocols, he had not gotten clearance from the ethics committees and the layers of university and federal bureaucrats — and the politicians to whom they were beholden.

"Let's just do it!" he'd finally decided at the end of the meeting with his core group. "If it succeeds, then our transgressions will be forgiven."

The members of the team had laughed at the joke — hoping he was right.

THE IMPLANTS WERE IN PLACE, and Daulby was fitting the piece of skull back into Chimp Donnie's head when the phone rang in the OR. Betty Reed took the call. They were short-staffed tonight — just the core team, for security — so work paused for the moment.

"Oh God!" she said, stumbling back against the wall. She looked across at Daulby, the color draining from her face. "It's for you, Dr. Daulby. It's about your wife."

"A divorce lawyer at this time of the night?" he joked, hiding his concern.

"It isn't that. Two policemen are outside to see you."

"Jesus! Get that fetal tissue out of sight," Martinson said. "Don't let the cops see that."

"That — that's not the problem," Betty said, slumping against the wall. "They found your wife's car, and she's — she and Jenny. Oh God!"

SEXY SALLY

San Diego, California.

THE JOURNEY TO HAUENFELDER had begun a month earlier in San Diego, the final day she worked with Sexy Sally.

"*But I don't want to go!* I like it *here!*" Sexy Sally said. "I like partying and drinking and screwing. I don't *want* to go, and you can't *make* me."

"But that life as Sally is finished," Kate Remington said gently. "It finished in the car crash. Now you must leave so that Linda can be healthy. Your mother and sister are waiting to guide you over. Just relax and let it happen."

"Sally" was stretched out on a recliner chair in the darkened office, while Kate—Katherine Remington, Ph.D.—sat at the edge of the room. Her doctorate was in psychology and counseling, with a specialty in what was termed Dissociative Identity Disorder, also known as Multiple Personality Disorder.

Kate was 32, tall and lean, with an attractive, gentle face, striking high cheekbones, warm brown eyes, and shoulder-length dark hair. She wore one of her trademark jogging suits, today pink. Jogging suits were comfortable to wear, and comfortable for the clients to be around.

Kate's friendly smile and easy manner put patients at ease, so rapport built sooner. She gave no indication of the way her life had been shattered a few months earlier when Karen, her twin sister, was mugged outside her apartment. Days later, Kate's fiancée was killed in a drive-by on his way home from the hospital.

KATE HAD BEGUN THE SESSION by leading Linda through the usual hypnotic induction, first relaxing her until she was almost oblivious to her present body and the present time, back to when it had all begun: A stepfather she called "Newdaddy." A little girl, then aged eight, who hated the things Newdaddy did to her.

Then that little girl, the child Linda, found herself outside her body, watching what was happening. It didn't hurt now, didn't shame her any longer, because now it wasn't happening to her.

Now it was happening to someone else, to someone who called herself Sally. Sally didn't mind the things Newdaddy did. Sally was always ready to step in when Newdaddy was doing the bad things. Once Sally arrived, Linda could go away.

"Now I'd like to speak to Sally," Kate said.

"The hell you want?" came the reply from Linda, but it wasn't Linda's voice, nor was it Linda's tone. Linda's normal voice was soft, so gentle and sweet it could barely be heard. This voice was brassy, the pronunciation coarse. This was the voice associated with the Sally personality.

"How long have you been with Linda?" Kate asked.

"You heard her, ever since Newdaddy started messing around with her."

"Why did you come to Linda?"

"The hell you think I came for? To have some fun again, get drunk, get laid."

"Where were you before you came to Linda?"

"Don't know *where* the hell I was. Lost somewhere, all confused, like some crazy dream."

Kate held a mirror in front of Linda's face. "Sally, I'd like you to open your eyes and look into the mirror. Is that your face you see?"

She pulled back from the mirror. "Hell, no, that's not me, not really me. That's Linda."

Kate eased back to her chair. This was the crucial step in bringing them out. "Tell me about the last time you saw your other body," Kate prompted.

"It was all . . . all tore up in the car, all bleeding and twisted. My – the face – it went through the windshield, and the head, it got turned almost clear 'round to the back."

She broke off and sobbed, convulsing in the chair. "It hurt so much at first, it was terrible. It was like I was being just tore apart. So I just kinda let go, y'know what I mean? Then it didn't hurt no more."

"I'd like you to look again at the body there in the car," Kate said. "Why is the head twisted around?"

"I don't *want* to look. That's *my* body, my *old* body. It's weird seeing it all tore up like that, a real bad dream."

"I'm sorry, but it's very important for you to look closely. Why is the head twisted around?"

"I think the neck's broke. But it *can't* be. I mean, I feel all right. My neck's not broke, *hell no!*"

"Now go in closer, and look at the eyes of the person in the car."

"No! I can't look at them eyes — they're . . . awful. Spooky!"

"What is it about the eyes?"

"They don't focus, they're just staring off into space!" She rocked with sobs. "Oh God! There's nobody *there* behind the eyes! It's *empty!*"

"Watch Sally's body there in the car. What happens next?"

"The men, they come'n put me—I mean, back then, after the accident, they put that body onto a stretcher and. . . " She broke off sobbing.

When she got control again, she went on, "And they put a sheet over it all, even up over the face."

"Do you understand what that means?"

Moments passed, and Kate was about to repeat the question when the reply came, "It means she's dead, don't it? But how can that be? *I'm* Sally, and *I'm* still alive."

"Look around you," Kate suggested softly. "Do you see any people you know?"

"Yeah," she said, and now her voice was softer, brighter. "Yeah, I see my mom. And my sister. They're there, just like —" She shook her head. *"But that can't be!* They're *dead*! They been dead for years! *The hell's going on?"*

"Ask them why they're there."

"Something about they've come to guide me."

"Guide you where?"

"Across, to the other side — that's what they tell me."

She jerked in the chair. "But I don't *want* to go! I like it here! I like having fun. I like partying and drinking and, hell, I like screwing. I don't *want* to leave here! *I don't want to go!"*

"But that life as Sally is finished," Kate said gently. "It finished years ago in the car crash. Your mother and sister have come for you."

"You stop this! I don't want to go, and you can't make me! Leave me alone!"

"Is anyone else with them?"

"I don't *want* to go! I don't! I *don't*!"

"Do you see a tunnel? Do you feel the energy pulling you into the tunnel?" Kate asked.

"It's pulling me, it's pulling me, and there's a light way up at the end. Mom has her arm around me now, and it's so good to see you again, Mom. It's pulling me up and —"

MULTIPLE PERSONALITIES

AFTER THE SESSION, Kate stopped by her office to check messages. Only one: a call from a Dr. Rausch of the Grafton Foundation. She had never heard of either Rausch or the Grafton Foundation, but foundations funded grants, and she desperately needed a grant.

She was on contract at the Clinic, and the contract was up for renewal next month. Not a good time, with talk of major cutbacks coming soon. Her approach to treating Multiple Personality Disorder, also known as Dissociative Identity Disorder, was controversial, and likely would be one of the first to be cut . . . unless she could come up with independent funding.

When she returned Dr. Rausch's call, he mentioned that he was intrigued by what he had heard of her "unorthodox but very intriguing therapy for Multiple Personality Disorder," and "believed they had some shared interests, based on her very interesting work."

He suggested lunch on Friday to "discuss some career possibilities that you may find of extreme interest."

IT HAD BEEN the prospect of a way to provide for her twin, Karen, that clinched it when Rausch made the offer at that first meeting.

"You haven't told me where the project is located," Kate had said after he had offered her a one-year contract, at a salary nearly half-again more than she was earning at the clinic.

"You will work in Austria," she had heard him say. She was sure he'd said Austria.

"Austria? I don't speak German, not a word."

"The other staff members speak English. It is a very scenic area, nicely secluded. The American media will not be forever looking over our shoulders, as they do in this country."

That was when it all fell apart. She couldn't leave Karen behind. Even though there really wasn't much *of* Karen left to leave. "Unfortunately, there's a problem. I can't—"

Karen had been in a coma since the mugging, an empty shell of the person that Kate had always felt was her alter ego. Even for identical twins, they had always been particularly close, each intuitively aware of what the other was doing and thinking.

The doctors told her there was no hope of recovery: Karen had come back as far as she ever would, and that was barely more than a vegetative state. For Kate's sake, for her peace of mind, they told her, the best thing would be to release her to an institution and get on with her own life.

But that was out of the question: she could no more sign Karen away to an institution than she could sign away half of her own body. They were identical twins, from the same ova. It almost seemed like a single personality spread across two bodies, so close, so attuned that they had often thought and said the same thing at the same moment.

But now Karen never spoke. Was she even capable of thinking now? There was no way to know.

Kate couldn't release her to an institution, and she certainly couldn't leave her behind and go work in Austria. But the insurance was running out: what then?

"Cannot leave your sister behind?" Rausch said. "Of course you cannot, we understand that, and have provided for it. We will have her flown to our clinic in a hospital plane, and she will be there with you. Your work will be in a hospital setting where we are exceptionally well-equipped to care for coma patients. Indeed, part of our research there focuses on therapy for coma patients and others with similar handicaps. Our past successes lead me to believe that we may be able to help Karen very significantly. All of her medical expenses will be taken care of, naturally."

Kate felt relief, and even something like happiness for the first time in what seemed a very long while. She smiled. "It seems I really don't have a choice, do I?"

"Exactly so," Rausch said.

A COUPLE OF DAYS after Kate arrived at the Clinic, an early morning jogger noticed a damaged guard-rail at a park along the Danube.

Police divers found a red Volkswagen, a rental car, on the bottom a couple of hundred yards down-river, with two suitcases in the trunk, and a purse wedged under the seat. The passport bore the name of Katherine Ann Remington, of Kingston, California. The car had been rented at the Vienna airport by woman showing ID as Katherine Ann Remington.

The door on the driver's side was open. They dragged the river for a day, but no body turned up. At nightfall, the search was called off. They had found from experience that the body might float to the surface in a few days as the gasses built up inside.

Unless, of course, the body caught on something underwater. When that happened, they were never found. That was not unusual in the Danube.

The American consulate was notified of the accident and missing driver. The information was cabled to Washington. A clerk pulled a copy of Kate's passport application to find who she had listed as her emergency contact.

As Kate and Karen had no close family still living, the contact was Debbie Whalen, her best friend.

At first, Debbie couldn't believe that Kate was really gone. She checked back with the State Department a couple of times over the next week, expecting to hear that she had turned up alive.

Finally, she notified the lawyer who had drafted Kate's Will only a few days earlier, and learned for the first time that Kate had released Karen to the care of the Grafton Foundation.

DANGEROUS DOORWAYS

Hauenfelder Clinic

ON THE MORNING Kate Remington arrived at the clinic, Dr. Rausch and Dr. Langwein took her on an orientation tour of the work in progress.

It went well, until she saw Vehicle 27.

She was stunned. Horrified. Sickened. Her flesh crawled as the Vehicle stared back at her with its vacant eyes.

She backed away from it until she felt the wall behind her. "This isn't *at all* what I expected when I agreed to come here! This—*whatever* it *is!*—isn't even human!"

"Vehicle 27 is advancing medical science," Rausch said.

"This isn't *science*, it isn't *medicine*. It's something . . . It's the kind of thing . . ., the kind of thing that *Mengele* might have done at Auschwitz!"

"Your comment is out-of-order," Rausch snapped, then walked out of the room, turning back to add, "I would remind you that you—and your sister—are *guests* here. You must keep that in mind."

Not guests, *prisoners*, she wanted to say, but cut it off. Already she knew that this was a strange place, an *evil* place, from the vibrations she was picking up. Karen, her twin, was vulnerable.

Dr. Langwein took over the orientation.

Langwein was short and puffy, with thick glasses that he polished constantly on his necktie. His eyes bounced around behind the thick lenses, unable to meet and hold contact with hers. He spoke English reasonably well, though in an accent inflected with what she sensed were traces of both German and Spanish.

Overall, a strange person. A creepy person. *Beyond* creepy.

He explained what her role would be, and how her experience with Multiple Personality Disorder tied in with the work at Hauenfelder.

"But don't you understand? You're opening very dangerous doorways!" she pressed. "Once those doors are open, there's no telling what kind of . . . what kind of *things* might come through!"

"Your twin sister is comfortable here at Hauenfelder, yes?" Langwein replied, then walked out, leaving her alone with Vehicle 27. It sat at the table, staring at her with empty eyes. She turned and ran to get away from the thing.

CHIMP DONNIE

He's in the kitchen at home when he hears the front door open.

"Daddy? Daddy, where are you?" Jenny calls. "We're back!"

"Here," he tries to say, but no sounds come.

Jenny finds him and hugs him around the legs. He lifts her up and kisses her. She smells as sweet as before.

"Oh, Daddy, it's so good to be with you again. We missed you so."

His mouth is dry, and he still can't speak. He hugs her tighter. He'll never let her go again.

Then Jackie appears at the door. He steps toward her. She backs away.

"I can't believe it," he finally manages to say. "I thought— I thought you and Jenny were . . . gone. Forever."

Jenny squeezes him. "We were visiting Grandma and Grandpa. They told us stories about when you were a little boy."

"But Grandma and Grandpa Daulby are dead. They've been dead for years, dead since way back when I was in high school."

"Oh, Daddy, you're really silly! We were just with them!"

He looks to Jackie for an explanation. But there is something different about her. It's the look she has when there is Important Business to discuss.

He sets Jenny down, and reaches for Jackie.

She shakes her head and backs away. "There's someone else in my life now, Doug."

"Someone else?"

"I'm sorry. You weren't there when I needed you."

"Is. . . is it anyone I know?"

"The only people you know are at the University, Doug. And yes, it is someone you know." She turns to the door and calls, "Donnie? You can come in now."

A chimpanzee, the one they had called Chimp Donnie, bounds through the house and hugs Daulby around the knees, just as Jenny did.

Then Donnie holds out his hand, and says, "Good to see you again, Doug. No hard feelings, I hope?"

Then he's not in the kitchen at home anymore; he's in a bed in a hotel room somewhere, the phone is ringing, and his head is pounding from a night's determined drinking. The sunlight streaming through an opening in the blinds reminds him it's Florida, near Orlando. And Jenny and Jackie are dead.

He rolled his feet onto the floor and took a sip of water to clear his mouth.

He reached for the phone, then changed his mind. There wasn't anyone he wanted to talk to, not now, not ever. Another couple of rings and it would stop and leave him alone. He dropped back onto the bed, wanting to savor the memory of the moments with Jenny. Even a dream was better than nothing.

Then he thought of Jackie and the chimp she said had taken his place.

He didn't want to think about that part of the dream. He picked up the phone. "Daulby."

"Dr. Daulby? My name is Dr. Roland Rausch. You don't know me, but I am very familiar with your work—very *impressed* as well, I might add. As it happens, I am also here in Orlando, and I think it would be in our mutual interest to meet, as soon as possible. Perhaps you would be free to meet for lunch today?"

Daulby tried to place the accent: stiff, formal phrasing, definitely not American. German? Spanish? More like a combination of both.

But what difference did it make? Anything has to be better than this. "Sure, why not?"

DR. RAUSCH turned out to be a tall, pale man, elegantly dressed in a classic European-cut black suit that looked hand-tailored. The clothing, as expensive as it was, did nothing to overcome the man's awkwardness. He struck Daulby as someone who seemed out of place in his own body.

As they talked, Daulby was surprised at how familiar Rausch was with his work, and quickly realized that this impromptu lunch was a strange sort of job interview. The offer came at the end of the meal, a one-year research contract at a salary triple what he'd been earning at the University.

"I'd need a few weeks to clear things."

"Naturally," Rausch said. "But we do have an urgent short-term need. Perhaps you could spare us ten days now on a consultant status at our facility in Austria? It would give you a chance to assess our operation, and us a chance to gain some of your expertise more quickly. For those ten days, we can offer an honorarium of $100,000."

"For ten days?"

The University had cut off his salary when the scandal hit the news. The house was in foreclosure, his medical license was in jeopardy, and he'd done nothing to save either. In these weeks of aimless wandering and drinking, he'd run his credit cards close to the limit.

$100,000 would get him back on his feet. Even better, the idea of ten days in fresh surroundings, with new faces and new challenges, and something to think about other than regrets, seemed ideal.

"How soon can you leave?" Rausch asked when Daulby agreed. "Perhaps today?"

"Today? That's imposs—" Then he thought, Why not? The sooner the better. Anything to get past this.

"We respect the value of your contribution, Dr. Daulby, so you will travel by private jet, a very comfortable Gulfstream. Will that be satisfactory?"

Daulby nodded, almost wondering if this was still part of a dream.

"Then I will need to take your passport now, in order to make the arrangements."

THE TOWER

AFTER THE LUNCH with Doug Daulby in Orlando, Dr. Rausch flew north for his monthly meeting with Parsons Couldsen. At those meetings, usually at Couldsen Tower, he briefed Couldsen on the progress at the laboratories in California, as well as the work at the Hauenfelder Clinic, where the real work was done.

Couldsen Tower was the center of the various divisions of Couldsen's empire.

Couldsen saw himself as primarily a venture capitalist. He'd always had the knack of knowing where to put money, where the growth was to come . . . and when to clear out and let others take the ride back down.

He'd started in the early '80's in Silicon Valley, back before it was known as the epicenter of tech startups. He'd had the knack, and he met the right people early. He put money—his own and investors'— into the little ventures that grew big, very fast, and success grabbed the attention of the investment media, and hence of the public. His reputation and fortune grew exponentially.

Then the dot-com bubble burst in the spring of 2000. It ruined a lot of the quick fortunes, and scared away a lot of other money.

It educated Couldsen, but didn't scare him, only broadened his horizons.

That bust, in his view, had been precipitated by two factors. First, the new tech market was over-extended, no doubt of that. It had come too far, too fast. A pullback was in order, and a natural event, opening the way to new growth.

But it was the second factor that caused him to see the world in a different way. The media—forever on the lookout for crisis headlines as a way of drawing readers, and hence advertisers—had (probably unwittingly) blown what could have been a manageable normal correction into what in the media termed a "tech cataclysm".

BY THAT POINT, Couldsen had plenty of money—not enough, there could never be enough—but plenty to invest in those fresh horizons. He shifted his focus from tech to power—the powerful media outlets, the shapers of the opinions of the masses—that he had seen operating with inordinate effect.

Most of them—print media, TV, even some early internet publications—were available for moderate prices. The real bargains would come later when the power of the internet to attract eyeballs, and hence advertising dollars. By then, Couldsen Media was firmly established and profitable.

Thus he now had two power bases—the tech world on Sand Hill Road and environs, where he remained a respected guru. And now the east coast, the "Boswash" strip from Boston to Washington, where the mainstream media and the political elite centered. From there, he could "nudge" news coverage and political direction.

BUT ALL THAT HAD TAKEN a personal toll. A couple of wives passed through, and children. Unfortunate, , but unavoidable.

The real toll had been on his health. Too many all-nighters working out deals, too much stress fighting and questing and pushing people to give 120%. Too many cigarettes and cigars and pep pills, and no exercise at all.

COULDSEN'S INVESTMENT TEAMS, and his personal office, occupied the top floors of the Tower. Most of his investments were on a five-to-seven year trajectory: provide seed money for a big cut of the whole, build up, sell off, move on to something new.

His media properties were an exception. He'd held onto the pieces as he'd acquired them, in part because they were profitable, but even more because of the platform they gave him to shape perceptions in the way he wanted them. These included the main studios of the television network he had pieced together, along with the headquarters of Couldsen Media, which owned a string of newspapers, magazines, and internet and cable operations in the United States and overseas.

The various other Couldsen enterprises—the sports teams, the bio-tech and software firms and the like—were, for the most part, also run out of The Tower.

Forbes had called Parsons Couldsen "possibly the most influential man in the United States," claiming his control of so large a media empire gave him more power than even the President in influencing the thinking of Americans.

A congressional committee had begun an investigation targeting Couldsen's growing media power. The investigation withered away after the committee chairman and the chief investigator were killed in the unexplained crash of a private aircraft.

COULDSEN'S OFFICE occupied the southwest corner of the 79th floor of Couldsen Tower. Wall Street lay to the south; the Hudson and New Jersey to the west. In an interview in *Fortune*, Couldsen said the view down toward Wall Street reminded him to keep a watch on the dollars, while looking westward put him in mind of the need for broad, pioneering vision. It was pure bullshit, something he'd made up on the spot, but quoted in most of the pieces about him since.

Couldsen led the way to the arrangement of leather chairs and sofas by the corner windows. Even those few steps revealed to Dr. Rausch's eye how much Couldsen had failed in the past month. Not good. Not good at all. Things were not ready. Even though Remington, and now Daulby, were on board, it would still take time. Couldsen kept a fully-equipped EMT team with him around the clock, but there was always the risk.

SITTING THERE, with nothing but glass ahead, the effect was of floating above the world. The rain had stopped now, and the lights of the evening traffic flowed below, streams of small bright dots like streams of luminescent ants.

In his dark business suit, with his wavy silver hair and tanned chiseled face, Parsons Couldsen was an impressive man, photogenic enough that over the years he had made the covers of *Forbes* and

Business Week, along with *Fortune*. A decade ago, he had shared a *Time* cover with the President.

After his second heart attack, he quit smoking and dropped the 30 pounds that had built up over the years. Now, with his year-round tan, he looked like a life-long athlete.

But the appearance was deceptive. Rausch had seen him in the pool at Couldsen Farm, his spread in the Virginia horse country. In a bathing suit, with his hair wet, Parson Couldsen was just another soft, prematurely old man with a chest full of surgical scars.

Despite the weight loss and the swimming and the newly-ascetic life-style with no bourbon or cigars, and a diet of unvarying fruit, rice, vegetables, and fish, Couldsen had suffered a third major heart attack. Now he was living on borrowed time.

AT ONE of these monthly meetings, months earlier, Rausch had been forced to tell Couldsen that they needed two more specialists to assist with the Hauenfelder work: first, Kate Remington, the psychologist, now Dr. Douglas Daulby, a neurosurgeon and researcher "with some very intriguing ideas."

"Each person we bring in adds more risk."

"We are evolving a unique process. We are creating an entirely new technology. Indeed there are risks, but the payoff is infinite, yes?"

Rausch had shown Couldsen the Daulby file then, the result of a year's search to find the right person.

Couldsen looked first at the photographs. Even in the photos, Dr. Daulby seemed to dominate by his presence. It was something in the way he stood, as if charged with energy. Couldsen liked that. From his years in television, Couldsen wanted his people to have presence.

Rausch had the charisma of a brick, and he was a pain to be around. But he was necessary.

Daulby had been an athlete: that was obvious from the power of his arms and legs in the shots taken while he was jogging a month earlier. Though he wasn't heavy, his face and body had filled in from the college yearbook photos. A thatch of curly silver hair framed his face.

The file also contained Daulby's professional Vita, listing his surgical residencies and copies of the professional papers he had written or contributed to in the course of his career.

Most significantly, it contained a copy of an interview Daulby had given to *Discover* magazine, in which he speculated on the potential of brain research in the year 2035.

As Couldsen scanned the article, a broad smile cut across his face. "Goddam, you may just be right. Daulby *is* thinking on the right track. He just doesn't realize how far ahead of the rest of the world we are at Hauenfelder."

Rausch said, "As we speak, Daulby is in-transit to Hauenfelder."

COULDSEN LEANED BACK in the chair and took several deep breaths. Rausch could see how he was tiring.

Then Couldsen said, "I'm not sure you really understand the urgency of this."

"Of course. We—"

"Sometimes I get the distinct feeling that you're playing games with me, stringing me along while I pay the bills for your research." He was silent then, staring at Rausch.

"Not at all—"

"You see, Dr. Rausch, I feel I'm on a conveyor belt pulling me toward the goddam grave, and I want to—*goddam need* to—get off that belt. N*ow!*"

"Yes, of course—"

"And let me tell you, I just saw my doctor, and he tells me my heart has declined even more just over the last month, so that conveyor belt is moving me faster and faster."

"We are very close, and now—"

"You'd damned well better be close. Because if I don't make it, then, neither are you and all that rest of that bunch of goddam weirdos you've got working for you. I die, you all die, I've arranged for that to happen. I live, you all get to live on forever, lifetime after lifetime, just like me."

JOGGING ROBOTS

HE'S IN THE KITCHEN at home when he hears the front door open.

"Daddy? Daddy, where are you?" Jenny calls. "We're back!"

"Here," he tries to say, but no sounds come.

Jenny finds him and hugs him around the legs. He lifts her up and kisses her. She smells as sweet as before.

"Oh, Daddy, it's so good to be with you again. We missed you so much."

Chimp Donnie bounds in, pushes Jenny away, and takes her place hugging Daulby around the knees.

"No! No! Get away!" Daulby shouts.

Then he's awake, a hand touching him on the shoulder. "Dr. Daulby? You were having a nightmare."

He looked at her, a small brunette in a uniform. It took a moment to place her, to figure out where he was.

It came together. He was on the Gulfstream that Dr. Rausch had arranged. He'd been the only passenger, apart from the second crew that would be taking over when they refueled in Ireland.

"We'll be landing within the hour," she said. "Perhaps you'd like to freshen up? I'll have some coffee and your breakfast ready."

He looked out the window. Darkness, apart from a sliver of dawn on the horizon.

"I've never been to Ireland," he said, pulling himself out of the seat.

She smiled. "Sorry, you slept through Ireland. You must have been very tired."

"I haven't been sleeping well for . . . for weeks. I needed it."

He sipped some water to wash away the strange coppery taste in his mouth. Unusual taste. Something to make him sleep? But he was the doctor, and he hadn't ordered it. Nor had he been told.

DAWN WAS BREAKING when the plane threaded through jagged mountains and landed at a small airport. That didn't surprise Daulby; private planes were unwelcome at the busy international fields.

But this place seemed unusually deserted, forlorn. He caught a glimpse of a couple of shabby fighter planes, and some battered military helicopters, some with rotors off, as if this were an airplane grave-yard.

"I know we're in Austria, but where exactly?" he asked the flight attendant.

"Austria?" She frowned momentarily, then flicked the smile back on. "That you must ask the pilot."

The pilots stayed sequestered behind the cockpit door, and the attendant walked with him down the steps to the runway. Just as well she did, he thought, as his legs seemed wobbly—too much sleep all at once. His head felt woozy, and that coppery taste lingered even after eating.

That was not just from too much sleep. They had slipped something into his food. Definitely so. Troubling.

A black Mercedes waited, along with three bulky men in black suits. One of them transferred Daulby's bags from the plane to the car trunk. Two rode in the front; the third climbed into the back seat with him.

"Where are we?" Daulby asked.

"Not English," the man beside him said. "We not speak English."

DAULBY DOZED AGAIN, and woke when he felt the car stop. The sky was bright, but still dawn down here, as the area was ringed by tall, snow-capped mountains, the tops glowing in the clear morning sunshine.

They seemed to be at a guard post. He saw a wire fence glinting through the trees and shrubbery. Three strands of barbed wire topped the fence.

The metal gate ahead looked heavy enough to stop a truck, and bore two small black signs. The first said:

PRIVATKLINIK HAUENFELDER.
Hauenfelder Private Clinic. Entry Forbidden.

He squinted, trying to read the second sign, then realized the words were in an unfamiliar alphabet. Cyrillic?

But Austria was German-speaking. They don't use Cyrillic characters in Austria, do they?

Why had the flight attendant had been vague when he'd asked if this was Austria? Dr. Rausch had said the clinic was in Austria. If not Austria, then where the hell are we?

A uniformed guard appeared from a small hut. He glanced into the Mercedes, then unlocked the gate.

The forest extended about 100 feet in from the fence. At the edge of the trees, the roadway rounded a bend and the view opened up, revealing an expanse of velvety grass, broken by trees and flowering shrubs leading down to a long white building, three stories high. A steeply-sloping red tile roof and scattered cupolas gave it a gingerbread-castle effect.

But beneath the facade, Daulby saw the stark framework of an old tuberculosis sanitarium.

A dense line of trees—and he guessed a fence hidden within them—circled the grounds from water's edge to water's edge.

Four very fit young men in shorts jogged along a path that circled the grassy area, just inside the trees. That jogging area was bounded by another wire fence that cut the track off from the rest of the grounds. The men ran in synch, one leading, the others matching strides. Military? Daulby wondered. Why here?

The faces of the three following faces seemed blank, devoid of expression, focused only on the area just ahead of them.

They were like automatons. Jogging robots. Zombies. Probably soldiers on punishment runs.

A couple played tennis on courts beside the lake, paying no attention to the joggers.

Beyond the clinic, the cobalt-blue water of a small lake sparkled where the first ray of sun cut through a gap in the mountain range.

The lake, still as glass, was cradled by a bowl of rugged mountains. The mountains thrust up from the water at a 45-degree angle.

The lower parts of the mountains were dark with pines, then slabs of grey granite thrust through the vegetation. The tops were still snow-capped.

A village nested at the base of the mountains, a mile or so away across the lake. The onion dome of a white church was visible even at this distance. A motor launch set out from the village dock, slicing the still waters.

But the village occupied only a narrow ledge between the water and the mountain slope. It was humbling to see how narrow the band of habitation was along the shoreline, contrasted with the height and majesty of the untamed mountains.

It seemed as idyllic as a photo on an Alpine calendar. Daulby was certain at that moment that he had made the right move in accepting Rausch's offer. Ten days in a setting like this, ten days with new faces and new challenges might be all it took to get past the guilt that plagued his nights.

GHOSTS

THE DRIVER pulled to the front of the main building. Daulby saw a face at a window, and a moment later a woman appeared at the door.

She was in her 40's, tall, large-boned, wearing a gray-blue wool dress so severely tailored that it seemed to be a uniform. Her brown hair was pulled back into an old-fashioned bun, accentuating her harsh, narrow face. A long, sharp nose linked cold, impersonal eyes with thin, unsmiling lips.

"So. You are Dr. Daulby, yes?" she said in heavily accented English. "Welcome to the Hauenfelder Clinic. I am Gerda, director of resident services. You must come with me now. I will show you to your quarters."

As they walked through the halls, Gerda sketched the history of the place. The Clinic was built in the 1920's on the ruins of an old monastery. Originally, it was used to care for tubercular patients, then later for mental patients from the families of the well-to-do. The families could warehouse them here in luxury, then with a clear conscience forget them. The German military took it over during the war to house the wounded.

It reopened after the war as a resort hotel, but then the stories began that it was haunted by the ghosts of the mental patients who had died there over the years. The resort failed.

She led him to the broad staircase in the center of the building, and started down to the lower floor. Then she paused, and said, "But surely you are not a believer in ghosts, are you doctor?"

"WE HAVE ALSO HERE a pool and Jacuzzi," Gerda said as they stepped off the elevator, and led the way down a hall. Daulby smelled chlorine in the air even before she opened the door.

The room was surrounded on three sides by large sliding windows that led to a deck overlooking the lake. A few swimmers were doing laps; the pool was large, though not Olympic size.

He looked more closely at the swimmers: two women, three men, and realized they were naked.

A blond woman, mid-30s, appeared from another door. She was naked, and smiled at him.

"Come, Sonja, you must meet Dr. Daulby. He has just arrived."

Sonja held out her hand. "Yes, yes, Dr. Daulby, we have all read of your work and look forward to working with you."

She held his eyes, but he was still conscious of her nudity. Sonja had been beautiful, that was still evident. But now she looked tired, worn. Despite the chlorinated air, he picked up a whiff of alcohol on her breath.

"We must go," Gerda said.. "Dr. Daulby has had a long journey and now needs to freshen up."

"Perhaps a nice swim will make you feel refreshed?" Sonja said. "I am about to swim."

"Perhaps later," Gerda said. "Now he must get ready for his meetings."

"Yes, yes, of course. But, Dr. Daulby, please, I hope to see you again, yes?"

From her accent, he guessed that Sonja was Russian. He had the sense this had been set up and rehearsed for his benefit.

He had the sense, as well, that Sonja had not been at all comfortable playing this part. Maybe vodka had made it easier.

SUCH IS THE POLICY

"YOU WILL BE ALLOWED to use the pool and Jacuzzi as soon as you pass your physical examination," Gerda said as they stepped onto the elevator.

"Physical exam? I'm here as a doctor, not a patient."

"This is the policy. All staff must be certified in good health before they are allowed to use the pool and sauna. The patients are not allowed to use the pool area at any time, of course."

She walked on down the hall then, saying, "You have had a long journey. Your baggage will be in your room by now."

"I don't understand. Why are the patients not allowed in the pool? Not even for therapy?"

"Is it not obvious?"

"I don't understand."

"They claim that the chlorination protects against the SIDA virus, but why should we gamble on that?"

"SIDA?" Daulby responded, his tired brain slow to make the translation.

"You Americans refer to it as AIDS."

"AIDS? This is an AIDS clinic?"

"Has it not been explained to you?"

"Nobody mentioned AIDS. What am I doing here? I'm a neurosurgeon, not a virologist."

"It will all make sense as soon as you have been briefed," Gerda said, beckoning him into an elevator. "We have AIDS patients here, yes. But our focus is not on curing their illness."

"Then what *is* the focus here?"

"I am not a doctor," Gerda replied, turning away. "I leave that question for others to answer in your briefing."

THE LARGER ROOM in his suite had been set up as an office, with a bedroom and adjoining bath. The furniture was modern and comfortable, and seemed more appropriate to a luxury resort than a hospital. A large private balcony overlooked the lake.

Gerda pointed out the small refrigerator in a corner. "You see? We have here for you every convenience. Dinner is normally served at seven in the main dining room downstairs. If you prefer, you can ring the desk and have a tray brought up to you. That is a privilege shared by the senior staff."

He asked about visiting the small village he saw across the lake.

She shook her head. "But that is not possible. For you to leave the Clinic grounds, you must have the written authorization of the director, Dr. Rausch."

"Are you telling me I'm locked in here for ten days? You're not serious!"

"I am always serious. And, yes, you will be confined to the clinic while you work here. Such is the policy."

"That's crazy. What *is* this place — a research facility or a prison?"

"The Hauenfelder Clinic is a secure research facility," she replied. "That is why we have rules, to ensure that security is total. But life is very pleasant here. We are a totally self-sufficient community, with all the facilities of a luxury resort, and more. Anything you could possibly want is available here."

For the first time, she looked him directly in the eye. "Anything at all. You have only to ask, and it will be provided. *Anything.*"

Gerda was at the door when he said, "Where are we?"

Her eyes, expressionless, stared at him. "We are at the Hauenfelder Clinic, that is where."

"I was told I was coming to Austria. Is this actually Austria?"

"Dr. Rausch will be here soon, and will want to meet with you immediately. You must get ready now."

THE PHONE RANG as he stepped out of the shower. "This is again Gerda, director of resident services. Dr. Rausch has just arrived. You will meet him for coffee on the terrace in 20 minutes. Twenty minutes exactly. You must not be late."

"Wait," he said. He was groggy from jet-lag. He took a sip of water to clear his mouth. "When I flew here, the air crew held my passport. They forgot to return it."

"They did not forget. It is the policy to hold in a secure place the passports of all Hauenfelder staff."

"But I'm not staff. I'm here as a consultant only. For ten days. I want my passport back."

"Such is the policy at the Hauenfelder Clinic," she said, and hung up.

BUTTERFLY

A WAITRESS showed Daulby to a table on the terrace overlooking the lake, then brought him a silver pot of coffee.

Quite a clinic, he thought. All the amenities of a plush mountain resort. Along with all the charm of a prison.

The morning was sunny and crystalline, with air so clear it seemed he could pick out the individual branches of the pine trees across the lake.

The lake, glass-still and silvery-blue, reflected the mountains in reverse image.

He watched a butterfly float past. With each flick of its wings, it shot up a few inches, coasted, then flicked the wings again. It circled him once, then landed on the edge of his table.

He looked closely at the butterfly, the first time he'd really looked at a butterfly since childhood. He was struck by its fragile beauty: the big wings were light orange on the bottom, intense orange on the top, richly-patterned with stripes and dots. As he watched it, the butterfly hopped around to face him, each move accompanied by a slow flap of the wings.

"Ah, Dr. Daulby," Rausch said, appearing beside him. Daulby had not heard him approach.

Bizarre. Yesterday morning he'd met Rausch in Florida. Now he was here, yet he hadn't flown on that same Gulfstream. Had Rausch flown on another private jet? Where did funding of that magnitude come from?

AS HE STOOD to shake hands, Daulby realized even more than before what an unappealing person Rausch was: awkwardly tall and ungainly, with uncoordinated long arms and legs. It again struck him that somehow Rausch's body didn't seem to fit the person, as if the wrong body had come back from the laundry.

Rausch's pale face seemed made up of sharp edges, and the dark eyes burned with an unpleasant intensity. Though he was nearly bald, he had let the sides grow long, and combed the long strands across the top.

But again he was elegantly dressed; even his white lab coat seemed tailored.

"You are settled in now?" Rausch asked, as they sat. Before Daulby could raise the issues he had planned, Rausch continued, "Good. Now tell me this: In your view, what is life?"

What is life? A glance at Rausch's face showed that this was not just idle conversation. What the hell kind of way is this to start a meeting?

"Yes, what indeed is life? What is the unifying life-force?" Rausch repeated, gesturing at the butterfly that still rested on the table between them.

"Take this butterfly, for example. What force brings the individual cells together into the delicate marvel that it is? What force gives it energy to move, to fly? From whence comes the intelligence to find food?"

Daulby shook his head. "I'm a neuroscientist, not a philosopher. Those aren't the kind of questions for which I have answers."

"Surely you have speculated on these questions, yes?"

"I don't have answers."

"A remarkable creature, the butterfly," Rausch said. "A creature that has already lived one life, as a caterpillar. Then it undergoes a transformation, a period of rebirth in a cocoon. Then it emerges to a brilliant new life. A first life, as a caterpillar tethered to the ground. Then it emerges free, brilliant, boundless."

Daulby nodded, puzzled.

"In a very real sense, the process by which the caterpillar transforms into a new, better life is very much analogous to the transformation we bestow on our patients here at Hauenfelder."

Rausch paused, as if waiting for a response from Daulby. When there was none, he added, "I expect you have heard the saying, 'What a caterpillar calls death, we call a butterfly'? That is what we do here."

What the hell are you talking about? Daulby wondered. What the hell am I doing in this place?

RAUSCH PICKED UP A TEASPOON and abruptly swatted the butterfly, crushing its head. The big wings twitched slowly a couple of times, then were still. Rausch set the spoon on the table, and took a sip of coffee.

Daulby stared at the still body of the butterfly, stunned. The butterfly was beautiful and harmless. As Jenny had been. Why kill it?

"A moment ago," Rausch said, "the butterfly was, as we say, alive— whatever 'alive' means. Now the protoplasm that formed it—the wings, eyes,—remain. Indeed, most of the individual cells will remain alive for a while. But the unifying life-force that made it a butterfly is gone. So tell me: Where did that unifying life-force go?"

Daulby shook his head. "*Go*? It went nowhere. It terminated. It ceased to be."

Rausch added more sugar to his coffee, stirring it with the spoon he had used to kill the butterfly. "Each day, millions of exquisite butterflies are created by nature. Yet, to this point, we scientists have never been able to bring a single one of them to life in our laboratories, nor even to return life to the body once the force has gone."

"Why did you kill that butterfly?"

"To open your thinking. To prepare you for what you will see and do here at Hauenfelder."

What in hell have I gotten myself into? Daulby wondered, feeling a growing sense of unease.

RAUSCH SCRAPED the remains of the butterfly off the table onto the stone of the patio. "A fortuitous coincidence that it should land precisely when it did, yes? Were you aware that in the original Greek, the word *psyche* meant both 'soul' and 'butterfly'?"

Daulby wanted to ask why the hell it was necessary to kill the butterfly to make the point. Life, he was realizing more than ever, since losing Jackie and Jenny, was too damned precious to waste.

But he said nothing. Just shut up, do what had to be done, take the money, and get the hell out of here.

"In our researches at Hauenfelder, we avoid the religious connotations of the word 'soul,'" Rausch said. "Here we prefer the term 'Conscious Essence' or 'Animating Essence' to describe the life-force."

Daulby felt Rausch's eyes boring into him for a reaction. He was determined to give none.

Rausch continued: "Tell me, Dr. Daulby: What of the more interesting issue of life after death? Are you a believer in a life after the death of the physical body?"

Daulby shook his head, wondering why Rausch was asking this question, at this time. "It's a nice idea, but I've never found any convincing evidence." I wish I *could* believe, he almost added, the images of Jackie and Jenny flashing across his mind.

Rausch nodded, then said, "I must confess that we got you to the Hauenfelder Clinic on false pretenses."

Daulby stared at him, feeling a flash of vertigo. "False pretenses?"

"Our research here focuses on the issue we have just been discussing: the question of life after death."

Rausch paused, as if giving that time to sink in. Then he added, "More specifically, our interest is in finding a practical way of ensuring that life—particularly the *conscious* aspect of life—continues after the death of the physical body."

Daulby stared at him, at a loss for words. Finally he managed, "Life after death?"

"No, better than that: we offer life after *life*. Without death. The fact is," Rausch continued, "we are very close to achieving our objective—renewed life. Put differently, we are engaged in finding a remedy for death. Only one final hurdle remains."

A remedy for death—the phrase echoed in Daulby's mind, "And that is?"

"A hurdle that we believe only you can help us cross."

"Me? How?"

Rausch stood. "Enough talk. Now it is time to meet the first of your patients."

TEDI

THE FAMILIAR WHITE DOCTOR'S COAT felt alien, though it was the uniform Daulby had worn through his professional career. He'd last worn one on that final day at University Hospital.

The day of the experiment on Chimp Donnie.

The day Jackie and Jenny died.

"The Perfect Scandal"—the media called it. Perfect for the media, at least.

In the morning, the news focused on the tragic murders of Daulby's wife and daughter.

By noon, the police investigation turned up the fact that at the time of the kidnaping, Daulby and his research team had been performing an unauthorized experiment in the University Hospital, transferring brain tissues from an aborted human fetus into the brain of a young chimp. They called it Chimp Donnie.

If he'd had the heart to fight, he could have argued that the experiment was—arguably, at least—within the protocols established by the grant he was operating under. But, shattered by the deaths of Jackie and Jenny, he couldn't summon the will.

That first day, about 200 protestors marched outside the University Hospital. By evening, it was double that, and double again by the following morning. The President and Board made it clear that the University's image had to be maintained. Daulby submitted his resignation.

After the funerals, he got in his car and drove, never checking back for messages.

He still didn't understand how Dr. Rausch had found him in Florida. He'd asked, but hadn't really gotten a clear answer. It didn't matter; he was here now.

THE FIRST STOP was Ward A on the second floor. "Surely you do not fear AIDS patients, do you, doctor?" Rausch asked as they logged in at the nursing station. "There is little risk, so long as the proper precautions are taken."

"I've operated on AIDS patients," Daulby replied. "But why AIDS patients here? Where do I fit in? I'm a neurosurgeon, not a virologist."

"It will all be clear as soon as you meet your first patient—rather, your first *pair* of patients. His name is Tedi Beckwith. He pronounces it in that absurd manner—'Tee-Dye'—for a reason known only to himself. Perhaps a pathetic attempt to invest himself with a sense of uniqueness."

Along the way, they passed a half-dozen men sitting in a sunny common room watching television: gaunt figures in bathrobes, slumped in wheelchairs. They looked up with hopeless eyes as Daulby and Rausch passed.

"It's odd," Daulby said when they were out of earshot. "Something about the way those patients were sitting there— the facial expressions, the wasted bodies—reminds me of photos of the inmates of the Nazi death camps. The same skeletal bodies, the same dead eyes."

Rausch stopped in his tracks. "You are in *Europe*, doctor. Be careful about speaking of the war and the camps. People here are still sensitive about those issues. *Extremely* sensitive."

"You told me the Clinic was in Austria, but I'm getting the sense that may not—"

"Austria? You are mistaken. I never said Austria. What I may have said was that the climate here is *similar* to that of Austria. You misunderstood," he said, walking on.

TEDI BECKWITH was even more wasted than the men they passed in the hall. His face was a layer of parchment covering a skull, and he lacked the strength to turn his head on the pillows as they entered the room. Only his black moustache showed that he had ever had a life outside the hospital.

"Thank God you're finally here, Doc," Tedi said in a voice so weak that Daulby had to lean forward to hear it. He spoke in English, with what seemed to be a South Boston accent. "I've hung on all these weeks, waiting for you to finally get here. I'm counting on you, doc, counting on you to give me a second chance at life." His eyes slowly shut, and Daulby wondered if he had died.

"I can't save him," Daulby said when they were in the hallway. "What's he talking about? 'Making it across'— is he delusional?"

"No, not delusional at all. And yes, we do think you can save him. You have the power to give him another chance at life."

"Another chance?" Daulby said, suddenly aware of how quiet the Hauenfelder Clinic was, with none of the quiet bustle of a hospital— no elevators chiming, no food carts rolling down the corridors, no nurses' shoes squeaking along polished floors, no phones buzzing.

Tedi's eyes opened. "Have you seen me, Doc?"

"Seen you?" Daulby responded.

"The *new* me. The new me they've got waiting for me in the other ward."

"That poor fellow is days, maybe hours from death," Daulby said when they were out in the corridor. "He's delusional, that 'new me' fantasy. There's no way I can save him."

Rausch shook his head. "Now you must come upstairs and see how."

VEHICLE

RAUSCH WAS SILENT as they walked through the dark halls to Ward B, then unlocked the heavy door by punching a code into an electronic lock.

"One never knows how best to introduce a new person to our work," Rausch said. "Some prefer to be taken step-by-step through the process as we developed it. Others find it best to begin with the end-product and work backward, showing how we arrived there."

"Let's start with the results," Daulby said, thinking. Let's get this over with so I can get the hell out of here.

Rausch nodded, then walked through the ward to a closed room at the end of the wing. Like the other ward, it was strangely deserted, as if this were the middle of the night instead of mid-morning.

Take me to the cannibals, Daddy. Please!

He turns. Jenny is running down the corridor toward him. He bends down and scoops her into his arms. Jackie comes behind, a strange smile on her face.

Take me to the cannibals, Daddy. Come with us. Please?

I can't tonight, Jenny, not tonight. Tonight I have to work, tonight is the only time I can try that experiment. It's very important.

Exper'ment? More important than coming to the cannibals with us? Chimp Donnie is more important than Mommy and I?

"Dr. Daulby! You must pay attention!" Rausch snapped.

Daulby looked around, shaken. Jackie and Jenny were gone, of course. They were dead, had been dead for months. But this was so incredibly *real*. Not just a memory, more like a flashback, the tactile sense of holding Jenny again, total recall of that last time he saw them, when he chose not to go with them.

He turned away so Rausch wouldn't see the tears welling in his eyes. "Sorry, jet-lag, not enough sleep."

But *still* that feeling lingered, the sense that Jenny and Jackie were right here, someplace close. Watching, playing hide-and-seek, waiting to be found.

There had been no chance to say good-by. That quick hug in the hospital corridor before they went off to the carnival had been the last he'd seen them. Later, after the police found them in the burned car, the bodies had been too charred for viewing.

If only he'd gone with them to the carnival that night, then nothing would have happened. They'd be alive. He'd still be at the University. The Chimp Donnie experiment would never have taken place. Everything would be as it had been.

"Dr. Daulby, you *must* pay attention. There is much work to be done."

Two men and woman hunched over microscopes in an open lab along the way. One of the men rose and accompanied them. Rausch introduced him as "Herr Doctor Langwein—Hubert Langwein."

Langwein held out his hand. It was soft and damp. He was pudgy, perhaps 50, with a shock of unruly white hair, sleepy eyes, and a puffy face. He wore silver-framed glasses with bottle-thick lenses that made his eyes small and beady. But the eyes were unable to hold a gaze; they would make contact, then dart away before coming back for an instant. Was he just shy, Daulby wondered, or did he live in a state of perpetual guilt?

Rausch, ungainly as he was, at least tried to look crisp; it seemed as though Langwein had slept in his clothes. He wore a silk necktie in a mustard and maroon pattern that looked like something from a vision test. His lab coat was too long in the arms, and too tight around the stomach. His shoes were scuffed, and one had come untied.

"Dr. Langwein is my second-in-command," Rausch explained. "He has been working with me for many years."

RAUSCH LED the way to a room midway down the ward. The room contained what seemed to be a child sleeping in a giant glass tube.

Daulby recognized the tube as a hyperbaric chamber, normally used in hospitals to stimulate healing by flooding body tissues with oxygen under pressure. Burn patients healed about 40% faster in hyperbaric chambers than those in control groups left at normal atmospheric pressures. According to rumors, Michael Jackson had slept in a hyperbaric chamber in the hope that it would lengthen his life.

Rausch nodded to Langwein, who released the pressure and shut down the system. He opened the hatch and assisted the patient out.

The patient was small, about the size of a boy aged 10 or so, but he wore a neatly-trimmed black moustache. A couple of days' beard stubble covered his small face. A small boy with a moustache?

Daulby stared at the figure, realizing how much he resembled Tedi Beckwith, the AIDS patient he'd just met downstairs on Ward A. Was this Tedi's son? Or a younger brother?

But why in a hyperbaric chamber?

"Dr. Daulby, meet Vehicle 27," Rausch said.

"Vehicle 27? Does he have a name?" Daulby asked, but no one responded.

With Langwein's guidance, the patient walked over to sit at a table in the corner. He moved clumsily, with odd, slow, sleep-walking movements. His eyes were open, but unfocused.

Langwein opened a refrigerator and took out a bowl of green jello. He put the bowl on the table, and slipped a spoon into the patient's hand.

With the same dreamy movements, the patient reached into the bowl and fed himself. His expression was vacant as he followed the spoon from bowl to mouth and back.

"I don't understand what I'm seeing," Daulby whispered. "Should we go outside to talk?"

"That is not necessary." As Rausch spoke, the patient turned to look at him, but his eyes remained blank. "His hearing is perfect and he follows the sounds. But he does not yet have the mental capacity to understand language. Would you care to venture a diagnosis?"

"The first thought that comes to mind," Daulby said, "is that he may be a recovering coma patient. He exhibits indicators of being in PVS—Persistent Vegetative State—principally the semi-consciousness with vacant affect. But, conversely, he shows no evidence of the repetitive reflex movements that are typical of PVS. He also seems to exhibit an unusual degree of purposeful motility."

Daulby shook his head. "I've never encountered a condition like this."

"There is something else unusual about Vehicle 27," Langwein said. "How old would you estimate him to be?"

Daulby approached the patient, who turned and stared at him with no change in facial expression. He was used to the vacant expressions of coma patients, but there was something unsettling about the utter blankness of this one, something he found oddly repulsive.

Daulby held an index finger in front of the patient's nose, and the eyes converged to focus on it. He moved the finger, and the eyes tracked it to the left, then to the right, up, down.

The skin was white, as if it had never been in the sun—unlined, unmarked by a scar, a freckle, or even an enlarged pore. The hands were as soft and uncreased as those of a baby.

"He is a very unusual specimen," Daulby said at last. "At first, judging from his size, I guessed between ages 10 and 12. But there is something in the face . . . this is not the face of a child. The moustache and beard stubble suggest that he has entered puberty. I'm picking up contradictory indicators. His skin is exceptionally fresh, almost like that of a new-born. How long has he been hospitalized?"

"Vehicle Twenty-seven has been with us about a year. That would make him one year old. Or six months, depending on what point you measure from."

Thinking Rausch misunderstood, Daulby repeated, "But how old is he?"

"As I said, one year from inception, six months past full physical development."

"What are you telling me?"

"Vehicle 27 is an exact replica of Tedi Beckwith, the AIDS patient whom you met a few minutes ago on Ward A."

Tedi: Have you seen the new me, doc? The new me they've got waiting for me upstairs.

MOVING VEGETABLE

"*EXACT GENETIC REPLICA?* You're telling me that— that this is a *clone* of Tedi Beckwith? But this *can't* be Tedi's clone. This is an adult, there wouldn't have been time—"

"That is *not* what I said, doctor. You jumped too quickly to an assumption. I did *not* say it was a *clone*. This is *not* a clone, not at all."

"Then what the hell is it?"

"An *engineered Vehicle*. We did not *clone* Vehicle 27, we *engineered* it."

"I don't understand what you're telling me."

Rausch and Langwein withdrew to a corner of the lab for a whispered conference.

Daulby continued to stare at Vehicle 27 as it spooned jello into its mouth. He was fascinated by the creature, yet appalled.

He was familiar enough with what had been done in the fields of tissue and organ engineering and regenerative medicine. Human noses, ears, skin, blood, cartilage even bones had been grown in labs, then moved onto living humans. In many cases, the new growth came from cells donated by the ultimate recipient, so there wasn't the issue of organ rejection.

In some of these projects, the living cells had been grown in dishes, then spread over a biodegradable "scaffold" that provided shape while the cells grew and form, then dissolved away.

In other cases, viable human organs had been grown in pigs and sheep, and work was under-way, perhaps already even performed, to implant those organs into humans.

But never had he heard, even rumors, of a full array of human organs being grown and then pulled together into a viable, moving whole that, at least physically, resembled a full human being.

RAUSCH AND LANGWEIN RETURNED, but were silent, staring at him.

To fill the silence, Daulby felt compelled to say, "It's remarkable, amazing, what you've done. But it strikes me that Tedi, as sick as he is, is a human being—a thinking, talking human being. But this, this—"

He stopped, unable to come up with a word to describe the vacant creature staring idly at his empty dish.

"You are perhaps trying to say that the Vehicle seems to be nothing more than a moving vegetable, yes?" Langwein offered.

Daulby nodded. "Something like that."

"Speak freely. You will not offend us. Indeed, at this point, Vehicle 27 *is* nothing more than a moving vegetable. As someone else phrased it, the Vehicles are 'bodies without souls.'"

Langwein paused. Daulby had so many questions that he didn't know where to begin. Finally he said, "But this—this *creature* —seems barely aware of us, of his environment. It's a human *body*, but is there human *consciousness* there?"

"Ah, consciousness," Rausch said with what seemed to be mock respect. "But what *is* this phenomenon we term consciousness? Is it memory?"

"Memory is part of it, of course. Along with insight—self-awareness. Personality. A variety of factors."

"Exactly, so," Langwein said, "and soon, with your assistance, Tedi will move his CE—our abbreviation for 'Conscious Essence'—into this Vehicle. Then you will see the Vehicle change from vegetable to full human."

"With *my* assistance? I don't —"

"The cell samples from which we began cloning the Vehicle brains weighed only a few grams," Langwein said. "In the course of replicating the brain, those cells multiplied millions of times. With the benefit of hindsight, perhaps we were asking the impossible to expect that the memories and education could survive that much cell dilution."

Langwein paused to clean his glasses, and Rausch spoke: "For a time it seemed that all of our work had been wasted. After all, of what use was an exact copy that was mindless?"

"Of no use at all," Langwein answered for him.

"Then we learned of your work in planting the seeds of memory."

"Seeds of memory. But I don't see how—"

HE WAS INTERRUPTED by the ringing of a red telephone on the wall. Rausch and Langwein froze in place for a moment. "Not now!" Dr. Langwein exclaimed. "Not now! It must not be so soon!"

THE SEEDS OF MEMORY

DR. RAUSCH picked up the red phone. The others sat, silent, frozen in place. Rausch listened a moment, his face grave. "Then you must bring him to the operating room now, and prepare him for brain surgery."

He jiggled the receiver, then dialed another number. "Bring Vehicle 27 to the OR at once, and see that he also is prepped for brain surgery. There will be a double operation."

He hung up the phone, then turned back to the others. "Tedi Beckwith suffered cardiac arrest a few moments ago. They defibrillated and restarted, but he is failing rapidly. We must operate immediately."

Rausch then turned to Daulby. "This is very short notice, I realize, but you will lead the operating team."

"*Operate*? You recruited me to come for ten days, to consult. Nothing was said about operating. For that matter, what *is* the operation? What's to be done? I have no idea."

"We had naturally planned more time for you to become oriented," Langwein said. "But Tedi does not have the luxury of time. For him, it is now or never."

Daulby hesitated, Langwein said, "Our Dr. Von Schwalbenbach is himself a very skilled neurosurgeon, and will be working alongside you, learning from you."

"Then Dr. Von Schwalbenbach should lead the operation. He's familiar with the surgical team and equipment in place here."

"But you are the innovator. You lead the world in this work. Von Schwalbenbach needs to learn from you."

"We must be realistic," Rausch added. "Without your help, Tedi will be dead in 24 hours, perhaps less. But if you operate, and it is the success I am confident it will be, then you can take satisfaction in having given Tedi a new life, a bright, shining new opportunity."

He shrugged. "But even if Tedi does not survive, then at least you will have given meaning to his life."

"*I* am to give meaning to Tedi's life? How?"

"By enabling him to make a contribution to our work."

"Just what is it you want from me?" Daulby said, groping for a way out.

Rausch stared at him, his eyes unblinking. "But, doctor, you of all people should understand, because it was your work that prepared the way for what we are about to do."

It seemed as if the floor suddenly slanted away beneath his feet, and Daulby grabbed the edge of a table to steady himself. "My work had nothing to do with this, nothing at all."

"The short article you wrote in *Discover* magazine intrigued us, and—"

"*Discover*! But that was just . . . just a speculative piece, just playing with ideas."

"Oh, we read your other writings, your professional papers, of course. But when we saw your visionary article in *Discover* we began looking at the work you were doing in transplanting the seeds of memory—most recently in the case of Chimp Donnie."

THE SEEDS OF MEMORY. The insight that shaped most of Daulby's research over the past decade had come to him one Saturday night during emergency surgery.

He had been called in to treat a gunshot wound to the head, a messy injury with chunks of bone, hair, and hat pulled into the brain with the bullet. All that foreign matter had to be removed before he could begin repairing the damage. Hopelessly damaged brain tissue had to go, as well.

But as little brain tissue as possible. He was debriding the area, suctioning away the junk, when the old brain-surgeons' joke came to mind: "Oops! I took too much—there went the guy's eighth grade! Oops! I just sucked away high school!"

But that's not true at all! Daulby had suddenly realized, pulling the suction away to think through the implications. If Karl Pribram is right, then high school could not be sucked away, because the learning from high school was like a *hologram—everywhere* in the brain, not at any specific spot.

It went back to the old question, Where were memories stored? In the brain, so it seems. At least that was what everyone took for granted.

But exactly where in the brain is a specific memory? Is there a precise spot a surgeon can point to and say, "There—those cells hold your mental map for the route to grandmother's house, and the cells over here on the other side contain the French you learned in high school?"

Lashley's experiments, going back a half-century, found that parts of the brains of rats could be cut away in stages, yet so long as any trace of the brain remained, they retained memories of the mazes they had learned. It seemed that there could be no "place" in the brain for a mental map, yet the rats, with barely any brain-matter left, somehow still retained that map.

The result remained a puzzle until Karl Pribram, a professor of neuroscience at Stanford, proposed that memories are like holographic images. Cut away a part of a holographic slide, and the part that remains will still contain the image of the whole, not just the half that remains.

Thus, Pribram suggested, perhaps as in a hologram, every portion of the brain (no matter how small the trace) carries the memories stored in the whole brain.

But if Pribram is right, Daulby had thought as he stood holding the suction unit in the operating room that Saturday night, then I don't really need to be concerned with suctioning away this patient's high school, because high school is in the hologram—which suggests that those memories are everywhere in the brain, and not at any specific spot.

The learning acquired in high school, or the ability to ride a bike, or the how-to of baking a cake, or the memories from a honeymoon, would remain somewhere in the brain even if we were to suction away half or more of the volume. The recall might be weaker than before, so it might take more effort or more prompting to remember. But the memories would still be there.

From that point, the next step—an enormous leap—was obvious: it should be possible to move memories from one brain to another.

If Pribram's theory was right, that *every portion of the brain held the potential of all of its memories*, then perhaps by transplanting tissue samples from Art's brain to Barbara's, then Barbara could "recall" Art's memories and learning.

Spread perhaps a dozen of these tissue specimens in corresponding areas of the brain of the recipient. Plant them like seeds, knowing that a gram of brain tissue contains as many interconnections among its neurons as all the telephone systems in the world, put together. Before long, the brain cells from each insertion would grow outward, "wiring" themselves into the new brain as the neurons of the implant interconnected with those of the host.

The seeds of memory.

Other researchers had tried, with some success, to implant human stem cells into brain tissue to help rebuild the areas damaged by stroke. But those stem cells were "blank"—raw tissue, with no memories attached. Daulby was the only one to suggest seeding memories.

He had been taking a step in pursuing those explorations the night he tried moving human fetal tissue to Chimp Donnie. Although the tissue of the human fetus had no memories to carry across, success in transferring language capabilities to the chimpanzee would open the door to further research on his insight.

MERE LEGALISMS

"TEDI HAS only a weak hold on life," Langwein said. "He could die at any moment. Remember what he told you when you met: he is counting on you, Dr. Daulby, to give him another chance at life. He is terminal, as you saw for yourself. He has nothing to lose, and a new life to gain if we are successful."

"I still don't understand what you want me to do."

Rausch stared at him, then finally said. "Ah, but I think by now you do understand. You have suggested that the brain is like a hologram, that memories are everywhere in the brain, not just in one isolated place. We want you to move some samples from Tedi to his Vehicle, Vehicle 27. In short, we want you to transfer tissue from the brain of Tedi Beckwith to the cloned brain of his Vehicle, as a way of planting the seeds of Tedi's memory in his new body."

"But moving tissue from Tedi, a living person, to that—the Vehicle. There are ethical—"

"Tedi is dying. You heard him for yourself. He has no interest in mere legalisms, his concern is on having another chance at living."

"But has the patient—"

Rausch cut him off. "A life is at stake, doctor. There is no more time for academic discussions. We must act now if we are to give Tedi the second chance at life he so desperately wants."

What the hell have I gotten myself into? How do I get out?

WHILE THE PATIENTS were being prepped for surgery, Daulby found his way to the dining room, set up cafeteria-style during the day, and made himself a salad and sandwich.

He'd lost count of how many hours since he'd last been in a bed, back in the States, in Florida —was it only yesterday morning? —when Rausch had called with the offer.

He took the food out to the broad terrace overlooking the lake, and settled at a table in the sun where he had a view across the rich blue lake to the mountains beyond. A small tour boat passed a few hundred yards offshore, slicing perfect waves in the glass-still water. He looked more closely. Not a tour boat, a military boat, with guns.

But he couldn't get the empty eyes of Vehicle 27 out of his mind.

He was stuck in a Damned-if-you-do and Damned-if-you-don't. The medical ethicists were still arguing over what was permissible with clusters of artificially-inseminated eggs: could the left-overs be reused for other experiments, or should they be destroyed?

But Vehicle 27 was a lot more than just a cluster of cells in a lab; Vehicle 27 was, to all appearances, a fully-formed human. Except that it was mentally vacant. It was a Vehicle, a body, as Rausch put it, without a soul. Or a mind. What were the ethics of experimenting on that?

The thing to do, the right thing, the *smart* thing would be to walk away. Refuse to have anything to do with this bizarre work.

But that was easier said than done. What if I were to refuse? Gerda said that this place is "a secure research facility." Meaning the gates are locked, apparently to keep me in as much as to keep others out.

A secure research facility. With, apparently, its own code of ethics—that there *are* no ethical limits.

And I'm already stuck in it, about to get immersed up to my neck.

Daulby tried to eat, but had no appetite. The view, down the grassy slope to the lake and the mountains behind, was spectacular, but his mind was filled with the pleading eyes of Tedi, and the spooky, empty eyes of Tedi's Vehicle.

Other staff-members passed by his table, ignoring him to sit at the larger tables, where the conversations were in German.

One other person sat alone, a tall, lean woman in a pink silk jogging suit, who seemed to be staring at him. He picked up anger in her expression before she looked away.

He finally got some salad down, then stood to go back to the operating room. He glanced over and again caught the woman staring at him.

TEMPLE

DAULBY WAS SURPRISED to find that the clinic's facilities were nearly as well-equipped as he'd used at the University Hospital, with a state-of-the-art operating room, as well as CT, PET, and MRI scanning equipment. He wondered how a place as remote as this, tucked away in the middle of nowhere, could afford such an array of state-of-the-art equipment.

While they scrubbed, Rausch introduced him to the other neurosurgeon on staff, Jose Von Schwalbenbach, a dour man of 45 or 50 with swarthy skin and incongruously flaxen blond hair. A strange combination of genes, it struck Daulby. A strange combination of names, as well: Jose—you can't get much more Spanish than that— along with a barely-pronounceable Germanic surname.

Von Schwalbenbach bore a short, deep curving scar on his cheek. It reminded Daulby of photos of the dueling scars prized by German university students before the war. But hadn't dueling and dueling scars gone out of fashion when the Nazi era ended? In any case, Von Schwalbenbach was nowhere near that old.

As he briefed Daulby on the set-up, Von Schwalbenbach made no attempt to disguise his resentment of Daulby's presence.

But that seemed natural enough. Daulby knew he'd feel the same way if he'd been the one bumped aside by a newcomer. You had to be an egomaniac to be a brain surgeon. If you didn't believe you were a unique gift to the human race, then you had no business cutting into a living brain.

A PAIR OF TABLES had been set up, head-to-head in the operating room. Tedi was on one. His clone, Vehicle 27, on the other. The heads of both were held firmly in place with metal braces.

Fresh MRI and CAT images, prepared while the surgical team was scrubbing, gave Daulby exact maps of both brains, so he could remove the small plugs of brain tissue from Tedi's brain, pivot to the other table, and position them in the precisely corresponding position in the brain of the cloned Vehicle.

He worked on Tedi, while Von Schwalbenbach led the team working on the Vehicle. It was virtually the same set-up as that last time at the University.

He opened the skull, lifted the bone out, then cut through the dura. Von Schwalbenbach had been keeping pace with the Vehicle, so they were ready simultaneously.

At Daulby's signal, Von Schwalbenbach stepped aside, the anger in his eyes visible even behind the mask and protective goggles.

From this point, timing was crucial. Brain tissue could survive at most four minutes deprived of oxygen: after that, it was useless. The window of opportunity might be even shorter with brain tissue from someone as far gone as Tedi.

Daulby measured off ten insertion points in the brain of the Vehicle, then pivoted and did the same with Tedi's brain.

Working through a magnifier, he teased away the first specimen from the verbal cortex on the left side of Tedi's own brain. Each specimen was the size of a pea, weighing about a gram.

He pivoted again to the other table, and fitted the implants into the corresponding point in the soft matter of the cortex of the Vehicle, then sutured the new tissue into place. The thread was too fine to be visible to the human eye, and he worked through a magnifier. Each plug required only two stitches. The tissues would begin growing together within hours.

AS HE WORKED, Daulby again felt the sense of awe that overwhelmed him each time he opened a skull and observed a living human brain.

In its three pounds of wet tissue were packed 100 billion nerve cells, which interconnected with each other through 100,000 miles of dendritic branches, to form 10 trillion synaptic connections, capable of storing an estimated one quadrillion bits of information.

He'd read, years back, that a computer capable of approximating the memory and computing power of a single human brain would require a building as large as the state of Texas, and 100 stories high. But computers had shrunken since then, even as their power increased: perhaps now, to match the power of one human brain, a computer would only need to be 50 stories high, and only as large as Pennsylvania.

Two hundred different neurochemicals operated within the brain as its personal chemical messengers. Every second, 100,000 different chemical reactions were taking place within the brain, without any need for conscious intention by the brain's owner.

Most marvelous of all, the brain managed itself automatically, beginning to "rewire" itself within seconds to reflect new learning, or to repair damage.

One of Daulby's professors of neurosurgery had once said, "When I operate on a human brain, I feel like a priest privileged to worship in a temple."

Daulby had quoted it to his own students each year, back before he'd lost his professorship.

SUMMONS

WHEN THE OPERATION finished, Rausch called Parsons Couldsen with a report on the operations on Tedi and his Vehicle.

They had matching scramblers so the call was secure. "This phase is a success," Rausch said, as soon as Couldsen came on the line. "Tedi's brain tissue has been moved, and both he and his Vehicle are doing well. Now we must wait for—"

"Here's what I want you to do," Couldsen cut in. "Once I heard the operation was a Go, I arranged for you to fly over here to show me the videos. The pilots are on alert, waiting to hear from me. I'll call them now, and—"

"You ask me to fly there! Impossible! It is already night here," Rausch said. "I was there only yesterday. I have had a very long and difficult day, and there is much other work to be done."

"As I was saying, the plane will be at that little airport near you in an hour to pick you up. You can grab some shut-eye on the way over, and I'll have one of my cars waiting to bring you to the Farm. We can have a late dinner, talk some, then you head back."

"That is absurd! My place is—"

"Understand this," Couldsen said. "I'm paying the bills, and your place is wherever in hell I damned well say it is!"

Rausch choked back his anger. They were so close now. Soon Couldsen would be irrelevant.

"We're what? Six, seven hours behind you here, so if you leave in an hour it'll still be only nine, ten at night here when you arrive. I'll take a rest now, be fresh when you arrive. We can talk a couple of hours, you'll be off again at midnight, and back at Hauenfelder early tomorrow afternoon. You can sleep both ways on the plane."

"All this takes me away from—"

"It's not just Tedi we need to talk about. First of all, our team — the investors— they've been making noises about going over there to see the progress."

"They will be a distraction, a very grave— "

"And there's something else. Seems a little problem has developed on my end."

"Problem?"

"Things aren't so good with me. I'm not feeling up to par. Saw my doc this morning. We're going to have to push the schedule forward. Forward a whole hell of a lot. Fast. Because if I die, then your project dies."

Couldsen paused. Now he didn't look so tired and sick, and he added, "And you, and your whole goddam team, will die. I've seen to that."

THE NEXT PHASE

COULDSEN FARM

Couldsen Farm, Virginia.

It was ten that night, east coast time, four in the morning in central Europe, when the Citation jet carrying Dr. Rausch landed in central Virginia. A limo came out onto the tarmac for him, and swept him across through winding country roads to Couldsen Farm.

Couldsen pulled himself to his feet when Rausch was escorted in, then walked over to shake hands.

Rausch knew that one of Couldsen's strengths was the ability to make you feel that you are the most important person on earth. At their first meetings, nearly a decade ago, he had assumed that Couldsen's apparent fascination was real and personal, and reflected respect for himself and his work.

Then he saw how easily Couldsen could turn that attention on and off. When Couldsen lost interest, which could happen in an instant, you ceased to exist in his world. For that ability to charm, then turn, Couldsen had been dubbed The Smiling Serpent.

That was just one more reason that Rausch hated Couldsen. But he couldn't let that show—not yet, not while the research still depended on Couldsen's funding.

A black steward in a starched white jacket brought herbal tea in a silver carafe. The mugs bore one of Couldsen's favorite "Couldsenisms," a line he had snapped off without thinking at a staff meeting, then found he liked enough to adopt as a kind of internal corporate slogan:

When You've Got Their Brains Caught in the Tube,
Their Hearts and Balls Are Sure to Follow!

"Well?" Couldsen said, pouring himself a cup of the herbal tea his doctor allowed. "What's the status?"

"I have some very good news," Rausch said. He slid a disk into the player.

"It'd better be good news, because I've got some damned bad news for you."

The tape opened with a shot of Tedi Beckwith the day before the operation, emaciated, barely able to speak. Then it switched to several scenes of Tedi's Vehicle, Vehicle 27, working out on the exercise machinery at Hauenfelder, obviously a superb physical specimen. But even in the video, the Vehicle's eyes were vacant, his movements like those of a sleep-walker.

When it moved on to the operation, Couldsen took the remote control and fast-forwarded the tape. "Spare me the goddam blood and gore." He paused the tape to check that the faces were those he expected: Tedi, Tedi's Vehicle, Dr. Daulby.

"Okay, I'm satisfied," Couldsen said when the tape finished. "Looks like you guys are finally moving. The question is, How soon do we find out if it's really going to do the trick for this Tedi character?"

"As soon as Tedi and his Vehicle recover from anesthesia. Dr. Remington will begin working with them tomorrow to guide the transfer of the Conscious Essence from the old, Donor body to the Vehicle."

"AS I SAID, there's another reason I brought you over," Couldsen said, a little later. "To give you some bad news. You're going to have to move faster— a hell of a lot faster."

"Scientific revolutions cannot be forced."

"Fact is, you're making progress just in time," Couldsen continued. "It seems that my heart is deteriorating faster than they thought it would— that's what my cardiac guy is telling me. I can feel it myself. The time has come for you and your crew to quit screwing around and start producing— while I'm still around."

"It is too early for you. The process is still experimental."

It seemed too early to risk operating on Couldsen until the methodology had been refined. The plan had been to run at least a dozen AIDS patients through the full cycle. But if he was declining this rapidly, there was obviously not going to be time for that level of testing.

"Too early? Hell, if you don't get a move on, it's going to be too late to do me any damned good. Keep in mind that if my heart stops, your money stops."

"There will be questions when you adopt your supposed bastard son."

"Leave me to deal with the other problems. Just you focus on speeding things up. Move faster with those goddam queers you're keeping in your private zoo. That's what they're there for, to be guinea pigs, so let'em earn their keep.

DREAMS

Take me to the cannibal, Daddy. Please!

Jenny's words tear at him, but it's too late to change things now. Jenny and Jackie are already at the carnival. He should have gone with them. But now he can't.

He pushes the thoughts away and forces himself to focus on the tiny creature on the operating table. Chimp Donnie.

The implants are in place, and he is fitting the piece of skull back into Chimp Donnie's head when the phone rings in the OR. Betty Reed takes the phone call. They are short-staffed tonight—just the core team, for security— so work pauses for the moment.

"Oh God!" she says, stumbling back against the wall. She looks across at Daulby, the color draining from her face. "It's for you, Dr. Daulby. It's about your wife."

"A divorce lawyer at this time of the night?" Daulby jokes, hiding his concern.

"It isn't that. Two policemen are outside to see you."

"Jesus! Get that fetal tissue out of sight," Martinson says. "Don't let the cops see that."

"That—that's not the problem," Betty says, slumping against the wall. "They found your wife's car, and she's—she and Jenny—Oh God!"

He dragged himself out of bed, threw on a coat, and went out to sit on the balcony. Another damned dream, another in the series that had haunted him all these months, since the murders.

Now the dreams were worse than ever, even more vivid. Like this one, an exact damned replay of that final night before his life shattered.

PHASE TWO

"YOU NEED THE OPERATION quickly, but is the paperwork finished for Couldsen II?" Rausch asked.

The steward had served a light dinner, the usual tasteless mix of rice, steamed vegetables, and fish. The joke at Hauenfelder was that even the worst prisons served tastier and more varied food than Couldsen was allowed. But tonight Rausch found no humor in it tonight: when dining with Couldsen, everyone was confined to his diet.

For lack of a better name, they were referring to Couldsen's new Vehicle as Couldsen II. No one had yet thought through the etiquette of naming a clone.

Couldsen snapped open a briefcase, and handed Rausch a thin file. "It's all set. My people found a bastard kid born in New Zealand whose date of birth fitted with one of my visits down there. The kid died a year later, over in another part of the country. I sent my man, Mr. Jenkins, down to take care of the situation. He stole the death certificate out of the courthouse files. Then he found the mother and shut her up."

So that makes victim number 15 for Mr. Jenkins, on this project alone, Rausch thought. How many others has Jenkins killed for Couldsen? More to the point, is Jenkins careful enough? Can he be relied upon to cover his tracks?

"This is the scenario," Couldsen continued. "When word gets out that I've been operated on for a brain tumor, the price of shares in Couldsen Communications will drop to hell and gone. After the stock has bottomed out, I'll hold a press conference acknowledging him—my clone, my Vehicle— as my illegitimate son from New Zealand. If they want to bother checking, they'll see the birth certificate from 21 years ago. If they go looking for the mother, they'll find she died a few months back in an accident— what *looked* like an accident. They'll never think to look for a death certificate for the real kid, since he'll obviously be alive. Nobody will ever be able to trace a damned thing."

Couldsen took the file back from Rausch before he had a chance to look at it closely. "In short, to answer your question, the paperwork is finished. I've legally adopted him. My lawyers got it sealed so nobody but them and the judge knows about it. I adopted him in the name of the New Zealand kid, but later on I'll get his name legally changed to Parsons Couldsen, Junior."

Couldsen leaned back in the chair and chuckled. "Isn't that the damndest thing? I've created a valid identity for a damned clone, and now I'm about to turn him into a billionaire many times over!"

"I'LL PUT OUT A PRESS RELEASE," Couldsen continued, "and it'll say that as a result of my failing health, I'm appointing my adopted son to step into my shoes immediately and start running Couldsen Communications. That'll cause another panic. The stock markets, the hot-shot investors—they'll figure I've gone soft in the head because of the supposed brain tumor. They'll start selling Couldsen stocks like mad, and prices will drop some more. I'll leave standing orders to buy them all up. With a little luck, I'll probably get them at half of today's price."

Couldsen chuckled again. "Before long, they'll begin to see that Couldsen Junior is a chip off the old block, a goddam business genius. Then they'll start buying the stock again, but this time they'll be buying back from me, and paying through the nose for it. I'll triple, maybe quadruple, my net worth in no time. I'll go from $30 billion to $60, who knows? maybe even $90. Hell, the sky's the limit if I'm starting over again at 21 with all this savvy under my belt."

"You'll be richer than ever, and starting over at 21 with the lifetime savvy and wisdom of a man my age. It's everyone's dream. Just keep in mind—"

"I damned well do keep it in mind that you made it happen for me, you and your team. I appreciate that, and I'm going to reward you in a really big way. That's why we need to begin talking about Phase Two."

"Phase Two? There *is* no second phase. This is all we agreed on. You fund the research until we accomplish the transfer into your Vehicle. At that point, you give the Foundation an endowment sufficient to let the work continue indefinitely. That is the agreement we made. I expect you to follow through with that endowment, or . . ."
He left the sentence hanging.

"You'll get your funding, don't worry about it. Provided, of course, I live. Provided I survive long enough to make it across into Couldsen II." He paused until Rausch was forced to say that he understood that.

Then Couldsen said, "This Phase Two is a whole new deal I'm proposing. It's an opportunity I think you'll really want to be part of."

WHEN HE'D HEARD Couldsen's idea, Rausch sat back, stunned by the potential. Even if Hitler had succeeded beyond his wildest dreams, he wouldn't have had an opportunity like this: unlimited power for an unlimited number of years, lifetime after lifetime.

NEED TO KNOW

DAULBY SNAPPED AWAKE, terrified. He didn't know where he was, but there was someone in the room, someone who hated him. Someone evil. Someone who'd been harboring anger and malevolence for a long time, and was ready to vent it now.

He groped for the light, expecting blows to hit at any instant.

But there was no one there, no one he could see. But he still felt the malevolence.

He jumped out of the bed, and looked in the bathroom, the closets, balcony, even under the bed.

The door was locked, from the inside.

He settled back onto the bed, his heart still pounding, still aware of that presence, almost like a lingering odor.

AT DAWN, drained by nightmares and troubled sleep, he pulled himself out of bed, resolved to have nothing more to do with the Hauenfelder work. He'd return the consulting fee. Money didn't matter now, now there was no need to build up an education fund for Jenny. Just get the hell out of this place, fast.

He found Gerda already at her desk, and told her he needed to speak to Dr. Rausch immediately.

"But that is impossible. Dr. Rausch is unavailable, and I do not know when he will return."

"He's away? He was here yesterday, for the operation."

"So? He is not here now."

"Then I need to speak to whoever is in charge. Is that Dr. Langwein?"

"What is this concerning?"

"It's urgent."

"As I said, Dr. Rausch is away. You will be informed when he returns, and has the time to meet with you."

HE WENT UP to the Recovery Area to check on Tedi and his Vehicle, and found Langwein and Von Schwalbenbach already there.

"I need to talk to —"

"Yes, yes," Langwein said, again refusing to meet his eyes. "Gerda already phoned me. Dr. Rausch will talk to you, when he has time. Now we must focus on our patients, yes?"

Both Donor and Vehicle were doing well, despite heads that were heavily bandaged. Tedi was conscious, and his Vehicle showed the same kind of semi-conscious, dreamy awareness that it had when Daulby first saw it mindlessly eating jello.

Although the Vehicle now had the implants from Tedi's brain, there still seemed to be no sign of conscious awareness behind the eyes.

Daulby asked about that.

"The awakening of consciousness in the new Vehicle comes next in our process," Langwein replied. "That depends on the work of our Resident Witch, Dr. Remington. Today—"

"Did I hear you say 'resident witch'?"

"Ah! A small joke. Today she will begin helping Tedi's CE— is Conscious Essence—move across to the new Vehicle."

"Move his consciousness? How?"

"That is not your concern," Von Schwalbenbach snapped. His index finger reached up and caressed the dueling scar on his cheek. "As you have been told already, we operate at Hauenfelder on a need-to-know basis. You do not need to know anything more than what we choose to tell you."

EVEN MORE TROUBLING

AFTER A QUICK BREAKFAST, Daulby headed back to the recovery area, hoping to examine Tedi and his new Vehicle without Langwein and Von Schwalbenbach looking over his shoulder.

Now the room was empty: both Tedi and his Vehicle were gone, along with their beds, and the attending nurse had disappeared. He checked the chart: Dr. Von Schwalbenbach had signed both patients out to Dr. Remington.

He found Von Schwalbenbach in the dining room. "We decided that the time had come for Tedi to begin working with Dr. Remington," Von Schwalbenbach said.

"He's too weak for any kind of work. He needs rest."

"His contribution is more important than rest." Von Schwalbenbach stood and walked away.

Less than 24 hours ago, Rausch had persuaded him to lead the operation on Tedi, claiming that Tedi was hours from death. Now Tedi was well enough to "work," whatever that work entailed.

HE FINALLY TRACKED Tedi to Room 127 in the basement of the clinic. A technician in white appeared and blocked his way, then agreed to tell Dr. Remington that Daulby was there inquiring about his patient.

Daulby recalled Langwein's reference to Dr. Remington as "Hauenfelder's Resident Witch," and he waited, wondering what he would encounter. Why "witch?" Supposedly only a joke, but a joke with an edge. For whatever reason.

Minutes passed before a tall woman emerged, wearing a Wedgewood blue jogging suit. He recognized her from the cafeteria yesterday, the woman who'd been staring at him. She had seemed angry then, and still seemed hostile.

A witch in a jogging suit? A pair of large, dark-framed glasses rested in her long brown hair. He guessed she was perhaps 30, 32 at most. Why was she angry at someone she had never seen before?

"You're Dr. Daulby," she said with the warmth she might use in speaking to a bag of garbage.

He nodded. She didn't offer her hand, and seemed to keep a distance from him, even in the small room.

"I'm Kate Remington, Doctor Remington. We were at a crucial stage of the maneuver just then. What is it you want?"

She was American— that was a surprise, the only American he'd encountered here. With high cheekbones in a thin face, she was unusually attractive, with an almost luminous quality about her. He got no sense of the weirdness that seemed the norm among the others at Hauenfelder.

Yet she obviously loathed him on first sight.

"I went to check on my patient— rather, patients, plural, Tedi and his clone—correction, his 'Vehicle' in the jargon of this place. I found they had been signed out to you."

She stared at him for a moment, then turned and led the way through the door from which she had emerged. "He is here, yes. Both of him. Both versions of Tedi, old and new. I have some time now, I might as well show you now and get it over with."

IT LOOKED LIKE THE CONTROL ROOM of a radio station, with a microphone and an array of tape recorders set up below wide windows that overlooked a pair of adjacent rooms.

Tedi Beckwith lay on a bed in one of the darkened rooms, earphones fitted around his bandaged head, the IV drips still in place. He wore a sleep mask.

In the other room, Tedi's Vehicle lay in a bed, also wearing headphones and a sleep mask. Beside the bed was what seemed to be a large white plastic cylinder, about eight feet long and three or four feet high.

"That's Tedi himself in the bed in Room A. His Vehicle is in Room B. We're not using the flotation tank yet, of course."

"Flotation tank? Out of the question. We can't have water touching those fresh incisions."

"Agreed. Even Dr. Von Schwalbenbach agreed not to use the tank yet. That has to be the first time he's ever agreed with me on anything."

"I don't understand — why a flotation tank?"

"The flotation tank, in case you've never seen one, is that thing in the room that looks like a giant white cucumber. The plan is to use it as an environment to assist the donor in moving his CE—his Conscious Essence—across to the Vehicle. After, of course, the incisions have healed."

He waited for her to explain. Finally he said, "You're giving me credit for knowing more background than I do. Langwein told me you were beginning to move the Conscious Essence, whatever they mean by that—to the clone, to the Vehicle. But this patient—correct that, this *pair* of patients—just had surgery. They should be resting, not working with you."

"On that, at least, we agree," she said, again seeming to scrutinize him. "It definitely is too soon. But I didn't make the decision, nor was I consulted. Dr. Rausch has made it clear that there is no time to lose on this work."

She shrugged. "In any case, the guidance tape is running, and both of the Tedis will be finished here in about a half-hour. Then they can rest until the evening session."

He was silent, not knowing how to respond.

She stared at him, and he had the sense that was looking through him in search of some inner essence. "You really haven't been briefed on these things?"

"On none of this. My involvement was strictly with the surgery, and that only because it was an emergency."

"Emergency?" She shook her head. "That's not true, not at all. Tedi's operation has been planned for weeks, to take place as soon as you got here. It was hardly an emergency."

"As soon as I got here? That's . . . that is very peculiar. The first time I ever heard of this place was the day before yesterday, I think, when I was back in Florida. So how could they have been waiting for me?"

She stared at him. "I don't know. But I also find that disturbing. *Very* disturbing."

Her hostility seemed to have faded a little, now replaced by concern. But concern for what? "The red phone rang yesterday, when I was being oriented, and Dr. Rausch said an emergency operation was needed. I didn't feel I should be directly involved in the surgery, but . . . But they twisted my arm."

"You really have been kept in the dark, haven't you?"

"Yesterday was only my first full day here."

"What's your schedule for the next few hours?"

"Nothing, so far as I know."

"I'm free, as soon as I finish with Tedi. I can show you the tank, and brief you on at least that aspect of it—whether they like it or not. You should know what's happening in this place. Perhaps if we meet back here in an hour?"

He was down the hall when she called him to wait. "You referred to these as clones. They're not clones, you need to understand that. They haven't been *cloned*, they've been tissue *engineered* — as adults. Which I find even spookier. Even more troubling."

"ONE OTHER THING," he said. "Where are we?"

"Where *are* we? What do you mean?"

"I was told I was coming to Austria. I'm getting the sense this is not Austria."

"They told you that? That's what they told me, and then when I called them on it, Rausch said I had misunderstood the offer, that this was a place *like* Austria. They lied to us both."

"Then where *are* we? Do you know?"

"No one will tell me, but I *think* we're in a small country, one of the small elements in the former Soviet Union, one that apparently reverted to a dictatorship—a police state where everything is for sale."

NOT THE MONSTER

KATE REMINGTON stood at the door, watching Daulby as he walked back down the hall. He had not been at all what she expected.

A couple of weeks earlier, the staff had been briefed that he would be joining the Hauenfelder team. In the briefing, Rausch gave the background: Daulby had lost his position at the University Hospital because of his unauthorized experiment transferring aborted human fetal tissue to a chimp.

Kate had shuddered when she heard it. What a monstrous experiment! She was a member of PETA—People for the Ethical Treatment of Animals—and had demonstrated on behalf of whales, porpoises, and zoo animals, and against the use of animals as research subjects in testing cosmetics.

She could accept—with great reluctance—using animals for research on serious diseases. But Daulby's chimp-human experiment seemed to have no purpose other than to experiment for the sake of experimenting. The result, if it had been successful, would have been the development of a quasi-human — a very, very bad idea in her view.

Daulby will fit right in here, she'd thought back then when it was first announced that he would be coming to Hauenfelder. He'd been trying to develop one kind of quasi-humans, and Rausch and his crew are developing another kind. He and the Hauenfelder gang deserve each other, but the world doesn't deserve them.

That was what she felt then.

But the Doug Daulby she'd just met surprised her. He was not the monster she expected. He seemed pleasant enough, intelligent, and sad.

That sadness struck a chord with her.

In the staff briefing, Rausch had mentioned the murder of Daulby's wife and daughter, and how that event had caused Daulby's chimp-human experiment to be uncovered.

At the time, Kate had felt, Serves him right.

But now it was hard to hold any hostility toward him. I didn't ask for this to happen to Karen, and he didn't ask for his tragedy.

ACTING DIRECTOR

GERDA WAS WAITING for him when Daulby returned to the main floor after his talk with Kate Remington. "Where have you been, Doctor?"

"Downstairs. I went looking for my patient."

"You must call now to Dr. Langwein. He is in his office."

"Dr. Rausch is unavailable," Langwein said when Daulby phoned him back. "In his absence, I am acting director of the Clinic. You will report to me now."

"Report to you?" Daulby responded, not sure what he meant.

"Be in my office in five minutes."

Langwein's office was cluttered with piles of papers on every area of desk and shelf space, and most of one corner of the room.

"Given Dr. Rausch's absence, and the fact that we are waiting to see how well the operation on Tedi turned out, this is a good time to orient you to some of the other experimental work being carried on at the Clinic," Langwein said, then paused to clean his glasses on his necktie.

Daulby wondered if he wore the tie only to ensure that he had silk ready to indulge his obsession with clean glasses. Or did he clean the glasses just for the sake of something to do with his hands?

"Our plan," Langwein continued, staring at his desk, "was to begin your orientation this afternoon. However, it has come to my attention that you undertook to attempt this orientation on your own by venturing into areas that you have not been authorized to see."

Langwein still avoided eye contact, so it was hard to tell whether he was genuinely angry, or pretending anger to assert his power. Gerda was angry. Kate Remington had been angry. Is it something about this place?

"I went looking for my patient . . . rather the *pair* of patients, the two versions of Tedi. That's how I happened to meet Dr. Remington, because Tedi—and his clone, his Vehicle—were signed out to her. I happened to see the flotation tank. She offered me a tour, so I accepted."

I'm sounding defensive, he realized.

Langwein nodded. "Ah, the elusive Dr. Remington. Hauenfelder's Resident Witch."

"Resident Witch? You called her that before. Why? It may be an insider's joke, but there's a point to it."

Langwein flicked a quick glance at him before his eyes again darted away. "Because she is in charge of what one might call the *occult* side of our endeavors."

"Occult?"

"You are surprised that I use the term? It should be no surprise. After all, our work straddles the filmy border-line between the leading edge of medical science and what is often referred to as the occult."

Daulby stared at him, unable to formulate a response. True, Hauenfelder was at the leading edge of science in several areas. First, tissue engineering, not just of individual organs but of entire bodies. Now, with his help, neurosurgery. But for Langwein to speak of the occult as only a small step further along the continuum from established science? Absurd. "I find occult a peculiar word for a scientist to be using."

Langwein leaned back in his chair and smiled. "Someone once defined the occult as occurrences for which the scientific establishment has not yet discovered the reasons."

"How does your so-called Resident Witch fit into that?"

"Our Resident Witch works her magic by guiding the Conscious Essence, or 'soul,' or 'personality,' or whatever term you prefer, in moving from the old body to animate the new one."

SENSORY DEPRIVATION

KATE REMINGTON apologized when Daulby returned to Room 127. "Unfortunately, a problem has arisen with one of my other patients so I can't be here during your time in the tank." The hard edge of hostility seemed to be gone.

"Tank? That's news to me. What kind of tank?"

"A flotation tank, like the one you saw earlier. I assumed Dr. Langwein had briefed you."

"He didn't explain much, just chewed me out for talking to you without his permission."

"Ah, this place." She shook her head, and he detected a trace of a smile. "They're all petty tyrants, they're all *crazy*. There's no better word for it."

She giggled, then cut it off. "Instant psychoanalysis. In any case, it's up to you whether you want to do the exercise in the tank. Though it *is* a very interesting experience."

He shrugged. "I do have a choice?"

"As far as I'm concerned you do. Though I'm not in charge . . . *far from it*. I'd suggest rescheduling so I could be present, but now Dr. Langwein has gotten himself involved, and any changes in the schedule would get him bent out of shape."

"I'm here, let's do it." Hold off on making waves until it really matters.

She introduced him to her technician, Hans-Georg, the one who had blocked him earlier. He was in his mid-20's, chubby and soft, with a face so pale it seemed he never left the basement. His long blond hair flapped in his face. As soon as he swept it back with his hand, the hair slid down across his eyes again.

Daulby asked what he should expect in the tank.

"It's best to let you discover that for yourself," she said. "Instead, let me leave with you some questions to ponder. First question: What makes the difference between the real Doug Daulby sitting here, and one of the empty Vehicles upstairs?"

He paused, trying to come up with the words. "I suppose 'consciousness' is the best word."

"What's involved in consciousness?"

91

"Personality. Intelligence. Memories and experiences. Whatever it is that energizes the body."

"Where is that 'whatever' located? Where is your consciousness, your personality? Is there a spot where it's primarily centered?"

"In the head, obviously."

She smiled. "Why is it so *obviously* there?"

What was it about Hauenfelder, he wondered, that generated these bizarre discussions? "Because that's where the brain is. Consciousness is a function of the operation of the brain."

"'Consciousness flows from the brain?' Why not from the heart, or the spine, or the big toe?"

"What's your point?"

"For that matter, how can you be sure that consciousness isn't something outside the body that steps in and uses the brain— in the same way that a person sits down at a computer, logs in, and taps into its memory?"

"I'd have to give that some thought."

She stood. "I think you're going to have an interesting morning."

HANS-GEORG led the way to an adjoining room, dominated by the white fiberglass flotation tank.

It really does look like a giant white plastic cucumber, Daulby thought, recalling Kate's description. Or like a midget blimp.

He opened the hatch at one end of the cucumber: a shallow bathtub sat under the canopy formed by the fiberglass. "This is a flotation tank, based on work begun by Dr. John Lilly in America," Hans-Georg said. "Do you know Dr. Lilly?"

Daulby nodded. "I've heard of his work. But it's out of the mainstream."

From the 1960's onward, in *The Center of the Cyclone* and later books, John Lilly had written of his development of the flotation tank, and the series of experiments he and others had undertaken as they developed what evolved into the flotation tank. They had used the tank in some of the early LSD experiments.

"Have you ever been in a flotation tank?"

"Never even seen one before."

"It is a sensory deprivation chamber. You will float in unusually buoyant water saturated with sea-salts, heated to match your body temperature. You will have no sense of gravity, and it will be very dark, as dark as the darkest night, so you will see nothing. You will lose awareness of your body. Dr. Lilly and others have reported very unusual experiences once the senses stop sending input to the brain."

"What kinds of experiences?"

"Some have said it is like being a mind without a body. But it is best for you to be open to whatever may come. Our approach, here at Hauenfelder, is somewhat unusual. You will not experience total sensory deprivation. Instead, you will be receiving certain input through your sense of hearing."

"Input?"

"You will hear music, very faintly."

"Why the music? Why not total sensory shut-off?"

"Because zis is our procedure," Hans-Georg said stiffly, his German accent coming through more strongly for a moment.

"There is one other matter," he added. "Dr. Langwein talked to you about Out-of-Body Experiences—OBE's—yes?"

"I'm familiar with the term, but no, he hasn't talked to me about it. I haven't really been briefed."

Hans-Georg looked at him for an instant, then said, "Well, so. In any event, if you travel out of your body, you will want some objective evidence to prove that you have actually been out of your physical body, and not merely imagined doing so. Thus we have devised a simple test, based on the work of Dr. Charles Tart and others."

"I'm to travel out of my body?"

"Yes, perhaps so, if you are lucky," Hans-Georg said, then opened a file cabinet, and motioned to Daulby to select one of the large envelopes lined up in one of the drawers. He chose one, and Hans Georg pulled a large white card from it, told Daulby to sign the back side, which was blank. Then he slid it onto a small shelf just below the ceiling.

"You were not able to read what was on the front of that card, were you, Dr. Daulby?"

"No."

"Nor was I. Thus no one knows what the card contains. Each of these envelopes contains a card with a different combination of letters and numerals. Do you understand?"

Daulby nodded, wondering what the point was.

"Therefore, when you pass out of your body, you must try to read what is written on that card."

"I'm supposed to read that card while I'm here in the tank? How am I going to pull *that* off?"

"I think you will understand once you begin the experiment."

"How long will I be in the tank?"

"That is up to you. Now you must shower and enter the tank."

TRAVELS

THE DOOR OF THE TANK closed over him, and Daulby felt a flash of panic—claustrophobia, mixed with a flash of the pain he'd felt when he saw the closed coffins that held Jackie and Jenny.

Then he relaxed, feeling the peace of total darkness, total silence. Yet it was cozy in a way, and he realized that it was also a lot like being in the womb: it was warm and dark, with his body bathed in comforting warm liquids.

Before long, he lost awareness of his body, and was no longer conscious of the water. It seemed as if his body had dissolved— as if he had left the body behind, as if he were now pure mind, unfettered by a physical body.

Music begins softly. It seems to come from within his head. It sounds Oriental, something like a harp playing far away, as if drifting on the wind from the next mountain—a great jagged snow-capped mountain floated past.

Or did he float past the mountain? It didn't matter.

No, not a harp. A flute, but like no flute he has heard before; softer, warmer, more like a wooden clarinet in its lower register holding a single deep tone that seems to resonate within his core, and he is drifting through a lush green jungle.

Lush. Warm. Languid. Ripe green, green flecked with spots of color. Huge tropical flowers, red, violet, pink.

He drifts into the petal of one of the pink flowers, and enters a pink, peaceful world that shimmers softly, and tastes of ripe mango— mango and strawberry and the pink glow in the dawn sky just before sunrise— feeling, seeing, tasting, and smelling all blended into one experience.

He looks again, and sees there is no petal to blend into, no substance at all, no physical matter, only a feeling of energy, of a soft pink energy that envelopes him.

He floats back into the sunlight. The sunlight feels pink and yellow and blue, and it's like drifting through a rainbow.

It seems he can inhale the light, and it tastes of lilacs and baking bread and the warm cozy feeling of a fireplace after a day of skiing.

Skiing a long white trail down the mountain. Skiing through a stand of pine trees, some of the trees dark green, others vivid pink. The scents of pine and jasmine and new-mown hay hang heavy in the crisp, snowy mountain air.

After leaving the pine trees, the trail runs straight for a while through glowing white virgin snow. His skis cut cleanly through the snow with a soft hissing, a hissing that blends with the sound of a thousand harps and flutes holding a single soft note until the trail dips sharply away.

A voice says "Lift out," and he watches himself skiing away through the snow while he hangs weightlessly in the air watching his body floating below the white canopy of the floatation tank.

He drifts up to look at the shelf, but what's on the card doesn't matter to him now. He passes into the next room and sees Hans-Georg reading a magazine.

I should go to my room, he thinks. The stairs and hallways pass as a blur, and he is in his suite here at the Clinic. He is surprised to see Gerda there. She looks up quickly, as if startled by a noise. She glances nervously around the room, then goes back to checking through the clothes hanging in his closet.

He notices a manila envelope on the desk which had not been there when he left the room earlier.

The hallways blur past, and he finds himself in front of one of the patient wards. But he feels strangely reluctant to pass through the door. The ward exudes a forbidding chill. He sticks his arm through the door, and pulls it back quickly. The arm feels icy now. It seems to carry an odor, a faint stench of decay.

He doesn't want to be there any longer. Back in my office, he decides, and he is soaring now, out of the clinic, across a cobalt-blue lake, over the snow-capped Alps.

HE IS IN HIS OFFICE at the University, in Chicago, but the room is different now. Different furniture, and different books fill the shelves. He sees a new fern by the window and a battered leather sofa that wasn't there when the room was his.

A man sits at the desk, reading a book. He moves into the man, assuming it is himself. The man jerks around in the chair as if he has been hit. Daulby sees that the man is Bob Perkins, from Oncology.

So old Perkins has taken it over. Good for him. At least now he has an office with a window.

It's time to head home for dinner, and he thinks how nice it will be to see Jackie, and maybe play a game with Jenny before tucking her into bed and reading her a story. That'll be good: there hasn't been enough time for stories lately.

He is in the house, and it smells as homey as always, the sweet blend of Jackie and Jenny.

But now he finds that the house is split down the middle by a pane of glass stretching floor to ceiling. He sees Jackie and Jenny, but can't pass through this barrier.

Jackie sits in her usual chair, the big soft one with the flowers, looking straight at him, her face troubled as he has never seen it before. She speaks to him, but he can't hear through the glass.

Jenny is coloring a book at her little table in the corner. Then she is a baby again in her rocker that used to be in that corner. Then she is already Jackie's age, and she is painting a canvas. She is crying.

"Why are you crying?" he asks.

"Because I'll never be like this," Jenny tells him. "I'll never know what my life might have been. They took me away too soon."

"Who took you away?"

"The men in the castle," she replies, turning her painting around so he can see it through the glass. In the painting, a solitary skier, one small dot in a field of white, heads toward a cliff. At the bottom of the cliff, far below, on the shore of an intensely blue lake, the Hauenfelder Clinic stands behind a stone wall.

"Be very careful there, Daddy. There're real cannibals in that castle."

NOW HE JOINS that painting with the solitary skier. He moves ahead of the skier, then slows and lets the skier blend into him just as they reach the edge of the cliff.

He soars out into the clear vanilla sunshine, and floats weightlessly down, the ski-poles now the handles of a parachute. The journey down takes a very long time, as he moves as slowly as a falling leaf. As he drifts down, he realizes he is hungry.

The roof opens to him. He floats down through the levels, watching the clinic staff going about their rounds. They seem unaware of him.

He passes through a room, and sees Kate Remington talking to someone in a bed, a woman, who seems to be asleep.

He looks again. The woman in the bed is Kate Remington. No, not Kate. It's Kate talking to a replica of herself.

He drifts through the floor to another level, feeling like a leaf floating gently downward. He senses Jackie and Jenny nearby. Are they hiding, playing a game? He calls to them, but no sound comes.

He pauses on his drift downward, curious. They are here, somewhere just out of his line of sight. He feels them, knows they are there. He follows the feeling. A doorway dissolves and he's in another of the wards of the clinic. He moves down the corridor, the feeling of them getting stronger, almost like their body-scents used to be early in the morning, after a night's sleep.

Through another door, and—

He feels pulled away, and tries to swim back to them, but he's helpless against the forces, and he's swept away, feeling as helpless as a leaf tumbling on the wind.

He sees the bulbous white tank again, but now there are others there, trying to climb into the tank. Not people, just indistinct forms. Get away! he says, and they fade away.

He passes a shelf and sees a card on which someone has printed what seems to be "BOOBZ," and he laughs.

He found himself back in the tank with a single flute playing very softly, far away.

BOOBZ

THE MUSIC FADED, but Daulby wasn't ready to leave the tank. He felt secure and relaxed in the enclosed warm darkness. He was still basking in the sense of closeness he'd felt to Jackie and Jenny. He savored it, wishing that it could be as real as it felt, yet knowing that this experience was no more substantial than a dream.

Finally, reluctantly, he pushed the door open and emerged, slowly, feeling as if he'd been drugged. Or detached from his body. His fingers were deeply wrinkled from the water.

Hans-Georg appeared and pointed him to the locker room.

He showered and dressed. Dr. Langwein arrived. "How long was I in the tank?" Daulby asked, guessing it had been about twenty minutes, a half-hour at the most.

"Slightly more than two hours," Langwein replied. "Some have been in six hours, believing it was only a few minutes. An interesting experience, yes?"

Daulby nodded. He didn't want to talk about it now. Especially not that sense of being close to Jackie and Jenny.

"And what of the message?" Langwein asked.

"What message?"

"The card on the shelf," Langwein said, pointing to the shelf by the ceiling. "Were you able to read it?"

Daulby printed BOOBZ on a pad while Langwein stood on a chair to reach the card.

"Interesting," Langwein said, reading what he had written, then handing him the card so he could see for himself: 80087. Daulby checked where he'd signed the card earlier: it seemed genuine.

"Close, but no cigar," Daulby said.

"Cigar?" Langwein asked, his eyes troubled.

Daulby suppressed a grin at Langwein's puzzlement. "A turn of phrase. I meant it was close, but not exact."

"But a very interesting juxtaposition, nonetheless," Langwein pointed out. "80087, BOOBZ— the B for the 8 and Z for the 7. 80087 which you saw as BOOBZ. I do not recall that we have ever encountered this kind of situation before. It is as if you saw, but not clearly enough. Or glanced too hastily."

"I'm not sure what it proves."

"It is one piece in a mosaic. Perhaps you would like to repeat the experiment another day, yes?"

"Maybe." He looked again at the card. At first glance, 80087 did look like BOOBZ— the sort of error you could make by not looking closely.

"But I—my eyes, my whole body—was floating in the tank. There's no way I could have read what was on the card," he objected.

"You are by no means the only person who has seen without eyes. Read the literature on Out-of-Body experiences, and you will find numerous instances like yours, even cases of blind people who have accurately seen while in an Out-of-Body state. Dr. Charles Tart in California conducted experiments like this as far back as the 1960's."

"But how could I have seen without eyes? It's a physical impossibility."

"In the conventional sense, yes, it seems impossible. Yet it happens. No one knows how, yet it is. Perhaps you will solve the mystery while you are here at Hauenfelder."

NOT PERMITTED

HE'D FORGOTTEN that sense of seeing Gerda nosing through his room until he spotted the manila envelope waiting on the desk when he returned.

It contained a schedule detailing what he was to be doing over the days to come, and a photocopy of a professional paper by Katherine Remington, Ph.D., "An Alternative Hypothesis on the Phenomenon of Alleged Multiple Personality Disorder." He put it aside to read later.

He checked through the closet and drawers; nothing seemed out of place.

He sat on the balcony for a few minutes, processing his experience in the tank.

The sky was cloudless, the lake mirror-still and silvery-blue. A pair of white swans glided effortlessly along the shoreline below. As effortlessly as he'd seemed to float around the world from the tank.

What really did happen in that tank? It *had* to have been an illusion, yet it had seemed as real as any waking moment.

Jenny and Jackie and the house . . . that was too vivid for comfort. Even the feel, the scent of the home was right.

But Jenny's painting and her warning about the "real cannibals" at the Hauenfelder "castle" . . . that troubled him, too. It was uncomfortably true: here they *were* "cannibalizing" parts from one body for the sake of the newer Vehicles. They *were* real cannibals here at Hauenfelder.

But, as one of his professors used to put it, All that might be interesting, but it wasn't evidence. It could all have been dredged up from the unconscious, things I knew at least latently.

But what about the things I *didn't* know?

Like the numbers on that card. Maybe they could have faked it, though beats me how. They could even have faked the near-miss mistake, BOOBZ for 80087. It seemed like my signature on the card, but that could easily have been forged.

But what would be the point? Why set up a hoax? I'm here on the payroll, for just a few days, and they don't have to convince me of anything.

Then he thought: there is one thing they definitely couldn't fake, and that's what I just "saw" in Chicago. Was Perkins really in my old office? Had he moved an old leather sofa in there? That would be solid evidence, one way or the other, and easily checked: just call Marge, she'll know.

"BUT IT IS NOT PERMITTED to make phone calls," Dr. Langwein told Daulby when he asked about calling Chicago. "The rule is necessary for security reasons. But not to worry, you will be going back to America soon, in a few days, and then you can call, yes? But there is good news. Dr. Remington is waiting to have lunch with you."

MOVING THE SOUL

HE FOUND Kate Remington reading at a bench by the lake. She looked up and waved as he approached. He saw a hint of a smile on her face.

In the mid-day sun, he noticed for the first time the undertone of auburn in her shoulder-length brown hair.

Apparently her dark-rimmed glasses were only for reading, as she pushed them back into her hair when she closed the book. Her eyes were deep brown and serious, with a glint of sly humor, but her face tended to relax into sadness.

They found a spot on the patio outside the dining room, where they could eat in the shade of an umbrella. She ate only fruit, explaining that she had been a vegetarian since college.

The warm sun baked the flower-boxes lining the patio, and the air was sweet with the clear aromas of flowers, grass, and pines. A boat passed a couple of hundred yards off shore, its prow slicing through the blue of the still lake. Puffy white clouds hung over the tops of the dark mountains, as if unsure in which direction to move.

"That's not a tourist boat, you realize that, don't you?"

"No, what is it?"

"Look closely. See the machine gun on the stern? It's police. Or military, though actually I don't think there's any real difference in this country."

SHE BROKE THE SILENCE, SAYING, "In the days that we work together, I'll be taking you through an abbreviated version of the program I've developed to train the donors to move their Conscious Essences into their Vehicles. Your introduction to the flotation tank was the first step toward learning to project your Conscious Essence."

She shook her head. "Incidentally, don't blame me for the awful jargon— 'Conscious Essences' and 'Vehicles.' Yuk! I just work here."

"I understand where Rausch and Langwein fit in— to develop the cloning process," Dalby said. "I understand my role— assuming they're telling the truth—which is to transfer the so-called 'seeds of memory' from the donor to the clone."

She nodded. "But you're wondering what's a nice girl like me doing in a place like this?" Her clear laugh was a delight.

She took a deep breath and held it, then said, "Like you, I don't know how much of what they tell me I can believe. The way I've pieced it together is this: they didn't develop the tissue-engineering methodology, by no means. From what I gather, most of it was cribbed—stolen—from reputable labs and researchers. But engineering organs, as you know, is increasingly common. Their unique contribution has been to find a way to put the pieces together into a complete human body."

"Which is mind-blowing."

"But totally useless."

"Useless? It's phenomenal."

"But the Vehicles are empty," she said, "just bodies without souls, so to speak. They're physically identical to the original donor bodies, even—they found in autopsies—even to the exact shape, size, and configuration of the ridges of the cortex of the brain. Yet they lack the memories and other aspects of personality that comprise consciousness as we know it. They are only automatons, not conscious beings."

She added, "They *look* like the donor, but they lack the donor's wealth of memories, and they lack that spark of personality and consciousness that forms the essence of the person. It's as if the Vehicles' brains are like batteries, waiting to be charged."

"Brains as batteries waiting to be charged—interesting analogy."

"In short, they found they could develop carbon copies, in the physical sense. But those copies lacked two key elements: the personality or consciousness, and the memories. They were 'empty'— empty of what makes us human. They brought us here to supply those missing elements. You, by transferring the seeds of the memories, the memory bank. Me, by guiding an aspect of the personality or soul or 'Conscious Essence' across to animate it."

"Move the soul? How?"

"The experimental methodology I've developed is based on a combination of deep relaxation and guided visualization. Later steps in the work build from what you experienced in the tank this morning."

He shook his head. "Sounds more like Voodoo than psychology," he said, instantly wishing he could call the words back.

"Look," she responded, her tone suddenly somber. "I don't like doing this. It wasn't my idea. I've been developing the approach because I *have* to—because it's *my job* here to do it."

"But you—" Daulby began, then decided it was better to let her tell it her own way.

"True, I did choose to come here, so I have only myself to blame. But I didn't realize then what I was getting into. They misled me. Now I'm here, and there's no leaving. So I have no choice but to do this, as dangerous, as *wrong* as I think it is. Frankly, I'm very concerned that this work is opening doorways to some extremely dangerous possibilities."

"What dangers? What possibilities?"

She started to say something, then stopped and looked at him. Again he had the feeling that she was somehow looking through to his core.

Then she shook her head. "We can talk about that another day, perhaps. Right now we need to focus on what you experienced in the tank."

AS HE TOLD HER of his time in the tank, he got the feeling his experiences were typical.

But her expression changed when he mentioned seeing her standing by a bed containing a replica of herself.

She shook her head, fighting to keep her voice steady. "For someone who's never done anything like this before, you do have an uncanny ability. Really remarkable. Men don't usually . . ."

"They say good surgeons have intuitive fingers. Maybe my intuitiveness has spread."

"Could be." She still couldn't condone what Daulby had done with the chimp, but she was sensing a decency about him that she hadn't expected.

She stared out across the lake for a while, then said, "I don't know what you actually saw. That's something that only you can tell. But let me give you some background. I have a sister, a twin sister. Karen. We were always very close, closer even than most other twins. So close that we always felt that we were two aspects of the same person."

She took a deep breath, and he sensed she was fighting back tears. "That's how it was with us, often thinking the other's thoughts. But then Karen got hurt a few months ago, mugged on the street, beaten up for the few dollars she was carrying. There was brain damage, permanent damage. She's been in coma since. Technically, PVS, Persistent Vegetative State. The doctors say the coma is irreversible at this point, that there's no hope of recovery, no hope of her ever again being the person she was."

She blew her nose. "And I feel incomplete, very, very incomplete without my twin." She turned away, wiping her eyes.

She looked back at Daulby, then added, "I guess I'd better tell you the rest now, and get it over with. Karen is here at Hauenfelder. *She* is the hold they have over me."

"Hold?"

"I made a bargain with the Devil to get Karen here, believing they could help her. I had no idea of the trap I was getting us into."

Thank God, Daulby thought, thank God they don't have that kind of hold over me. He almost told her about that sense he of feeling physically close to Jackie and Jennie. Another time.

Instead, he said, "I understand what you're feeling. I lost my wife and little daughter a few months ago. They were killed by . . ." He couldn't finish the sentence.

"I know," she said, looking away from the pain in his face. "They told us about that before you came. I'm sorry about your loss." She shook her head. "But 'sorry' can't help much, can it?"

"When I agreed to come here," he said, "I thought it would be a way of getting away from it— from the pain and guilt I was feeling. I thought throwing myself back into work would be a way of breaking free from the— from thinking about it. But not *this* work, not *here*, not with *these people*. It's not what I expected. I'll be glad when my contract is up so I can get out of here. I don't think I'll renew."

"How long is your contract?"

"Ten days."

"Just ten days? That's amazing. They signed me up for a full year, and I don't think—"

The way she had cut herself off troubled him. "You don't think what?"

She looked at him, saying nothing. Finally, she said, "I'm wondering if they will let me leave here when my year is up. Already I know too much."

ATTACKS

BEHIND THE DOOR

"DADDY, DADDY, we're here, right here with you!" Jenny says, popping her head over the railing at the top of the staircase. "We're here, right here with you, come and find us!"

She disappears back into the shadows. He tries to run up the stairs but everything is heavy and he can hardly move. He can't lose her! He can't let her go away again!

Still half in the dream, Daulby struggled to get free of the sheets and run after her. Then he remembered where he was, and slumped back into the bed, devastated. It had seemed so real, Jenny *so* close. *"Daddy, daddy, we're here, right here with you!"*

HE TRIED AGAIN TO SLEEP, but the thoughts returned, the same dead-ends that had plagued his sleep for months: the If-onlys, he'd begun to call them.

If only I hadn't operated on Chimp Donnie that night, then Jenny and Jackie would still be alive.

If only I hadn't been so driven, so damned ambitious.

If only I'd spent more time with them when I had them. A lot more time.

If only.

But there were some new worries as well, worries unique to Hauenfelder.

The mood of the place, not just a pervasive depression in the air, but something even more oppressive, something dark.

Kate's comment: they might already know too much to be allowed to leave Hauenfelder.

Most troubling of all: the obsessive secretiveness of the place.

HE STEPPED OUT onto the balcony. The air was fresh and sweet, and he settled into one of the chairs to think things through.

He heard a vehicle coming with lights off, an SUV. It pulled up to the side entrance. Two men in white jumped out, popped the rear door and hustled what looked like four picnic coolers into the building.

Strange time of night for that, he thought. Nearly two in the morning. He recognized the men in white: Technicians he'd seen around, but didn't know their names or their specialties.

HE SETTLED BACK. Thinking time was a strange luxury for him. For years, from med school onward, his life had been lived flat-out, always more to do by a factor of ten than there was time for it. Thinking was something to be done on the run between other obligations, or at night, bone-tired, driving home.

There's no rational explanation for what I saw in the tank. I *couldn't* have seen that message on the card, yet I got it almost right. BOOBZ was too close to 80087 to be just coincidence.

There was no way I could have known that Kate Remington had a twin in this place, yet I "saw" them together, and I was right.

But if I was right about Kate and Karen, then what about that sense I got of being near Jenny and Jackie?

What about this dream? "Daddy, daddy, we're here! We're here, right here with you, come and find us!"

Right here with you! Come and find us! Why not? At least I can try!

He dressed quickly, then took the bedside flashlight and the emergency candle and lighter from the desk.

The Clinic was divided down the middle by the main staircase, and he hurried to the third floor, where Ward B occupied one side of the old building.

Rausch had punched a code into an electronic lock at the entrance to the Ward: either 4927 or 4928.

Daulby paused outside to listen at the door. Nothing. He punched in 4927 and nudged the door. It didn't move.

He tried 4928 and heard the lock click. He stepped inside, holding the door so he could retreat in a hurry. But he heard no sounds.

He switched on the flashlight. The batteries were nearly gone, and the weak yellow beam threw strange moving shadows on the walls as he moved through the Ward. A prickling sensation moved up his spine, and he wondered if that was the feeling that comes just before you're hit by lightning.

A hallway lined with a rainbow of doors. What was behind them?

Only one way to find out. He felt his breath coming fast, his hands clammy, and knew he was more afraid of encountering one of the zombie-like Vehicles than of being caught snooping by Rausch's people.

He tried the first door. A laboratory filled with electronic gear.

The second door opened to a storage closet.

The flashlight batteries were fading quickly. He lit the candle, then tried the third room, feeling the pressure of time. Get this done fast, find out what in hell is here, then get out.

The door opened to a large room. He saw the outlines of a half-dozen of the big glass hyperbaric chambers like the one Vehicle 27 had been in.

Something moved in one of them, a face looking up at him with dull eyes and a flat expression.

Other faces rose, as if awakened by the flickering candle-light. Some of the faces were still only half-formed, characterless smears of flesh covering skulls.

High-pressure oxygen here! he realized, and quickly snuffed the candle.

Stupid! Holding an open flame around high-pressure oxygen! Too close! If there had been even a small oxygen leak, the candle-flame would have set off an inferno.

But the image of the vacant faces stayed with him, and his flesh crawled with fear.

He heard a click behind, then the hiss of pressurized air escaping. He spun, flicking on the flashlight. One of them was climbing out of its chamber. He heard a moan, and realized it was his own cry of terror.

The Vehicle answered with a series of angry grunts. The pressure valve in the glass chamber hissed, feeding pure oxygen to fill the vacuum created by the open door.

Daulby sprang for the door to the hallway, but the Vehicle got there ahead of him, and blocked the way. Daulby backed away. He bumped into another chamber, and felt the Vehicle stir inside.

The first Vehicle stumbled toward him, clumsy but driven. Daulby was trapped against the wall. The Vehicle's hand reached out and gripped his arm. Its face was still a characterless blur of flesh, but its hands were formed and strong. The hand was icy.

He tried to shove the creature away. He tripped and fell. The Vehicle kicked at him, the foot connecting with Daulby's solar plexus, knocking the wind out of him. The flashlight rolled away under one of the tanks, and the light quit.

His hand closed on the lighter. It was tempting. The flame would hold the creature back. But with the oxygen hissing out of the open chamber . . . He didn't want to think what might happen.

A second Vehicle was out of its tank now, stumbling toward him.

Daulby scrambled around the back of one of the chambers, and ran for the door to the hall.

An explosion caught him, searing his eyes.

"Get up," a voice said. There had been no explosion; it was only the beam of a flashlight in his eyes.

"Get up, I said. On your feet, your hands over your head."

He recognized Von Schwalbenbach's voice, but the glare of the powerful light blinded him.

"What are you doing here?"

"What do you think?"

Compressed oxygen continued to hiss out of the open hyperbaric chamber. "You idiot!" Von Schwalbenbach screamed. "You took a lighted candle into a room with oxygen! You could have killed us all!"

"I didn't know there was oxygen. I snuffed it at once, so—"

Von Schwalbenbach stepped into the room. The Vehicle, waiting behind the door, slammed a chair across his head. Von Schwalbenbach dropped to the floor. The gun and flashlight skittered across the tile floor.

Daulby dove for the gun and grabbed it, then spun around to see the Vehicle coming at him with one of the broken chair legs, ready to use it as a club.

"Stop!" Daulby yelled, but the Vehicle kept coming. The light cast by the flashlight illuminated the other Vehicles, shadowy figures now all awake and trying to climb out of their tanks.

The first Vehicle loomed over him now. Daulby fired, but the shot went wide. He fired again and again, the explosions deafening in the room. One of the other glass chambers shattered, the pieces flying around the room like shrapnel.

The Vehicle stumbled back, blood spurting from its head and abdomen. Then it came at Daulby again. He fired two more rounds; the Vehicle slammed back against the wall, then slid to the floor and lay motionless.

The room seemed to explode, and Daulby threw up an arm to protect his face, thinking the gunshots had ignited the high-pressure oxygen.

Again no explosion, it was the overhead lights coming on: the Vehicle had hit the switch as it slid down the wall.

Another hyperbaric chamber clicked open, and a Vehicle threw his leg over one side and clambered out and lumbered toward Daulby, its arms slowly flailing.

Daulby tried to back up, but felt the wall blocking his escape. The Vehicle wobbled toward him, arms outspread, malevolence in the eyes despite the vacant face. It was huge, even taller than Daulby, and already well-muscled.

Daulby waved the gun, but the Vehicle kept coming. He pulled the trigger; it clicked, empty. He pushed back along the wall. Something blocked his way. A fire extinguisher. He grabbed it and hit the trigger. Foam spurted across the Vehicle's face, and it bellowed in shock, grabbing at its face. Daulby slipped past the creature, heading for the door.

"Drop the gun!" Rausch screamed, bursting into the room, his hair disheveled. He wore a robe, and also carried a large black pistol. Langwein arrived seconds later, also carrying a pistol. Both were out of breath.

Langwein led the Vehicle back to its glass chamber.

"The guards called me," Von Schwalbenbach said, struggling to his feet. Already red welts were growing where he had been hit. "Someone was tampering with the lock on Ward B. That was a few seconds before the power outage. I caught Daulby in the—" His eyes flicked to see who else was there. "He was in a restricted area."

Daulby felt Rausch's eyes sear into him, and realized that there was a force there that he hadn't realized before. He had underestimated Rausch, because of the physical awkwardness, because of the pomposity and arrogance. But this was not just an egotist. This, he saw, looking into those dark eyes, was an exceptionally strong and unpleasant personality.

"We operate on Vehicle 31 tomorrow, regardless," Rausch said. "We will rest now in preparation for that. We will discuss this incident when the work is complete."

Then they heard a scream, a single long wail at first, then *"Ach, mein Gott! Nein! Nein! Hilfe!"*

MISSING PERSONS

THE SCREAMS CONTINUED, then were drowned out when the building's main fire-alarm suddenly cut in. Daulby followed the others as they ran downstairs.

Elizabet, one of the nurses, her face chalk-white, sat slumped in a chair at the end of the corridor, puffing nervously on a cigarette. She was in uniform.

Rausch pushed through the crowd to talk with her. Then he stumbled back against the wall. It took him several seconds to recover, his mouth opening and closing as if he was gasping for air.

Then he waved one hand. "Von Schwalbenbach! Langwein! Come! Come now!" The three conferred, then hurried down the hall.

Kate came to stand beside Daulby. She was wearing a sage-green silk jogging suit, but her hair was still rumpled in the back.

"You must all go back to your beds," Gerda called. "There is no cause for concern."

But no one was ready to sleep again. Within minutes, the story was being passed around. Tedi's Vehicle had apparently committed suicide. Elizabet had come into the room to check him on her nightly rounds and found the bed empty and the window open. The body lay motionless on the stone terrace below.

"But the Vehicle had been operated on, only yesterday," Daulby said. "How could it have had the strength to get out of bed? It must have been helped."

"But that is absurd. None of us—"

"What about Tedi himself? Has anyone checked on Tedi?" someone called out. There was no response, so two of the nurses ran to Ward A to check Tedi's room.

Then the screams began again. "He's been strangled! Tedi's been strangled in his bed!"

"Tedi's other Vehicle? Where is it? We must find it!"

"*Other* Vehicle?" Kate asked. "You mean there was a *second* new Tedi? Even Tedi didn't know that!"

Another scream, a long icy wail that echoed through the halls of the old building, filled the air. It came from the upper floors. They raced up to see what had happened now.

A body hung from one of the old rafters, swaying gently on the end of a rope. The face had blackened with congealed blood, and the mouth was locked open in a rictus, an obscene parody of a smile, exposing the teeth.

"It's Tedi's other Vehicle, Vehicle 28," Daulby said.

"Oh God!" one of the nurses screamed. "There's a killer here, killing us one by one!"

"It's not killing *us*!" another nurse said. "It's killing the *Vehicles!*"

"But some of the Vehicles just tried to kill me," Daulby said, but no one heard.

ALTERNATE EXPLANATION

DAULBY SLEPT TILL NINE. The clinic seemed unusually quiet. Apparently everyone was in shock after last night.

He got a coffee, and headed out for some fresh air and a walk around the grounds.

The property was massive. A grassy lawn sloped down to the lake front. The forest resumed on each side of the lawn, and the tall wire fence obscured by the trees extended 50 feet or more into the water. From the way the fence was placed, it seemed there was a sharp drop-off just off shore.

He put his hand into the lake water: it was icy, probably glacier-fed.

He followed one of the trails back from the water, and passed a double tennis court. Beyond that, obscured by the forest, he spotted a row of garages. He looked in the windows: three Mercedes sedans, a couple of work trucks, and a beige ambulance.

In the woods on the other side of the main building he came on the housing for the security force, a long, low barracks-like building that seemed to have been newly-built.

Odd, he thought, that they would build separate housing for the security types when there was so much empty space in the main building. Then he realized he had never seen security people anywhere in the main building, except in the dining area.

At the lake-shore, he found a small aluminum rowboat chained to a tree, along with oars tucked under the seat. Interesting.

KATE REMINGTON was in the dining hall, and waved and smiled when she saw him. But when the smile passed, he saw concern on her face.

"Did you hear the news?" she asked. "They discovered who strangled Tedi."

"Who?"

"Tedi!"

"I don't follow."

"Tedi strangled Tedi."

"Strangled himself? You mean he hung himself? But he couldn't have. He didn't even have the strength to get out of bed, let alone—"

She shook her head. "He didn't hang himself. It seems that his clone—his Vehicle—somehow found his way into Tedi's room and strangled him with his bare hands. They could tell it from the scratches on his hands."

"There's more," she went on. "Vehicle 28 found his way to the room where Tedi and Vehicle 27 were recuperating from the operation. 28 strangled Tedi, then opened the window and guided his twin clone—Vehicle 27—to come over and jump. Then 28 went up to the attic and hanged himself. What a place!"

"Still," she said after a moment, "in a way things have worked out for Tedi. He got his wish—to be allowed to die."

"He wanted to die? Not when I met him that first day. The first thing he said was how glad he was that I'd arrived. He said he'd hung on for weeks, waiting for me to give him a second chance at life."

"That was before the heart-stoppage that nearly killed him. He had an NDE, and didn't want to come back from it."

"NDE? He had a near-death experience? I hadn't heard that."

A couple of his patients had claimed to have that sense of leaving the body and going toward light or toward a tunnel. One had supposedly encountered his dead parents before being pulled back to the body. Some researchers claimed it was perhaps what it seemed— a foretaste of death. Daulby had written it off as an hallucination induced by oxygen deprivation. But that was then, back at the University, before Jackie and Jenny were taken, before that strange experience in the immersion tank.

"He told me about his NDE when I visited him last night. He said he wished they hadn't brought him back, that they had just let him die then. Even after the transfer to his Vehicle, he was still wishing he'd died."

"You're saying Tedi engineered his own murder—and his suicide?"

She threw up her hands. "I don't know. I just don't know."

She went for more juice. When she returned, she said, "There is an alternate explanation, one I like even less."

"Tell me."

"What if an outside entity took over the body of Vehicle 28, and did the killings?"

"Outside entity? You mean a ghost?" *"Surely you are not a believer in ghosts, are you, doctor?"* Gerda's strange comment that first day, as they walked through the building.

She shook her head. "I wouldn't want anyone— any *thing—to* get ideas. But there is a possibility, a truly terrible possibility. Truly terrifying."

"Which is?"

"I think this place has opened some very dangerous doorways. And now something — rather, some things, plural—are finding their way through those doors!"

THAT WAS WHEN Kate told him about the unconventional therapy she had developed to help victims of Multiple Personality Disorder, like Linda Fraley, who had been taken over by a personality that called itself Sexy Sally.

Daulby listened, puzzled why she thought this related to what happened to Tedi last night.

"A classic case of MPD, that's true. But my approach to treating MPD is definitely not the classic, the mainstream approach. Did they, by any chance, give you my paper on MPD–the paper that caught Rausch's eye and got me here?"

"Gerda dropped it off in my room yesterday, while I was in the tank. Sorry, I haven't gotten to it yet."

"Bear with me if I restate what you already know, but we do come from different disciplines. As you're doubtless aware, there are a variety of theories on the causes, as well as appropriate treatments, for MPd. Which is also termed Dissociative Identity Disorder, or DID."

"It's not . . . not something I've encountered in my practice."

"In a nutshell, my theory, based on considerable experience in treating MPD victims, is this: I am convinced there are discarnate entities or personalities looking for an entry point back to the material world. When these personalities find a vulnerable individual, they 'take over' that person's body and control it for a while as if it were their own. In effect, they live in that borrowed—or *stolen*—body."

"Discarnate? I'm not clear . . ."

"Discarnate—as in lacking a physical body. As in discarnate spirit. And I can understand why you'd be . . . dubious, skeptical."

"It sounds like you're suggesting there are ghosts out there, looking for bodies."

"Exactly! Though 'ghost' isn't the word I'd use. Still, that does convey the point: that there are entities, ghosts, lost souls—whatever you call them—out there, looking for bodies to inhabit. I think the consciousness that called itself Sexy Sally was one of those lost, bewildered souls, looking for an entry back to the life it knew, and it took over Linda's body. Linda became vulnerable because of the sexual abuse, and Sally stepped in to fill the void."

Daulby was silent. He had a sense where she was going with this, but wanted her to say it in her own words.

"As I said, I fear that this place has opened some very dangerous doorways. These Vehicles—empty bodies, waiting to be animated—they offer doorways for these other entities, other consciousnesses to enter and take over. Now it's happening. This place is full of 'ghosts'—using your term. I think they're hanging around looking for bodies to inhabit. And the bodies are here, ripe for the taking."

TRANSGENIC WURST

HE WAS HUNGRY NOW and went up to the counter to get food: A pair of fragrant wursts just off the grill, potato salad, a couple of rolls.

Kate came back to the table with a bowl of fruit salad and a cup of yogurt. She froze when she saw him slathering mustard on the wursts.

"You're not . . . " She shook her head. "Let me start again. It's none of my business, but you *do* know those wursts contain pork? Pork grown here, as part of the Hauenfelder experiments?"

"I didn't know the place included a farm, no. Why does that matter?"

"They use the pigs on the farm to grow internal organs for implantation in the developing Vehicles."

It took a moment to sink in. "These are from transgenic pigs?" He set the wurst back onto the plate, suddenly nauseous after one bite.

"Blastocyst complementation, that's the technical term I've heard buzzed around here. They take induced pluripotent stem cells from the Vehicles, or maybe from the donors, then inject those cells into pig embryos. The pigs mature, bearing the pancreas and liver and whatever other organs. At a certain point, the pigs are slaughtered, the organs are harvested and moved over here to the operating rooms where they are implanted in the Vehicles."

The image flashed in his mind of the SUV pulling up last night, lights off, and the two men in white carrying in the refrigerated boxes. Most likely, Rausch and the others were waiting to implant the parts.

"And after the organs have been harvested, what happens to the rest of the pig?"

"What happens to the rest of the pig? Wurst case, pardon the awful pun, it's right there on your plate, slathered with mustard."

MOVING CORPSES

GERDA CAME UP TO THEIR TABLE, visibly annoyed. "Where have you been, Dr. Daulby? We have been looking for you. You must report immediately to Ward D."

He'd been caught exploring Ward B last night. "Why? Why the urgency?"

"You will be told when you get there. Now you must go there immediately, yes?"

The Ward door was locked when he arrived. He knocked. No response. He settled in a chair in the hallway.

Kate had told him she'd heard that the Vehicle that attacked him in the Ward had died of the gunshot wounds.

Maybe they were going to pretend it hadn't happened. But now they'd be watching him more closely.

And they would try to pretend, too, that the Vehicles had not climbed out of their tanks to attack him. That was "impossible"— impossible according to the Hauenfelder official rule book. They didn't have an explanation, so the easiest thing was just to try to wish it away.

Dr. Langwein arrived a minute later, puffing from the exertion of the stairs.

He made no offer to shake hands; instead, he pulled off his thick glasses and polished them on his silk necktie.

Then he said, "So, let us begin, yes?"

"Begin? Begin what? Gerda told me to report here, she didn't say why."

"We begin today your orientation to the process of developing the Vehicles— the orientation you undertook covertly in the middle of the night."

It had been a mistake to have gone snooping last night. Knowledge was a dangerous thing: the more he knew about the work here, the more dangerous he could be to them when he finally got back into the real world. All the more reason for them to keep him locked up here.

"Look. There's no question, I was out of order. I shouldn't have gone snooping. You don't owe me a tour. Let's just forget about it."

Langwein shook his head. "No, no, the decision has been made. We value your contribution, and want you to be fully aware of the work, so that you can be even more creative in your contribution."

He nodded. There was no point in refusing now: that would make them even more paranoid.

At least there was a bright side: it was Langwein doing this, and not the obnoxious Rausch, or the arrogant Von Schwalbenbach. Langwein was nerdy, a little creepy. But at least he was bearable.

"We will begin with the tissue engineering process, as that is my area of particular expertise," Langwein said.

He led the way to a long sunny area set up as an exercise room and rehabilitation clinic on Ward D.

But the room reminded Daulby of the practice room in the ballet school where he had sometimes taken Jenny for her lessons, and he felt a pang of sadness for that room. It was part of the life that was gone forever.

Two of the Vehicles pedaled energetically on exercise bikes, their expressions characteristically vacant. Beside them, two others worked mindlessly on Nautilus equipment. Each of the Vehicles seemed oblivious of the others and the surroundings.

The faces of these Vehicles were fully formed, not like the grotesque, still-unformed masks on those he had seen in their hyperbaric chambers the other night. So how many of the things were here? he wondered. The four or five he had seen on the ward last night, plus four more here. So there were at least ten, maybe more, all of whom needed nursing and medical care. It was a major undertaking.

Langwein paused, and he had a chance to examine the four working out here. It seemed like any health club filled with young athletes— except for the mindless, mechanical way these creatures moved through their exercises.

They really *are* moving vegetables, Daulby thought.

Or moving corpses.

A REMEDY FOR DEATH

"BUT NOW TO BUSINESS," Langwein said, leading the way to a table. "Tell me: are you familiar with the literature on cloning and tissue engineering, Dr. Daulby?"

"Not at all. Cloning is not my field."

"But you do know what a clone is, of course: an exact genetic replica of the original." When Daulby nodded, Langwein went on. "Identical twins, as surely you know, are nature's own clones—two separate bodies, yet genetically identical."

Daulby nodded. Identical twins as nature's clones—that much he had learned in medical school, a long time ago, and an immense amount of research had been done in the field since.

The breakthrough had come with Wilmut's cloning of Sheep Dolly in Scotland in 1997. But that, like the others, involved cloning at the egg stage, before being implanted in a surrogate mother for normal gestation.

Langwein shook his head. "But we at Hauenfelder were too impatient to be satisfied with cloning only to the ova stage. We were not willing to wait two decades for our Vehicles to be ready. Nor were we much interested in a process that forced the personalities to endure childhood and adolescence and education, and all that wasted time.

"So we developed a procedure that enables us to clone to the full adult stage, bypassing infancy and childhood. This saves at least 21 years. Thus one can move into the Vehicle when it reaches its physical peak, yet with all learning and all memories intact. Strictly speaking, we do not *clone* the Vehicles, we *engineer* them."

"Engineer? As in tissue engineering?"

"Exactly, though on a much larger scale than mere body parts."

By the early 1990's, Organogenesis, a firm in Cambridge, Massachusetts, had developed a "living skin equivalent" for use in skin grafts for burn patients. This test skin was a living substance grown from a base of living human skin cells which looked and felt like natural skin, and would even tan when exposed to sunlight. Researchers at Johns Hopkins developed a methodology for cultivating human brain cells in a test tube, the first reported cloning of human brain cells. The cells were developed for treating Parkinson's and Alzheimer's patients.

Over the following few years, researchers had found that virtually any kind of human tissue could be grown in culture, and a new specialty called "tissue engineering" had grown up to explore the possibilities. By setting up a "scaffold" of bio-degradable material, then "seeding" it with cartilage cells, replacement noses and ears had been grown for people who had lost their own to fire or cancer. Other labs were growing cartilage for use in knee replacements. Valves to replace the originals in hearts and bladders were being grown artificially from a base of human cells.

Researchers had even experimented with some success in causing the bodies of laboratory animals to grow artificial organs within their bodies, referred to as "neo-organs," or "organoids." In this procedure, a small piece of Gore-Tex fiber pad was coated with natural factors that stimulate rapid cell growth. It was then inserted into the test animal's body to serve as a scaffold on which the body cells could arrange themselves and grow.

At Harvard, "surgical/tissue engineers" had begun growing replacement organs for lab animals, including new bladders, windpipes, kidneys, even hearts, with the eventual goal of developing a methodology for producing spare parts for humans.

This newly-formed tissue then spontaneously grows blood vessels, as well as cells similar to natural nerve tissue. If it is placed in the body at the spot where the liver would be, for example, the neo-organ will secrete hormones appropriate to the liver.

"But those projects focus on growing merely parts of bodies," Langwein said. "None have even imagined what we have already accomplished: growing complete bodies, to the young adult stage."

ONE OF THE VEHICLES climbed off the bike and sleep-walked over to a water cooler in the corner, drank from a paper cup, and went back to the bike. The Vehicle, wearing only shorts, his skin coated with a light film of sweat, had the build of a well-conditioned athlete. But the eyes were empty, the face vacant.

"As you see, the Vehicles emerge from our cloning process at their physical primes, roughly equivalent to 21 years of age. In some ways, they are even more physically perfect than normal 21 year-olds, since they have no bad habits, no addictions, no unhealthy eating patterns. Their veins and lungs are clear. If the donor's genetic life expectancy was 70 years, you can effectively begin counting those 70 years from this point. The first 21 years have not been wasted in childhood and gaining an education."

Langwein shook his head, then continued: "But of course long before the new body is worn out, a new Vehicle will be waiting for them, so they can begin all over again. They can have life after life after life "

Langwein waited for Daulby's response. When none came, he added, "The priests and their churches promise the fantasy of eternal life somewhere up in the sky. We at Hauenfelder offer the reality— and I stress *reality*—of infinitely renewable life on earth, for lifetime after lifetime. We offer life after life! We offer a *remedy for death!*"

ARTIFICIAL SOUP

LANGWEIN SHOOK his head. "But with this talk of eternal life, we are straying from the point. The orientation plan tells us that today you are to learn how we create the Vehicles, yes? Enough of philosophy."

He took off his glasses again, and Daulby expected him to clean them still again. Instead, he rubbed the bridge of his nose where the glasses had rested. "Ach, if only it were possible in my new Vehicle to have better eyes. But such is not yet within our capabilities, to improve upon the original."

"You have a new Vehicle?" Daulby blurted.

Langwein nodded. "Yes, yes, under development. We all do— that is one of the privileges of Hauenfelder, to have a guaranteed life after death, our own remedy for death."

He set the glasses on the table. Without the thick lenses, his face seemed distorted now. The eyes that appeared small and furtive behind the thick lenses were actually unusually large, almost bulbous.

"What we have learned to do at Hauenfelder, and in the earlier researches that predated our work here, is fundamentally very simple. That is, we have learned to build upon the body's natural ability to heal itself and regenerate new tissue where needed. Let me make that clear: *our process is based on the body's own capacity for growth and restoration.*"

He put the glasses back on, then moved to the door. "But enough talk. Now you must see for yourself."

THE TOUR BEGAN in a lab lined floor-to-ceiling with tissue cultures stored in what resembled fish tanks. The tanks slid out individually for examination. Some of the cultures were growing in a cloudy liquid.

Langwein described the liquid as an "artificial soup of life." It was chemically similar to lymphatic fluid, though laced with additional nutrients, as well as a few additional components that had proven useful. "Thus each of these tanks is in effect an artificial womb."

"As the tissue cultures grow larger, they no longer need to be fully immersed in the fluid." Langwein said as they moved on to another group of cultures.

Some of these cultures were filmy white substances, like pieces of damp tissue paper. This was skin tissue, Daulby realized. Other cultures were obviously developing organs, thicker and darker, none larger than a raspberry.

It seemed the Hauenfelder researchers had copied the methodology developed by Organogenesis and the other researchers to grow skin and organ equivalents.

But growing individual body parts was one thing; pulling those parts together into a human cloned to the adult stage was another order of magnitude—yet these Vehicles were proof that they had somehow accomplished that.

As a scientist, Daulby wanted to know how they had done that; yet he knew that, for the sake of his safety, it would be better not to know.

THE GLASS BOXES in the next room were much larger. Here the tissues were also larger, and they rested on a latticework resembling nylon fly-screen. A vaporizing system misted them with the artificial soup of life, keeping the tissues moist and nourished.

"Notice the mesh beneath the cultures. You might think its function is solely to allow drainage, and it does that. But the mesh also serves another even more important purpose. Though it resembles fly-screen, it is in fact a grid of fine silver wires coated with a special plastic. The mesh distributes a faint electromagnetic current across the tissue."

"Why the current?"

Langwein smiled and rubbed his hands. Sweat beaded his forehead. "The human body has a natural ability to regenerate itself, but represses that ability. At Hauenfelder, we have found a way of *unleashing that repressed capability of the human body to regenerate itself!*"

He was shouting in excitement as he spoke, and spittle sprayed into the air.

Daulby waited while Langwein composed his thoughts. "You need not be concerned with the details of how we do this. As I say again, the essence of what we are doing is simple: we supply an electromagnetic field as a framework for tapping the latent potential of the human cells to grow together.

"After all," Langwein added when Daulby was silent, "as you know from your own experience as a surgeon, *you* cannot heal your patients. All that we as physicians can do is to put the elements together, and then step aside so the body can heal itself. That is what we do here: we put the body parts together, we give them nourishment and a little extra energy, then we get out of the way and let the growth occur."

LANGWEIN WALKED over to a large glass tank, the size and shape of a coffin, saying, "Now we move from the parts to the whole."

This was a larger version of the tissue culture tanks Daulby had seen in the other room. As in those smaller tanks, a steady spray of the artificial soup of life misted the tissue, which rested on the same kind of silver-nylon grid.

But in the large tank, the parts had been arranged within a pattern sketched on the mesh. The pattern resembled a crude human figure, like the police chalk-mark outlining a murder victim on a sidewalk.

"The figure you see outlined on the grid marks the shape of an electromagnetic field. As you may have noticed, it also outlines the shape of the human body we are cloning. The field serves as a temporary substitute for the nervous system. Within the framework provided by that electromagnetic field, the various tissue and organ cultures begin to grow together."

Langwein's voice rose as he got to the crucial sentences, and his eyes glittered with unusual intensity.

Daulby was silent, trying to absorb what Langwein was telling him. Finally he said, "I'm not clear exactly why—"

"You are aware of the work of Professor Harold Saxton Burr, a professor at Yale? Or of Dr. Robert Becker, formerly of the American Veteran's Administration?"

"Not really. I've heard the names, but this isn't my field."

"Dr. Burr discovered that there are electromagnetic energy fields around all living things— trees, animals, humans. Becker built from Burr's findings. He demonstrated that healing can be facilitated by supplying a slightly stronger electromagnetic field. Even the most stubborn bone fractures will heal rapidly when a healing EM field of the appropriate strength is set up."

Daulby was silent. Langwein went on, "We built from the work of Burr and Becker. The electromagnetic field you see here, outlined on the mesh beneath the array of cloned tissues, serves two purposes. The EM field both supplies additional energy for healing and growth, and provides a framework for the cells to grow together into an appropriate form."

This was going against all that Daulby had learned in his lifetime as a physician and scientist. But almost everything at Hauenfelder seemed to contradict the realities he had accepted as fixed. "You're saying that by flowing a faint current past the tissue, the cells both multiply faster, and grow together into the form of a human body?"

"Exactly so. Though to achieve this, it is necessary to use precisely-modulated electromagnetic currents, as well as to add the special nutrient solution— our 'artificial soup of life.'"

Daulby shook his head.

"You shake your head and think it impossible," Langwein said, "But that is only because you have been conditioned by the medical establishment to accept presumed limits as unchangeable fact."

"I *was* the medical establishment, not so long ago," Daulby said softly.

BODIES WITHOUT SOULS

"WE LOOKED at what others had done, and asked ourselves, How can we springboard beyond this to something truly revolutionary? The progress that we made attracted the interest of private funding sources, primarily Parsons Couldsen."

As he said the name, Langwein's eyes flickered, and Daulby wondered if he had caught himself saying something he should not have. Odd. Why would he hide a sponsor's name?

If it was an error, Langwein covered it adding, "We built from that work, and now have carried it several steps further."

As they passed from tank to tank, Daulby saw the effects of additional developmental time. It was like being able to look in at the development of a dozen fetuses in the womb, each one a couple of weeks older than the one in the previous tank.

But here they developed in glass boxes, not hidden away in a mother's body.

The human fetus grows to around nine pounds over a nine-month period. In the Hauenfelder Clinic's labs, through the combination of electromagnetic energy and Langwein's mysterious nutrients, these Vehicles apparently grew from inception to small adults in barely half that time.

In the process, Langwein explained, the Vehicles were gradually weaned from the glass tanks to spend increasing amounts of time in the hyperbaric oxygen chambers. The mild current was continued there, supplemented by high-pressure oxygen to further enhance growth.

In time, the spraying of nutrients onto the tissues gave way to intravenous feeding as the Vehicles' circulatory and digestive systems developed.

During the final month, the intravenous feeding was supplemented by solid foods.

Initially, the Vehicles had to be fed like babies by the nursing staff. But that became unnecessary as their muscle control developed, enabling them to hold spoons. Then they could feed themselves, though as mindlessly as Vehicle 27 had spooned jello into his mouth.

In time, as they developed more, the Vehicles would begin spending hours each day in the high-pressure hyperbaric oxygen chambers like those in which Daulby had first seen Vehicle 27.

But even the fully-developed Vehicles had strange, waxy faces, eerily empty like the faces of the wax figures at Madame Tussaud's: perfectly formed, yet utterly empty.

"IT'S ASTONISHING how much you've accomplished, to have brought the process this far," Daulby said. "But the Vehicles are still not . . . How can I say it? They're still empty. *Empty—that's* the only word that fits. They lack . . ." He shrugged, searching for a way to express it. "They lack any real consciousness."

Langwein nodded. "Yes, yes, exactly so. As one of the other people put it, the Vehicles are bodies without souls."

Daulby waited for him to go on. When he did not, he echoed, "bodies without souls?"

"The next few days are going to be very busy, but once we are past that, when you both have some time free, our Resident Witch, our occultist, will you teach you to move your own Conscious Essence— your `soul,' if you will—out of your present body."

"Move my CE? Why would I want to do that?"

"Because it is part of the work here."

"But I don't—"

"Don't what, Dr. Daulby?" Langwein asked, his eyes glittering behind the lenses.

"I don't need to know this" he improvised. "Knowledge here is on a need-to-know basis, as I've been told several times. There's no reason I need to know about moving Conscious Essences."

Langwein smiled and shook his head. "We have discussed that, Dr. Rausch and I. And Von Schwalbenbach. You made the point. You are our number one surgeon. You do need to know what we do here, and how we accomplish it. You are one of us now."

You are one of us now. The words stayed with Daulby like an indictment.

LANGWEIN'S PAGER chirped, and he broke off the orientation to return the call.

"That was Dr. Rausch," he said when he hung up. "We will have important visitors arriving today, and preparations must be made. We will finish your briefing at another time."

Daulby was relieved; the tour had depressed him. Technologically, the breakthroughs were breath-taking. But the work left him with a bad feeling.

Part of it was realizing how close the Hauenfelder mindset was to his own in those final, obsessed months back at the University. Implanting human fetal tissue into a chimp in the hope of expanding the chimp's verbal abilities was something that—he was convinced back at that time—*should* be done if for no other reason than that it *could* be done.

He had never bothered to, or wanted to, think through the consequences of what might happen to that verbal chimp once it came into being, nor with what non-scientists might do with chimps that could be "harvested" with quasi-human capabilities.

His focus in those days had been to expand the limits of the possible. What happened after he had expanded those limits was not his concern as a scientist, that was someone else's job.

But now he was seeing the consequences.

AT THE CAFETERIA, he spotted Kate Remington at a table by herself. Again she brightened when she spotted him. He got his tray and joined her.

"You look like you've had a tough morning," she offered.

"Grim. Not from working, just from thinking."

"This place does that to you."

"What's the remedy?"

"I haven't found one yet. From what I see, though, alcohol, taken in large doses, seems to be the standard remedy for most of the others."

He glanced out the window. It was sunny. "Dr. Daulby's prescription is exercise. That blows away dark moods better than any pills. Are you, by any chance, a tennis player?"

Her broad smile surprised him. "Definitely!"

He was glad he'd asked. Whatever had troubled her about him at the beginning seemed to have faded. In this place, they could both use a friend. "Free this afternoon?"

She nodded.

THEY ARRANGED to meet at the tennis courts by the lake. Daulby was warming up, batting balls against a backboard, when he saw Kate wheeling her sister down the hill. She was strapped into the wheelchair by a band around the waist to keep her from rolling out.

Kate introduced him as if Karen was conscious, and he took her hand and felt a twitch. A signal that she had some level of consciousness?

Even now, with Karen's eyes vacant and her expression slack, there was a mirror-like resemblance between the two, and he shared the sense of loss he knew she was feeling. It would be like having half of yourself dead.

She wheeled Karen to a warm spot in the sun, held up a water bottle for her to sip from, then kissed her before coming over to the court.

They played an hour, and he was surprised to find just how much of his fitness he'd lost in those grim weeks drinking his way across the country after the funerals. Maybe, just maybe, coming to Hauenfelder had saved his life.

Kate, tall and lean, was more than his match today. He resolved to get back into shape fast.

THEY BROKE OFF, and Kate rolled Karen to sit beside them on a bench by the water. The mountains seemed bigger and closer than ever in the bright sun and crystalline air. The lake was mirror-still, the icy blue waters split only by the wake of a small tour boat that passed off-shore.

"You're troubled by this place, too, aren't you?" she asked. "Moving brain tissue from a corpse to a clone! What in God's name are they up to?"

"More accurately, what the *devil* are they up to? There's another thing: they didn't come up with the technology overnight, and they didn't finance it out of someone's piggy-bank. They've obviously been working for years, probably decades, absorbing everyone else's research and building from it. Yet never, in all that time, has a word slipped out in the professional community of this work. They haven't published any papers on their work. There haven't even been rumors about the existence of this place."

"Rausch told me—implied, anyway, back when he was recruiting me—that this was a CIA operation," she said. "The CIA is in the business of keeping secrets."

"I can't begin to estimate the budget of this place, but it has to be tens of millions of dollars per year. At least. Then there's the matter of the equipment—you don't equip an operating room or scanning center by phoning an 800 number with your credit card handy. The manufacturer wants to know who's buying and how it's going to be used, and they send people to install and calibrate it."

"What are you getting at?"

"It's obvious when you look at it: they equipped this place through a cover operation," he said.

"That shouldn't surprise us. After all, the CIA does tend to operate under cover."

"But if it is CIA, then why are we the only Americans here?"

She shrugged. "Just lucky, I guess."

"So where does that leave us?"

"It leaves us trapped here, all three of us."

POLITICAL DIMENSION

THEY GOT in another set before a helicopter swept in from the lake and landed on the grassy lawn in front of the Clinic. They broke off to see what was happening.

The rotors stopped, and the copter's hatch slid back. Rausch and Langwein hurried up to greet a man as he stepped out— a big man with a deep, salt-water tan set off by a thatch of silvery hair. He was wearing a dark business suit.

"That's Parsons Couldsen!" Kate burst. "What's he doing here?"

"Couldsen? Should I know that name?"

She laughed. "Amazing! Neurosurgeons really *do* live in another world. What can I tell you? When you hear the name Couldsen, the tag-line 'Billionaire Media Baron' is usually attached to it. He made his first fortune with tech in the Silicon Valley boom. Then he broadened out. Now he owns a series of television stations around the United States, the lion's share of a couple of cable channels, and newspapers and magazines in various countries. The last I heard, he was buying up worldwide satellite TV channels. He also owns a baseball team. Or is it football? I forget, all professional sports teams are the same to me. Anyway, he's big money. And big influence."

After a moment, she added, "He's also a kind of venture capitalist, providing a lot of start-up financing. This may be one of his ventures. Probably is."

COULDSEN WAVED to the crowd of staff members who had come to greet him. Rausch, standing beside Couldsen, spoke into his ear, and pointed at Kate and Daulby. Couldsen waved them over.

"So this is the famous Dr. Daulby," Couldsen said holding out his hand. "Dr. Rausch tells me that you're a sculptor of the human brain, a true genius. We're looking forward to wonderful things from you."

Up close, Daulby could see that Couldsen was far less healthy than he seemed from a distance. He was still puffing from the slight exertion of stepping out of the helicopter, and his voice was weak and wheezy. Serious cardiac problems, Daulby recognized, probably coupled with emphysema.

Couldsen turned to Kate and took her hand. "And you must be Kate Remington. As lovely as your voice is, you're even lovelier in person."

He looked her up and down, before continuing. "Rausch refers to you as Hauenfelder's 'Resident Witch.' But such an *attractive* young witch you are."

Couldsen's attention seemed to bore into her. Somehow it felt overwhelming, as if an electrical charge exuded from him. Incredible charisma, she thought. He held onto her hand. The feeling was repugnant, and she sensed he was toying with her. "My voice?" she echoed. "I'm not sure what you mean."

"I've been listening to the tapes you made for us."

Couldsen glanced again at Daulby, then turned back to Kate. "I see the two of you have been playing tennis. Wonderful. Get rested. We'll be putting you to work soon, and want you at your best."

He turned back to Rausch, and the entourage headed toward the Clinic.

Couldsen walked slowly, and with each step seemed to bend over more. Finally he stopped, and Rausch raised his hand.

A technician ran over with a wheelchair from where he had been waiting out of sight behind some shrubbery. Another wheeled a cart containing an oxygen bottle and what Daulby recognized as a defibrillator kit for restarting stopped hearts.

Couldsen slumped into the chair, and they wheeled him the rest of the way.

KATE HAPPENED to glance back at the helicopter as the crowd of staff members drifted to the main building. Five men emerged from the copter. She pulled Daulby behind some shrubbery to watch. "I don't believe this! Will you look at who was riding with Couldsen! Incredible!"

Daulby recognized the U.S. Senator: he had made a short-lived bid for a presidential nomination. Kate pointed out that the second man was the leader of the opposition party in Britain: she had seen him on the evening news a few times.

"The others, I don't know who they are," she said. But there was something in the way they held themselves that conveyed that they were Important People, certainly in their own eyes.

They watched as Dr. Von Schwalbenbach hurried back from the Clinic to greet the five visitors, and walked with them to the main building.

"What are those characters doing here?" Kate asked. "I don't like it. The Senator is the kind of guy who gives even politicians a bad name."

"Like attracts like."

"Then what are *we* doing here? Are we becoming like them?"

WHEN DAULBY RETURNED to his room, he found a notice taped to the door: "The Hauenfelder Clinic is honored to host a special dinner tonight in honor of Mr. Parsons Couldsen. Your presence is expected."

He phoned Kate on the internal line. She had received the same notice.

"Want to sit together?" he asked.

"I thought you'd never ask!"

After what they'd seen earlier—the bizarre electrical effects and then the Vehicle attacking Dr. Rausch, they never wanted to go back inside the old building. They wanted no part of Hauenfelder and the ghoulish work being done there.

But they had no choice when the wind kicked up; they hurried inside to avoid the rain they saw moving across the lake.

They passed by the formal dining room, and heard voices coming from inside. That was a surprise: they thought the room had been abandoned after the attack on Rausch.

Kate peeked through the crack between the doors, then quietly led the way to a serving room off the main hall where they could eavesdrop.

Couldsen sat in a wheelchair in the center, under a huge crystal chandelier, surrounded by the upper echelon of the Hauenfelder staff. Rausch now was also in a wheelchair, his face and neck bruised and swollen. Normally the dominant presence, now he seemed shrunken.

Von Schwalbenbach had passed up the pool party he arranged in order to be present here. The two politicians and the three other visitors were present as well. Daulby wondered what they had made of the incidents earlier.

They stood close together, peering through the crack in the door. Daulby was conscious of her lean body standing close to his in the narrow space, and of her sweet fresh odor. He pushed the images away, feeling as if he had betrayed Jackie. But Jackie was gone. It's too soon, he told himself. Pay attention to what's happening in the other room.

"FACT IS," COULDSEN DRONED ON, "we're only just getting started! We've developed a technology that'll enable us to take over the whole damned world and run it the way we want it. That's why I'm calling it Phase Two."

Watching through the door crack, Daulby saw him pause to scan the faces. It was surprising that Couldsen had recovered so well from the shocks earlier; he was a tough old bird, that for sure.

"Life's funny," he continued. "You spend all those years building up a financial base and learning how the world works. Then, just about the time you're beginning to get it together, to understand what in hell life's all about—well, dammit, that's when your old body's shot to hell and it's time to go get fitted for a coffin.

"That's the way it is with me. I've spent this first lifetime learning my way around. Now I'm at the point where I've got the savvy to know what to do, and the power to do it with. I've got the money to buy off who I need. Or get past the ones I can't buy."

He shook his head. "But now that I've finally got it all together, I find I'm a not-so-old man with a prematurely worn-out old body."

He paused to sip some water. "But thanks to my having had the brains back then to invest in you folks and the work you're doing, I'm going to break the cycle. Pretty soon, I'm going to be a healthy, horny 21-year old again, and at the same time, I'm going to be starting out again with a lifetime's savvy already under my belt, ready to cash in."

He shook his head. "Guess I said that earlier, about coming back horny and full of savvy—it's an idea I really like, let me tell you."

He chuckled. The laugh developed into a rheumy cough. When he caught his breath, he went on: "And in another 40 or 50 years I'll pull another body switch and start all over again, life after life after life. Just trade it in, like you trade in your clunker of a car for a fresh new one that runs good and smells good."

Couldsen's eyes swept the circle around him, then went on. "But that means I'm going to be walking this old earth a hell of a while, several lifetimes, maybe forever. That being the case, you'd better believe I'm going to make damned sure that I'm living in the kind of world I want. That's where you folks and the Clinic come in, as part of Phase Two."

AGAIN HE PAUSED. The anticipation built in the heavy silence.

"What I'm saying is this: With all the media I own—and you can be damned sure I'm going to control a hell of a lot more the second time around—I can jerk the strings of the masses. That's easy. But one thing I've learned this lifetime is that to get anywhere in this world, you've got to buy off the so-called 'leadership'—the politicians, the big bankers, some of the generals—that whole bunch."

He laughed. "A lot of those types you can buy so damned cheap you can't believe it. They get elected, get themselves a title, it's giving them the key to the candy store, and they can't stop themselves from gorging."

Daulby glanced at the five visitors. They sat, faces frozen. This was obviously hitting close to home, but they weren't protesting. Couldsen had something they wanted, and this was part of the price they had to pay to play Couldsen's game.

"Once they get in, they milk the office for all it's worth. Once they start selling out, then it's just a question of haggling over the price. Some of them'll even sell out on flattery alone: you treat 'em like they're really one of the big boys, they'll eat out of your hand."

Daulby noticed the heaviness in Couldsen's lungs as he droned on. Too many cigars over the years.

Couldsen guzzled more water, then went on: "But what about those who don't want to sell out so cheap? Well, they're tough, they can be trouble. But just about everybody has his price. And let me tell you, what we have to offer is the most fantastic damned bribe the world has even known!"

Couldsen shook his head. "You can bet that not very damned many will be able to turn down the chance of having another whole lifetime, starting out again at age 21. After all, that's the carrot we held out for you folks— the chance of another lifetime. And what happened? You all bit for it, didn't you? Back then it was just a promise, just pie-in-the-sky. Now that we've succeeded, you better believe the big-shots of the world are going to line up, willing to do anything we tell them to do. Anything at all, just so they get our treatment."

"Good Lord," Kate whispered, "he might just be—"

She froze, the words hanging in the air, as she saw the door behind open slowly. Gerda stepped in, a large black pistol in her hand. She was grinning—a weird, lop-sided rictus, as if two different faces fought for control.

"Pretty soon we'll have whole damned *networks* of people we own!" Couldsen was saying in the background. "They'll make the decisions the way we tell them now, in this lifetime. Then when they come back for another lifetime, under another name, they'll help each other get ahead. We'll control a really old Old Boys' Network!"

Gerda signaled for them to follow her. She backed away slowly, and they followed her into the hall. She pointed to the open door to the formal dining room. She had left it open when she slipped out.

"Want to know something?" Couldsen was saying. "Up to this point, I wondered if I wasn't just pouring money down a damned rat-hole here. But now that we're ready to set me up in a brand-new Vehicle, I really feel I'm going to live forever. Nothing, *absolutely goddam nothing*, is going to stop—"

He cut off at the sound of crackling overhead.

Von Schwalbenbach sprang from his chair to shove Couldsen's wheelchair and send it rolling across the room. Then he dove out of the way just before an old chandelier fell on the spot where Couldsen had been sitting.

Shards of broken glass and crystal exploded across the room, spraying the others. They sat rooted to their chairs, some bleeding from the glass shrapnel.

The animal sounds coming from the corner at last broke into their attention— deep, gutteral growling like a couple of dogs gnawing a bone.

Couldsen lay rolled in a ball on the ground beside his wheelchair, the sounds coming from his open mouth as his arm flapped uselessly across his face. A pool of water grew from the dark stain on his trousers. Gerda ran in to help, leaving Doug and Kate in the hallway.

Langwein and two of the visitors rolled Couldsen onto his back. Von Schwalbenbach ran for the emergency cart that traveled with Couldsen. Gerda tore open his clothing, while Langwein fitted the oxygen mask to his face.

Von Schwalbenbach and Dr. Hoerschner, the anesthesiologist, fitted the paddles of the defibrillator to his chest. Rausch nodded, and the first jolt passed, lifting Couldsen's body in a massive spasm.

AFTERMATH

OLD GARDEN HOSE

WHEN COULTER COLLAPSED, Gerda forgot about Kate and Doug and ran in to the dining room, visibly panicked.

They stayed a few seconds, processing what had happened. Couldsen's three Vehicles riding bikes. The spooky electrical effects. Now this, a chandelier suddenly dropping, as if aimed at Couldsen by some angry force.

A look passed betweeen them. They hugged, seeking peace and energy, then hurried back to their rooms.

DAULBY'S PHONE RANG as he came through the door: Dr. Langwein, screaming that there had been an emergency and he must come at once to the operating room.

When he got there, he found that Couldsen's heart had stopped, though they were able to restart it within 60 seconds.

But it would be hours before the chemistry tests could confirm how much heart tissue had died. The risk of another attack occurring within 24 hours was high. As weak as Couldsen now was, a second attack could be fatal.

"Therefore," Rausch said, "as a precaution we will transfer Mr. Couldsen's brain tissue to his Vehicle on an emergency basis. It is not the best time, I realize, given his weakened state. But better to do it before the death of the donor body, yes?"

ACCESS TO WARD C had been restricted to certain staff members. Now Langwein brought Daulby there to help select which of Couldsen's three Vehicles would receive the implant of his brain tissue.

They anticipated that there would not be any physical differences among the three Vehicles, since they had been cloned at the same time from the same tissues. Still, if there were problems, it was essential to spot them now, before Couldsen's Conscious Essence found itself trapped in a defective new body.

Couldsen's three Vehicles had originally been referred to as A, B and C. Couldsen found that too clinical, and dubbed them Alfie, Bobbie, and Charlie.

Daulby ordered scans on all three Vehicles as a final check to ensure there were no neurological or other defects. The scans would help map the precise points for implanting the tissue samples from Couldsen's brain.

Parallel scans would also be run on Couldsen himself, so they could insert each sample into the precisely corresponding spot in the Vehicle's brain.

They worked intensely, focusing first on Alfie. In examining the images, their interest was mainly on the ridges of the cerebral cortex, the deeply-ridged outer section of the brain. That was the area in which the implants would be placed. The MRI scan produced a series of X-Ray images, each a cross-sectional slice of a different level of the brain.

Daulby was the first to spot the problem, a minute bulge in an artery within the brain that indicated a developing aneurysm. They sent Alfie through the CAT scan again, this time after a radiopaque dye injection. The dye would provide contrast, highlighting details.

This time there was no doubt: there clearly was an aneurysm deep within Alfie's brain, a balloon-like bulge in one of the brain's arteries. It was like a miniature version of the blister that forms on an old garden hose or inner tube just before it bursts.

If the wall of the artery gave way, a cerebral hemorrhage would result, flooding the area with surges of fresh red blood, compressing and killing the brain tissue in the area—a hemorrhagic stroke that could leave the new Couldsen paralyzed or mute. Or dead.

They called Rausch. He came on the run: this was a potential disaster.

"The defective artery is deep inside the brain," Daulby said in explaining the implications to Rausch. "There are ways we can get to it, but they're risky for the patient. I expect Couldsen wouldn't want to move into a Vehicle as damaged as that."

Rausch turned to Von Schwalbenbach for his opinion.

"I concur with Dr. Daulby," Von Schwalbenbach said. "There is no doubt of it: a serious risk of an aneurysm exists in Vehicle Alfie. There is no way to predict: the artery could blow tomorrow, or it could last the rest of this lifetime. Any attempt to repair it would almost certainly cause as much or more damage than a stroke. There is no point in proceeding with this Vehicle, since we have the others available."

"Yes, yes, that is so," Rausch said. "It is no problem, we will use Vehicle Bobbie."

Langwein phoned the Ward. His face drained as Daulby watched. Langwein hung up the phone as if in a daze.

"The nurse on the Ward says that Vehicle Bobbie is not there. She thought it was here with us."

"Vehicle Bobbie is gone? *Gone?* Gone where? Who signed it out?"

"No one. We were in such a hurry earlier that we did not sign out Vehicle Alfie, either. That is why she assumed it was with us."

"But this is impossible! A Vehicle does not go off on its own," Rausch snapped. Then, more softly, he asked, "Where? Where could an empty Vehicle have gone?"

No one had an answer.

"Do you want Vehicle Charlie brought here?" Langwein asked.

Rausch shook his head. "No, not yet. Vehicle Bobbie cannot be far. Alert the staff to find it."

It was going to be a long night once the operation got under way, so Daulby headed off to one of the nearby rooms to get some sleep while he had the chance.

"Find Vehicle Bobbie!" he heard Von Schwalbenbach shouting, just before he drifted off.

SACRIFICE

THE DOOR OPENED, and he felt a presence in the room. Someone climbed into the bed with him. He was too tired to resist; his body seemed paralyzed. The person climbed on top of him, very light, no heavier than a cloud. It felt as if his body spasmed, and he found himself standing beside the bed. He tried to shout, but his voice wouldn't come.

Then he watched himself as he threw back the covers and stood up. "But if that's me, then how can I be here, too?"

"Help! Help!" he shouted. "Someone's stealing my Vehicle!"

The door opened and light from the hallway streamed in. "Dr. Daulby, are you all right?" one of the nurses asked.

"I was sleeping, just a nightmare."

She left him, and he lay back in bed, trying to calm himself.

HE STOOD OVER COULDSEN holding something behind his back.

Couldsen opened his eyes and screamed, "No! No, please!"

Daulby looked to see what he had in his hand. It was a scalpel. "Sorry, Mr. Couldsen," he said. "It's better for everyone this way." He cut the oxygen line going into the oxygen mask that covered Couldsen's face, and Couldsen flopped on the ground like a fish out of water. Then he was still.

Daulby woke again, his body gasping on the bed.

Then he calmed. Couldsen is the key, he thought. If Couldsen dies, the funding will probably stop. Then these ghastly experiments will stop before things go any further.

But there was his oath as a physician: First, do no harm. He had taken that oath. He couldn't cut Couldsen's oxygen lines, and he couldn't do anything else to harm him.

But what if? What if Couldsen got into trouble on the operating table?

Is there an ethical line I can draw: This but no more? Or am I obliged to use every bit of my skill to save him?

Couldsen, like it or not, is my patient. If I operate, then I owe him. But owe him *what*? Do I owe him the opportunity to continue funding the evil that's here?

He checked his wristwatch. It was coming on one in the morning.

The events here rolled through his mind, and it was obvious: he already knew too much. He knew what they were doing here, he knew about the Vehicles, and now he knew Couldsen's link with the place. They would never let him leave. The ten-day contract he signed would never end— it would extend for the rest of his life . . . however long that life might be.

ESCAPE.

But how? Security fences block three sides, and an icy lake takes care of the fourth. Once out, where am I? Someplace in some dictatorship in middle Europe, with no money and no passport. And sure as hell, if I do get away, Rausch and all of his security people will come looking for me. And all of the government's people as well.

But I am not going to waste the rest of my life here. I'm going to find a way out, no matter what. Even if I die trying.

DAULBY WOKE AGAIN. It was not yet two in the morning. He splashed some water on his face and went to see what was happening.

He looked through the glass doors into the OR, and was surprised to see Rausch, Von Schwalbenbach, and Langwein in surgical garb bending over a figure on the operating table.

"Come in, come in," Von Schwalbenbach called on the intercom. "It is merely an autopsy. A few germs can do it no harm at this point."

The head of the cadaver had been cut open, and the face had been pulled away from the skull, distorting it beyond recognition. "It is Vehicle Alfie," Langwein explained.

"Alfie's dead? So quickly? Did the artery burst?"

Von Schwalbenbach shook his head. "We thought it best to examine the area of the aneurysm directly."

"You killed Alfie?"

Rausch, whistling softly as he worked in the head of the cadaver, looked up for the first time. He shrugged and said, "Come, come, doctor, you make it sound so sinister. We did not kill, we simply sacrificed a specimen. It was necessary. We needed to learn all we could before the operation on Mr. Couldsen."

Daulby walked over to the table. Alfie's flesh was still warm. The memory of the three Vehicles bicycling through the dining room last night flashed through his mind, and he felt a stab of sorrow for Alfie. Vehicle Alfie had never really lived, and now he was dead.

Daulby slumped onto one of the stools. "But he was otherwise in perfect health. It seems . . . it seems a waste."

"Waste? This was only a Vehicle, a laboratory specimen, a creature bred for a purpose. It was not a human being, not a person in any sense of the word. At that point, Alfie was nothing more than a sub-human species, specifically bred for a purpose."

Daulby turned away. He had lost patients before, dozens each year. With every one, he had felt a sense of failure, a nagging sense that if only he had been a little smarter or a little more innovative he could have saved them.

But this was different. By pointing out the potential aneurysm, he had given Vehicle Alfie a death sentence.

Daulby forced himself to look into the open skull. "Well, what did you find? Was it worth wasting him?"

Von Schwalbenbach reached in with his gloved hand and pulled back the tissue. Under the magnifier, the weakness of the arterial wall was evident.

"It is fortunate that you spotted the traces on the scan," Rausch said. "You averted what could have been a disaster."

"What are you going to tell Couldsen?"

Rausch glanced at the other two. "I think nothing. There is no point in worrying him unnecessarily, yes?"

Out of the corner of his eye, Daulby caught movement. He turned. A jar of alcohol bounced off Rausch's shoulder, then shattered against the wall.

Rausch turned to find the source, and Daulby got a glimpse of the fear in his eyes. Fear— but not surprise.

RED PHONE

THE RED PHONE RANG. Langwein answered it. He listened a moment, his face dissolving. He stumbled back and sagged into a chair.

"What is it, Langwein?" Rausch snapped. "For God's sake, tell us."

Langwein slowly replaced the receiver, then he looked up. He looked like he was going to be sick. Or to cry.

"He—he's dead. They found him in the hot tub. His wrists had been slashed. He bled to death."

"Dead! Who?"

"Vehicle Bobbie."

THE WATER IN THE HOT TUB was only faintly pink: the tub's filtration system had been running. But the chalky color of Vehicle Bobbie's skin showed that the warm bubbling water had drained all the blood from the body.

The kitchen knife used to cut the wrists rested on the bottom of the tub.

"An easy, painless way to go, so they say," said Sonja, the physical therapist. "In hot water, you hardly feel any pain, even as you cut the flesh. Then you lie back, and sleep carries you away."

Daulby wondered what deeper message she was conveying. Did Sonja also see death as the only way out of Hauenfelder?

"Who is responsible for this?" Rausch demanded. "A price will be paid!"

"It was not my fault!" Hertl, the ward nurse, screamed. "The procedures were not followed. Vehicle Alfie had not been signed out. I knew he was with you. There was no way for me to know that you had not also taken Vehicle Bobbie."

"The important reality is that neither Vehicle Alfie nor Bobbie can now be used," Von Schwalbenbach said. "Therefore, we must take extra precautions to ensure that nothing happens to Charlie. I have ordered him to be put on a constant watch."

"But what if Vehicle Charlie has the same aneur—" Langwein began, then cut himself off and looked around to see who was listening. "We must ensure that Vehicle Charlie is healthy."

"And if not? Then what?" Von Schwalbenbach demanded.

No one responded.

"True, we could generate more Vehicles. We have the tissue available. But that would take months, and Mr. Couldsen needs our help now. He cannot wait for months more."

"Do they— Do Mr. Couldsen and his guests know what has happened?"

"Mr. Couldsen is resting. The politicians, they are . . . being, uh, entertained by some of the female staff. They know nothing of this."

"It could not have come at a worse time, especially with— with our special patient arriving tomorrow," Rausch said. "We risk chaos."

Chaos! My best chance to escape this place, Daulby thought. Tonight's the night, now or never.

But I can't leave Kate here!

NOW OR NEVER

BREAKOUT

"CAN'T IT WAIT till morning?" Kate asked when he phoned.

"It's urgent, really urgent."

She met him wearing a thick white terry-cloth bathrobe. She seemed wary at first, then stepped back from the door and let him in.

He told her his plan.

She thought a moment, then shook her head. He was surprised by the pain in her eyes.

"I'd like to go, of course I would, and I appreciate your thinking of me. But I can't leave Karen."

"Once we get out of here, we can go to the police. It could all be over by noon tomorrow. Then Karen would be safe."

"You're forgetting where we are: in a dictatorship, a police state. It's very likely that Couldsen and Rausch have bought off the local police. Not just the police, more likely all levels of the government."

"It's a chance we have to take. Anything is better than being trapped here. At least let's give it a try."

She considered a moment, then shook her head. "It is kind, very kind, for you to invite me. But I can't. But *you* go, you *should* go. There's nothing holding you back."

"If I go, there could be—" He groped for the word. "There could be repercussions for you."

She shook her head. "It's a risk I'll take, a risk I'll balance against the chance you can bring help. But I must— I *want* to stay here with Karen. She's trapped. I could never leave her, not in a place like this."

She threw her arms around him and hugged hard, as if desperate for a last human contact. "But you go. Go and bring help for the rest of us, if you make it."

DAULBY SLIPPED out of the Clinic through the sliding door to the dining terrace. The night air was cooler than he had expected. He should have brought a sweater.

Keeping to the shadows, he jogged to the front gate. There was a chance, given the confusion, that the guards had left it unattended.

That hope died when he saw the shadow of a head outlined in the window of the guard shack.

So there was no easy way out. And dawn would here in an hour or so.

Maybe he could lure the guard out of the shack. Catch him by surprise, take his gun and the key to the gate.

Possible, but not likely. He was a surgeon, not a commando, and the guard probably *was* an ex-commando.

On to Plan B, the rowboat chained up on the shore. Break the padlock, row across to the village, find a phone.

It was nearly four now, not long till first light. There was no time to waste.

He jogged down to the lake. The boat was gone, along with the chain.

Scratch Plan B. Move on to Plan C, swim the icy lake.

The only question was whether to go left or right. There had to be other estates along the lake shore, but, stuck at the Clinic, he had no idea how close they were.

He chose left, and waded into the water near the fence on that side. He had expected cold, but he hadn't prepared himself for water so icy that it burned his skin. The muscles of his calves were instantly ready to cramp.

But now he was wet up to his knees; there was no going back. He pushed on into the water. The bottom fell away unexpectedly, and he went under. It happened too fast to catch a breath. Panic hit. His skin felt seared with the cold, and the little wind he had was knocked out by the shock.

He struggled to the surface and caught a breath. The weight of his wet clothes pulled at him.

He tried to swim on, but the cold was knotting his muscles, and he couldn't lift his arms in the familiar rhythm. He pushed on in a doggy-paddle, now trying to keep his head out of the water. As a distraction from the cold, he tried to recall what percentage of the body was comprised by the head. Twenty-percent came to mind, but he wasn't sure. In any case, it made sense to keep the head out of the cold— less heat loss that way.

He tried to remember the exposure tables. How many minutes did a body have in 35 degree water before hypothermia and unconsciousness? Two minutes? Twenty? The number wouldn't come. But the point wasn't to recall the numbers, the point was to distract himself from the cold.

He knew he was slowing down. His arms and legs weren't swimming now, just jerking forward, almost beyond his control.

Was it time to head to shore now? he asked himself. He turned to look at the shore, and knew he was going to die. The shoreline here consisted of sheer rock cliffs that rose fifty or a hundred feet from the water. There was no beach area, no place to come to land, no slope to pull himself up on.

"Push me, Daddy," Jenny giggled, her arms hooked around the yellow inner-tube. "Push me, let's go fast." He nudged her along with his head. "Come on, Daddy, faster, faster, push me faster. You can do it if you try."

He was nearly to the end of the cliffs, and he saw lights ahead along the shore. His arms were heavy, so heavy he could barely move them. He wanted to close his eyes and sleep. It was hard to keep his head out of the water.

He slipped under the still water without noticing it. The icy water coming into his bronchial tubes startled him, and he got his head up into the air to cough the water out and take a breath. He pushed on.

He slipped under again. He had no strength left. He let himself ease down, grateful that the struggle was over. He found himself in a blue cavern that seemed to have been carved out of the ice. He floated up into the cavern, and at the far end, a long way ahead, he saw a light. He didn't feel cold now, he felt warm and cozy. He floated toward the light, and the light seemed to draw him, and he was glad to let it happen. He was tired of the struggle.

Jenny was standing in the middle of the ice cavern, waving her arms. "Stop, Daddy, you can't come yet. Go back, go back, there're things you need to do before you can come with us."

Again he felt the icy water burning his skin, and his body was heavy and tired, and his lungs burned. But he couldn't let Jenny down.

He was out of the ice cavern, struggled toward the surface, but it was too far, and he felt himself sinking again.

"Just push off on the bottom like you taught me, Daddy. See? The bottom is right here. Now push, push, and uuuup! you go!"

He broke through the surface, sputtering and coughing. The air felt hot as he breathed it in, and it gave him the strength to push on..

Finally his feet touched bottom. He dragged himself onto shore and collapsed. He rested a couple of minutes, then sat up to see where he was. It looked like a small resort. He saw a long building: maybe hotel rooms. Off to the side was a dock, and tied to the dock were a couple of small fishing boats.

He made it to his feet. The ground felt good beneath him now, and he was getting his breath back. But he was cold to the core.

It took minutes to untie one of the boats: his fingers were numb, and it was like trying to work in mittens. Then the knot slipped, and he pulled himself into the boat.

He was quivering with the cold now. He pulled a life-jacket on: that might hold some warmth in. Exercise is the best thing. He slipped the oars into place and rowed out into the lake.

It was a strange time of the morning. The sky was light overhead, but it was still night down along the shore. The effect of the mountains: the sun may have already risen, but we won't feel it for a while. Good news. That much more time to get away from Hauenfelder.

The exercise warmed him, and he began to feel a little better. Now he was far enough from the shore to risk starting the little outboard. It was a small engine, just big enough to push the boat along for fishermen. At least it would be quiet.

His original plan had been to cross to the village across Hauenfelder, but when he got further from the shore, he spotted the lights of a larger village further down the lake. Farther from Hauenfelder, and bigger, more chance to hide.

SHELTER

DAULBY GUIDED the outboard toward the village's dock, scanning the shore for trouble. The golden sunlight of the dawn gleamed on the clouds overhead in the clear sky, but down here, ringed by the high mountains, it still seemed almost like night.

He eased back on the engine until it was barely moving along, and ran parallel to the shore. When the boat grazed the village dock, he grabbed the ladder and held the boat still in the water. He held the ladder with one hand, and with the other reached back to twist the engine's throttle, and pointed it out toward the middle of the lake. It was a still morning. The boat would go on until it ran aground somewhere, or until it ran out of gas.

Wherever the boat turned up, that's where Rausch's people would start looking. Here in the village he would be safe. For a while. For long enough to figure what to do from here.

I'm in a foreign country, a police state, a dictatorship, I don't speak the language, don't have a passport or a cent in my pocket, have just stolen a boat. And I don't have a clue where to go to get help. I could go to the police, but what if they don't take me seriously? Why are you soaking wet? And can you tell us anything about a certain fishing boat that was reported stolen?"

Worse, what if the police are on Couldsen's payroll? Almost certainly they were. Just before the chandelier fell, Couldsen had bragged about how easy it was to bribe politicians. No doubt, he's done that here, too: grease a few palms and ensure that the Clinic is left undisturbed.

He pulled himself up the ladder onto the dock and looked around. The area was deserted. He checked his watch. Ten to six.

He was still cold, but at least could function now. His fingers were stiff. His clothes were wet, but no longer dripping. In time, they would dry from body heat.

He walked on as if he knew where he was headed. He found a pathway along the water, and followed it. In a couple of minutes he came to the village swimming pool, perched at the edge of the shoreline.

He glanced around: no one. He pulled himself over the iron fence. It was easy to slip the cheap pad-lock on the locker rooms. From the men's locker room, he scaled the wall into the pool office. There he found what he needed: a couple of warm woolen emergency blankets, and a stretcher. He propped the stretcher between a couple of desks and climbed on, pulling the blankets over him.

He dreams that he's wandering in a desert. He sees Jackie and Jenny ahead and runs to catch up with them. But they are on the other side of a deep, rocky gorge.

He hears a motorcycle in the distance. He turns. It's coming toward him, a silver cycle without a rider. He catches it as it passes and hops aboard. He twists the throttle, and the cycle spurts ahead, soaring over the chasm.

He floats in the air, drifting light as a leaf to the other side, and Jackie and Jenny see him, and they smile and hold out their arms, and then he's holding them and they're all crying with joy at being together again after so long apart.

He snapped awake at the sound of voices. He checked his watch. It was after eight now, and he saw sunshine touching the tops of the mountains. The sky was azure blue.

The voices passed by. Good news: at least they weren't coming in to open the pool. Not yet. But they would soon.

He folded the blankets and replaced them and the stretcher as he had found them. Leave no traces: I might need to return here tonight.

He pulled the door open slowly and looked around. No one in sight. He stepped outside. Two men came for him from the side of the shack. He ran. Another jumped him from behind a tree. He pulled away and tried to make it to his feet the other two were on him now and he sniffed the familiar bite of ether as a white cloth came across his face.

THREE JOLTS

DAULBY WOKE just before noon, in his bed at the Clinic. His head ached, his mouth was cottony.

He showered, alternating hot and cold until he felt ready to face the Hauenfelder crew.

At least I'm alive.

At least they didn't lock me away in some dungeon.

But I'm still stuck here.

He saw Kate when he entered the cafeteria. She looked as tired as last night, and just as sad. He got some juice, fruit and cereal and joined her.

"Don't take this the wrong way," she said, forcing a smile, "but I'm sorry to see you back."

"I'm sorry to be here, believe me. They caught me."

"At least you tried." No point in adding, Now they'll be watching us even more closely.

"I'm not giving up. Next time, I want you to come with me."

She shook her head. "I'm the only hope Karen has. I must stay with her."

He ate some orange slices, then said, "What's the word on Couldsen— still alive?"

"They want him stabilized before they risk the operation."

"If they wait too long, he may surprise them and die."

"That *would* be the perfect solution, wouldn't it?"

"I had a dream," he began, then changed direction. "I'd rather not find myself in a life-or-death situation with him as my patient. It'd be too tempting."

"I'm a pacifist," she said, "and I'm vehemently opposed to the death penalty, and I'm a vegetarian because I don't think we should kill animals just for their meat. But with Couldsen . . . yes, it is a temptation. If his heart stops, then it's very likely that the work of this awful place will stop, as well. And that would be a very good thing."

She went for another glass of orange juice. When she returned to the table, she said, "There is something else. It seems that overnight some person or persons unknown went at the anesthesiology equipment with a hammer. Dr. Hoerschner is trying to see if it can be salvaged."

He felt a chill pass over his neck and scalp.

"Who did it?"

"That's the interesting thing, the spooky thing. They're trying to keep it quiet because of the visitors who came with Couldsen. But I overheard some gossip that shards of glass from the gauges were found —are you ready for this?—were found in the hands of one of the Vehicles."

He stared at her for a moment, absorbing what she had said. "You're telling me that one of the Vehicles somehow rousted himself out of his glass tube, found a hammer, and figured out what to do? They've been telling us that the Vehicles are mentally empty, waiting for some kind of jump-start. How in hell could a Vehicle *do* that on its own. . . before the so-called Conscious Essence moved in and took it over?"

She nodded. "Maybe the same way as the empty Vehicle that climbed out of the oxygen chamber and attacked you. The same way that Couldsen's empty Vehicle Bobbie somehow found his way down to slit its wrists in the hot tub. The same way Tedi's Vehicle took care of himself and Tedi. Seems to me there are what we might think of as ghosts looking for bodies, and here's where the empty bodies are, waiting."

"But . . . but at least Tedi's Vehicle had the implant of brain cells. And you had worked with Tedi, teaching him how to transfer his Conscious Essence across to the Vehicle. These others haven't had either the implant or the training. They're apparently doing it on their own initiative."

"Exactly. Which explains the sense of panic that's filling one of the conference rooms upstairs. Even Rausch and the others must be grasping by now that something is going very wrong here. Just as I predicted. They chose to open dangerous doors, and now they're having to deal with what's coming through those doors."

A WAITRESS HURRIED OVER to the table to say that Daulby was needed upstairs in the recovery area. That had become the unofficial command center since Couldsen's heart attack.

He went in, wondering what to expect after his escape. Obviously, they still needed him, or else he'd be dead or locked up.

Play along with them, tell them I've learned my lesson. Meanwhile, be alert for the next opportunity.

Couldsen woke and saw them standing around his bed. He seemed to have aged another decade overnight. "How am I doing?" he whispered.

Then his eyes went blank, and his head dropped back onto the pillow. The whine of the heart monitor filled the room. Von Schwalbenbach grabbed the paddles of the defibrillation unit while Langwein cleared away the covers.

This time it took three jolts before he came back.

The glance that passed among the others told Daulby that they understood just how bad things were. Couldsen was vulnerable. They might not be able to restart his heart next time . . . or the time after that. Besides, with each attack, the flow of blood to the brain stopped temporarily, risking further brain damage.

Rausch said, "I think the time is upon us that we must—"

The sound of a pistol shot. Glass fragments sprayed the room.

A light bulb had exploded behind Couldsen's bed. Electricity sparked from the elements.

"The oxygen!" Von Schwalbenbach screamed. "Cut the electricity before it ignites!"

When that was done, Rausch sagged back against the wall, obviously spent. His face was bleeding from a shard of glass in his cheek. Even Von Schwalbenbach looked drained. And frightened. "I have never seen such things happen. And so many."

"Nor I," Nurse Elizabet agreed. "Such strange things happen here, yes? It frightens me."

GERDA RUSHED IN, breathless, looking even more rumpled than last night. It was clear that she had not slept. "Dr. Rausch, you must come! The visitors, the politicians, they have been waiting all morning, and insist on seeing Mr. Couldsen now. They expect him to fly with them to Vienna in the helicopter."

"Tell them he is resting on the orders of his physician."

"But he is expected for a meeting in Vienna this afternoon. Then he and some new people are to come back tomorrow evening after the conference ends in order to see the experiments. Mr. Couldsen has invited some new people, as well. We must be ready for them. Somehow."

"It is out of the question. He is in no condition to travel."

"Then I think you must explain that to these men yourself."

"Terrible," Langwein said. "It is happening too soon."

The door slammed behind Gerda, startling them all. She turned, angry at the disturbance, and checked the hallway. It was empty.

"That door is very dangerous when it slams like that. It should be braced open. Or left shut."

Dangerous doorways— the term Kate had used. They are opening dangerous doorways and now have to deal with what's coming through them.

BLISSFUL CONFIDENCE

ALL OTHER WORK was suspended until Couldsen's crisis had passed. That was good news for Kate, as it freed her to spend the rest of the day with Karen.

She went to Karen's room, got her into a wheelchair, and took her for a "walk" earlier than usual. It was warm and pleasant, and they circled twice around the grounds before settling in at the shore of the lake.

A pair of large white swans glided past, barely rippling the still water. "Aren't the swans beautiful, Karen?" she said, gently turning Karen's head in hopes she would focus on them. "They just glide past, as if it were no effort at all."

It was hard to keep the usual one-way conversation going today because so many thoughts were running in her mind. She tried to push them away, so there wouldn't be a chance that Karen might pick them up in the personal telepathy they had always shared, but the questions kept returning.

Had she done the right thing, passing up the chance to escape with Doug Daulby last night? If the chance came again, should she go for it?

What future did she and Karen actually have here? Once she had perfected the methodology for transferring Conscious Essences, what then? Would she and Karen be expendable?

And what about Doug? Would they ever let him leave this place? He knew too much now.

Karen drifted off to sleep, and Kate almost envied her. It was as if Karen had reverted to infancy: no concerns, nothing to do but eat and sleep. No troubles sleeping, no worries about the future, just a total blissful confidence that someone would take care of her.

BALANCING RISKS

COULDSEN HAD STRENGTHENED a little, so Rausch decided to go ahead with the operation— transferring brain tissue from Couldsen to his Vehicle Charlie.

There were risks in operating now, given Couldsen's weakened condition. But the alternative was worse. Both of Couldsen's two other Vehicles, Alfie and Bobbie, were dead, so he was out of options. There was no point in worrying whether or not Vehicle Charlie shared the problem of the aneurysm; now there was no choice: Either use Vehicle Charlie and give Couldsen a chance of living on, or do nothing and wait for another cardiac incident to take him.

Dr. Hoerschner had managed to patch up the damaged anesthesiology equipment. His control panel was dented, and some of the gauges cracked, but it seemed to be working well enough.

Tension hung in the room as they worked, as if everyone were waiting for the next incident. Would something come flying through the air? Would an electrical apparatus short out in this oxygen-rich air? Would the power stay on?

But the afternoon passed without incident, and the tension eased. Maybe things had returned to normal.

Midway through the operation, word came that a new VIP patient had now arrived at the Clinic. He had survived the flight well, but was weak. Daulby was unable to catch his name.

"Then when we finish here, we must go check on his Vehicle, yes?" Rausch said, but his voice was softer than usual, as if he were tired, or depressed. Or seeing the whole enterprise beginning to fall apart.

FIRST ATTACK

THE MIRRORED OPERATIONS on Couldsen and his Vehicle Charlie finished by early evening, and both were taken to the recovery area.

Now, with a small window of time free, the doctors trooped down together to the Ward to examine the Vehicle prepared for the new VIP patient who had arrived today. That operation, moving brain tissue from the donor to this Vehicle was scheduled for tomorrow.

Like Couldsen's Vehicles, this Vehicle had a name—Ralph, or was it Rolf?—not just a number, like Tedi's Vehicles 27 and 28. Did that mean he was somebody important to them not just another experimental animal like poor Tedi?

Rausch and Von Schwalbenbach shouldered Daulby aside to lead the examination of the Vehicle. That suited him: the less involvement, the better. He drew back from the circle to observe the Vehicle from a distance.

At first glance, Vehicle Ralph seemed little different from the others—a young male, apparent age of about 21, in peak physical condition. But there was something different about this Vehicle.

What that was came to him as the Vehicle's eyes met his: these eyes were not blank and passive like the other Vehicles; these eyes were alert, savvy, even cunning.

But that's impossible, he told himself. This Vehicle hasn't had the operation yet, there can't be intelligence there.

He kept silent, watching the Vehicle as it submitted to the doctors' probes. The face was bland and immobile, but the eyes tracked the others as they moved around. There even seemed to be emotion—anger? hatred?— in the eyes.

There was something wrong, very wrong here. "This Vehicle—" Daulby began.

"Quiet! Can you not see that I am conducting an examin—"

Daulby heard glass shattering, and felt water spray on his neck. He turned. The pieces of a water glass littered the floor; the wall was wet where it had hit. Where did it come from? he wondered. How could it have broken that far up on the wall?

Then he heard the crunch of flesh on flesh. Rausch screamed.

Daulby turned. Rausch was backed into a corner, his hands up to protect his face. Blood spurted from his nose. Vehicle Ralph pounded him with a flurry of fists and knees.

"*Hilfe! Hilfe mich!* Help! Help me!" Rausch screamed.

Daulby and the others stood frozen. Rausch screamed Help! again and again.

Von Schwalbenbach was the first to move. He dove past Daulby, and knocked the Vehicle away from Rausch. One of the orderlies jumped in and grabbed Ralph in a hammerlock.

Daulby looked into the Vehicle's face again. He saw the same flash of intelligence in the eyes, along with an expression of mingled anger and triumph.

Then it quit struggling. The eyes lost focus and became blank again, and the face lost expression, becoming once again a vacant mask like the other Vehicles.

RAUSCH'S NOSE and some teeth were broken. They got the bleeding stopped, but he insisted on determining what had happened even before his injuries were treated. "We must stop this, whatever it is!"

Daulby told about the flashes of intelligence he had seen in the eyes of the Vehicle. One of the nurses confirmed that she had also seen intelligence in the eyes of the Vehicle as she struggled to subdue it.

"*That cannot be!*" Von Schwalbenbach said. "After all, we have not yet done the implant operation. It is *impossible* for there to be any intelligence in the Vehicle now— *totally* impossible."

"Impossible or not, it was there," Daulby said.

"Dr. Daulby is right," said Edith, one of the nurses. She was a tall, dark-haired woman with a long nose and thick glasses. "I also saw intelligence. I'm sure of that. There was intelligence and hatred in those eyes."

"But where could intelligence possibly have come from?" Von Schwalbenbach asked. "Intelligence implies a Conscious Essence— which of course these Vehicles lack at this point."

Daulby was surprised at how tired Von Schwalbenbach sounded. The crackling arrogance was gone now. Like Rausch earlier in the day, he seemed suddenly subdued. Or was he depressed? Or frightened?

"We don't really know about the CE, do we?" Daulby said. "All we do know for certain is that we haven't taken our usual steps to move either the brain implants or the CE from the donor. Maybe somehow the donor moved its CE spontaneously into his Vehicle. I understand the donor arrived here today."

"But that is not . . . not part of our program."

"Maybe they don't always play by Hauenfelder's rules," Daulby said.

"THEY HAVE FOUND the doorway," Sonja said from the back of the room. "Don't you understand? This means that the entities have found their own way through the door!"

"What door is this?" Von Schwalbenbach demanded. "Surely you do not truly—"

"Now these—these evil spirits—now they have found the door through to our world!"

Her voice choked with emotion, then she continued. "The empty Vehicles provide the door! We must stop this work now . . . before it becomes too late! We must close that door!"

"You know nothing about these things!" Von Schwalbenbach shouted.

"I know enough to know the trouble we are now in!" Sonja shouted back. "It's just as Dr. Remington wrote in her paper, the paper you all read. There are entities—spirits, whatever—around us here at Hauenfelder. I've felt them, we've all felt them. And now they're coming through the doorways we left open! We must stop these awful experiments before it is too late!"

"Find the Remington woman," Rausch said. "Bring her here. Let her tell what she knows about this."

SONJA LEFT the others, and walked down to sit by the lake, a dull sense of terror churning her insides. She was not a religious person—no one here at Hauenfelder was . . . or *could* be. But she respected nature, and what they had been doing was very contrary to nature—and now the price had to be paid.

She stopped at the commissary and picked up two bottles of Swedish vodka to take back to her room, hoping that would numb her to what was happening.

GERDA UNLOCKED THE DOOR and caught Kate stepping out of the shower.

Kate grabbed a towel to cover herself. "What are you doing here! Get out! Leave me alone!"

Dark rings circled Gerda's eyes; they glittered with strange intensity. She's beginning to crack, Kate realized.

"Dr. Rausch sent me to bring you to him. You must come with me now."

"Like this? In a bath towel, soaking wet? No! Get out, now! I'll come with you after I've dressed."

It didn't really surprise her when Gerda backed out of the room. She was a bully, but like most bullies, intimidated by strength.

GERDA LED KATE to the large conference room on the third level. She entered to find most of the senior staff sitting around the long polished table.

She was stunned to see Rausch bandaged, his face battered, teeth missing. "Dr. Rausch! What happened to you?"

"We ask the questions. You answer," Von Schwalbenbach said.

She spotted Doug Daulby down at the far end of the table. He looked grim. Was he in trouble, too? Or had he signed on to Rausch's team?

"You were brought here to assist the Conscious Essence move over to the Vehicles," Rausch said. His speech was slurred by swollen lips and broken teeth. "Now we find that these Vehicles are doing strange and dangerous things, and the finger points to you."

"Points to me? Why?"

"Because it was you who developed the methodology for guiding the Conscious Essences to move across to the Vehicles."

"Suddenly some of the empty Vehicles are taking on lives of their own, so to speak," Von Schwalbenbach said. "One of them attacked Dr. Rausch a short time ago. It appears that another Vehicle attempted to destroy the anesthesiology equipment overnight. Why? What have you done to awaken these Vehicles?"

"*Awaken* them? Nothing! The *last* thing I'd want to do is get these Vehicles moving on their own."

She looked around the table, her gaze steady. "As you all know, I've spoken out before against this. I had no idea what I was getting into when I agreed to come here, and now that I know, I think the work is very dangerous. I've been saying—literally since I first arrived here—that the existence of the Vehicles is opening some very dangerous doors, doors that—"

"Spare us your sermons," Von Schwalbenbach cut in. "If this is not your doing, tell us this: how could an empty Vehicle, without the transplant of donor brain tissue, operate independently?"

She had not been invited to sit, and felt like a prisoner standing before the Inquisition.

"I warned, from the very first day, that these Vehicles were dangerous doors. Apparently some kind of discarnate intelligences have begun finding their way through those doors."

"How could that be?" Rausch asked. He seemed subdued.

"I don't know. Nor can I explain what happened last night at Couldsen's dinner. I think we all know there was some force, some kind of strange energy in that room. We didn't know what it was, but it terrified us. What we're seeing with these out-of-control Vehicles may be another manifestation of that energy—or collection of energies."

She watched the faces as she spoke, and sensed both fear and denial in the same faces. What she said made sense, whether they liked it or not. But they wanted to blot it away: it didn't fit their view of things, so it couldn't be happening.

Her eye passed Doug Daulby's and he nodded his head ever-so-slightly, and she knew he was still an ally. He was a neuroscientist and may not accept the reality of what she was suggesting any more than the rest of them. But at least she could trust him. He was a good person; she was sure of it in that instant.

"You speak of 'energies' and 'intelligences.' What do you mean by that? What kinds of intelligence?" Dr. Hoerschner asked. He was a pale, slight man with a fringe of blond hair still ringing his bald head. She had overheard some of the nurses giggling about Hoerschner's antics in the pool. Apparently, despite his weak demeanor, he had an insatiable sexual appetite for whichever sex happened to be available at the moment. Now he looked terrified.

"I don't have a clue. I think no one, here or elsewhere, knows. I suspect it's the work of discarnate entities of some sort— that is, some form of intelligence that lacks a body, hence the term, discarnate."

"Ghosts, you are telling us?" Hoerschner asked, the bravado muted by the quaver in his voice.

"That's not a term I use," Kate replied. "But yes, something like that."

"What we're experiencing could be just mischievous, poltergeist-like activities. But this goes beyond the normal range of poltergeist activity. Slamming doors, blowing out candles— yes, that could be the work of poltergeists. But I've never heard of a poltergeist taking over and running a human body."

"Yes, yes, go on," Hoerschner said.

"Some of the physical effects—the events in the dining hall last night, the thrown bottles, the sounds, even the strange wind that we experienced—that could be what's popularly called a 'haunting.' One hypothesis to explain that is 'place memory'—that rooms, buildings, even natural spots can take on and hold the energy created by strong human emotions, just as a tape recorder can record sights and sounds on magnetic tape. Does anyone know of anything in the history of the Clinic that's relevant?"

The room was silent.

They know something, she realized as she looked out at the people sitting around the table. The faces were closed and frightened— like the faces of children harboring a guilty secret.

"The clinic has always been a medical facility," Langwein said. "Sometimes it was for tubercular patients, other times for mental patients. During the war, it served as a military hospital."

KATE CONTINUED: "Strong emotional energies may have implanted the residue of events here. Perhaps the youthful physical and sexual energies of the developing Vehicles amplify the place memories. But there is another aspect that—"

Von Schwalbenbach rose. "It is late. It has been a difficult day. It is time that we went to dinner, yes?"

Now he's suddenly trying to cut off this discussion, she realized. But why?

"I'm sure we're all hungry, doctor, but we haven't finished with this," she said. "Sure, we can walk away now, and pretend. But that won't stop these things from happening."

"This is just alarmist talk," Von Schwalbenbach said, forcing a laugh. "Perhaps you can tell your high-tech ghost stories at midnight."

Rumblings came from around the table. "Let her talk. Let us hear her ideas."

"Proceed," Rausch said.

"'Place memory'—the imprint of strong emotional forces left on the building or grounds could be one explanation— or at least a partial explanation. Poltergeist activity—usually playful discarnate entities could be another. But there's a third possibility, and that's the one that very much concerns me, because the work has opened some very dangerous doors—"

Von Schwalbenbach cut her off. "Enough of this nonsense of dangerous doors. Get to—"

He was interrupted by three loud knocks on the door behind.

"See who that is," Rausch said, and Langwein rose. Before he got to the door, it swung open.

Langwein checked the hall. When he turned, his face was white. "There was no one there! It seems the door opened by itself!"

"Get on with what you were saying," Rausch said. His voice sounded strange, as if he were having trouble getting enough air.

"Poltergeists seem to be less-than-human intelligences, more akin to the intelligences of playful animals. What we are experiencing is more complex. That suggests to me a third possibility: that we are encountering discarnate human intelligences, as in—"

"Are you telling us there are ghosts here?" Langwein interrupted.

She nodded. "As I said, ghost is not a word I use. But basically yes. After all, the idea of disembodied human spirits–'Conscious Essences'— as the term is here, is at the core of the work, is it not? We help the CE's of a patient move into a waiting new body. Well, it seems that someone else has been moving on their own into those fresh young bodies—and their intent seems to be working mischief."

She paused, then said, "Or perhaps their intent is to stop this work."

"MOVING INTO THOSE BODIES"—her phrase struck a chord with Daulby, and he recalled that—was it a dream? The door opened, and he felt a presence nearby. Someone climbed into the bed with him. He was too tired to resist; his body was paralyzed. The person climbed on top of him, they were very light. It felt as if his body spasmed, and he found himself standing beside the bed. He tried to shout, but his voice wouldn't come.

Then he saw himself, still in bed, throw back the covers and stand up. "But if that's me," he asked himself, "then how can I be here, too?"

"Help! Help!" he shouted. "Someone's stealing my Vehicle!"

"SURELY YOU CANNOT BE SERIOUS," Von Schwalbenbach said. "What proof do you have?"

"You didn't ask for proof when you recruited me here to adapt my ideas on Multiple Personality Disorder."

She waited. He didn't respond, so she continued: "But I think these cloned Vehicles are even more vulnerable than the usual victims of MPD. These are 'open' all the time. An outside entity coming in wouldn't even have to push aside the 'owner' of that body. The empty Vehicle is an open door, an open invitation back to this world."

LAST BREATH

SONJA DRANK FAST. She wanted to blot out everything. Everything at Hauenfelder, everything that had come before in life, everything that she knew was to come.

After a while she felt someone there with her, and he was above her, pushing in, and she was frightened by the anger and strength she felt from him. She tried to resist, but he was in now, and she felt her body move out of her control. Then it was as if she was on the outside watching her body spasm, observing how the anger and passion overwhelmed her until she was possessed by a searing, flaming rage more consuming than any orgasm she had ever known.

JOHANN ERHOFF was midway through his two-hour tour of night patrol duty of the Hauenfelder grounds, charged with ensuring that outsiders didn't sneak onto the Clinic, and that staff members didn't sneak away.

Like some of the others at Hauenfelder, he had been born in South America of primarily German ancestry. In his case, it had been his grandfather who had come to Paraguay in 1946, and it was the grandfather's connections who had gotten him this job. He was now 32, and had been here for seven years.

Like the other security guards at Hauenfelder, Erhoff was not allowed above the ground floor of the Clinic. He knew that classified medical research was being conducted there, but none of the details. He'd been warned at the start that it was best not to be curious about the work being done. Of the guards, only Brennerman, chief of security, knew what was really under way at Hauenfelder.

Hauenfelder was by far the best job Erhoff had ever held, and he couldn't imagine ever leaving. Like now, on the night shift, he worked ten hours, but since there were only two men on night watch, half of the time was just sitting at the security command center, up by the main gate. Even the other half, patrolling the grounds, wasn't bad— a helluva a lot easier than driving a truck, or standing guard around some oil rig in the desert.

The only sour note at Hauenfelder was that the security types weren't allowed to mess around with the women there. Erhoff and the others got two weeks off, an air ticket, and expenses, every six weeks. "You can do whatever you want when you're on leave. Just stay away from the women here," Brennerman had said.

"What if they come on to me?" Erhoff asked.

"Not very damned likely. But no matter what, don't mess with them. That's the orders from on high."

Erhoff had one more week to go before his next leave, and he was having trouble keeping his mind off it. It wasn't natural, asking a man to live like a monk. Especially in a place like this, where sex was in the air. He'd peeked in the windows at night to watch the regulars swimming naked in the pool, going at it in the corners, three, four, a half-dozen all rolling together. It was hard as hell to keep from jumping through the window to join in.

He had even tried taking cold showers, but they didn't help much.

ERHOFF COULDN'T BELIEVE it when he saw the woman in the woods. He swept the area with his flashlight to check himself. She was still there. She pulled her coat open. She was naked underneath. She smiled at him, and waved him to join her.

He knew what he should do: radio in to the command center about a suspicious woman. But why ruin a good thing? Probably one of the nurses out on the prowl for something kinky. This was too good to pass up.

The woman moved toward him, still smiling. He recognized her then, Sonja, the blond he'd talked to on the grounds a few times. When she was ten feet away, she let the coat slip to the ground, and stood naked in the beam of his flashlight, her tongue running over her lip.

She spread her coat on the grass, and lay atop it. She beckoned with her hand, and said what sounded like "Come."

Erhoff snapped on his walkie-talkie to radio in that all was well: now they wouldn't call him for a while.

It's too good to be true, a small voice inside said, but he didn't want to hear it.

She said nothing, and reached out to fumble with his equipment belt—the one holding his pistol, mace, handcuffs, and radio. The hell with it, he said, and finished the job for her. He tossed the belt out of the way.

"No," she whispered.

The smell of alcohol on her breath was almost overpowering. From the odor, she must have downed a barrel of the stuff. Her eyes were unfocused, dead. "Tonight we try something interesting." She pushed his arms back, over his head, then yanked the handcuffs off his equipment belt, and snapped them around his wrists securing him to the trunk of a small tree. He preferred it the other way, with the woman helpless, but he found this stimulating.

She slid his pants down to his ankles. "Now you are totally helpless," she whispered, straddling him.

"Maybe next time I do this to you," he said, his breath coming fast now.

"There can be no next time," she said. "So we make the most of this now, yes?"

He didn't like her smile, something about it frightened him. Her words were thick, and the alcohol on her breath was sickening.

She rubbed her body against his. "We enjoy it tonight, like there is no tomorrow, okay?"

"Okay."

"She smiled and leaned back. "Now I do something special for you, something you will remember the rest of your life. You want that?"

"Yes, yes, whatever," he said, already finding it hard to breathe between his excitement and the weight of her body on his. This would be a story to tell the others, all right. Except he couldn't tell it here at Hauenfelder, or Brennerman would hear and then there would be hell to pay.

She moved on him again, and he felt something snake around his throat. "What— what is this?"

"You have never tried this? It makes it more intense for you to come."

"Yes, yes, I know that, but not tonight, not here." He tried to pull away, but the tree held his hands over his head.

She smiled, that dark smile again, and now he was terrified. She wrapped the scarf around his throat and pulled it tight. He realized the scarf was attached to a piece of wood, as a sort of lever.

She moved on him, still smiling. He was terrified now, yet more stimulated than he had ever been before. His whole body tingled even as his vision dimmed. "Oh God!" he gasped with his last breath.

DAMNED!

"I CALLED YOU because Mr. Couldsen has been acting very strangely for the past few minutes," Rausch told Daulby when he got to the recovery area. "His Vehicle, Vehicle Charlie, has also been restless, in a strange way."

Daulby looked through the glass wall: Couldsen was thrashing around in the bed. They had strapped him down, and he was fighting against the bands.

Dr. Hoerschner arrived. "I do not understand this," he said. "Mr. Couldsen should be waking peacefully from the anesthetic. This is very strange, very troubling. Perhaps if I—"

The cry from the second recovery room stopped Hoerschner, and they ran to check. That was the room they were using for Couldsen's Vehicle Charlie.

As they opened the door, the Vehicle cried out again: *"Verdammt! Wir sind Verdammt!"*

"'*Verdammt?*' Did I hear right? Did the Vehicle say, 'We are damned?'"

"This cannot be," Dr. Hoerschner said. "Mr. Couldsen has not yet moved his Conscious Essence to this Vehicle. The Vehicle is empty. In any case, Couldsen does not speak German."

"Hilfe Mir!" the cry came now from Couldsen's recovery room down the hall. *"Bitte! Bitte! Hilfe Uns!"*

Elizabet translated for Daulby as they ran to see what was happening. "He's saying Help me! Please! Please! Help us!"

Couldsen gyrated in the bed, his face red with the strain. As they watched, he pulled one arm free of the bonds, and lashed out at the tubes that entered his arms. He was reaching to pull the bandaging and tubing from his head when they reached him and caught the arm.

"This cannot continue," Hoerschner shouted. "His heart is too weak to permit this."

"Then *do* something," Daulby said, fighting to keep hold of Couldsen's free arm. He had unexpected strength.

"What can I do? I cannot stop this. It is most—"

"Sedate him! Give him a shot!"

"But he is just coming out of—"

"Dammit, Hoerschner, you're the anesthesiologist. If you don't get him quieted down fast, we're going to lose him. His heart's no good."

"Yes, yes, perhaps so."

As Hoerschner fumbled to draw a sedative into a syringe, Couldsen began choking.

Couldsen's hand reached out and gripped Daulby's. Suddenly his unfocused eyes changed, and Couldsen was awake. But there was something different in them. "Dr. Daulby, you must help! They are again here killing patients! You are a physician. You have the power. Make them stop what they are doing! For God's sake, stop them!"

"Stop them? How?"

"Close the doors!"

Then the eyes closed, and Couldsen's grip loosened.

Elizabet checked to ensure that Couldsen's air passages were clear, then fitted a plastic airway down his mouth so he wouldn't suffocate himself. One of the other nurses taped the airway in place, then fitted an oxygen feeder tube over the end.

It was difficult for Hoerschner to find the vein in the old man's arm. Finally he got it, and eased the sedative into Couldsen's blood stream.

Shouting continued from Vehicle Charlie's room; they hurried back to tend to him. He had pulled both arms free, and flailed uselessly in the air. He also screamed that he was choking, that he was being gassed. But at least his tubes were still in place.

Daulby grabbed one arm, and Elizabet the other. Hoerschner sedated him, and gradually he calmed.

Dr. Hoerschner slumped into a chair. "This whole episode is— is impossible. The Vehicle could not have been speaking."

"But it *was* speaking," Elizabet said. "We heard it ourselves."

"*But it could not be so!* Mr. Couldsen does not speak German, not at all. I know that for a fact."

The door swung open. Dr. Von Schwalbenbach stepped in, pointing a pistol at Daulby. "You will come with me now."

WARD C

THE STAFF MEMBERS they passed in the hall averted their eyes when they saw Von Schwalbenbach's gun. None seemed surprised. It was clear that they didn't want to get involved. It was not their concern.

Von Schwalbenbach directed him to the small conference room on the second level.

He was surprised to see Kate already there, sitting on a wooden bench. She looked even more drawn and tense than earlier. Von Schwalbenbach motioned Daulby to sit beside her.

Dr. Rausch sat behind the table. Langwein and Von Schwalbenbach took chairs beside him. Gerda sat beside Von Schwalbenbach. Now Daulby had the feeling that he and Kate were facing an inquisition. They instinctively moved closer to each other until their bodies touched.

"It would have been better for all if you had left well enough alone and not gotten into matters that do not concern you," Rausch said. Daulby realized that Rausch's mood had changed again. The earlier tiredness and fear had vanished now, and he was back to his usual arrogance.

"Just bury our heads in the sand and follow orders— is that what you expect?" Kate said.

"It is entirely up to you. Obviously, it would be best for you to become full members of our working team. But before—"

"I'm not interested in becoming a member of your team," Daulby said. "I don't want to get in any deeper than I already am."

"Keep an open mind. I think you will see that it is very much worth your while to remain here, working with us."

"We can't be bought," Daulby replied.

"No?" Rausch replied. "Perhaps you have never been offered the right price."

"No price could ever be right."

"No? I think it is now time for you to visit some people on Ward C."

SONJA STUMBLED back to her room and changed into her white uniform, then headed for the Ward. A couple of the nurses passed her in the hallways and spoke to her, but she passed as if oblivious to them. They had seen her like this before, drunk out of her mind, and thought nothing of it. That was common among the Hauenfelder staff, a way of coping.

MOST OF THE SECRET RESEARCH work had been conducted on Ward C. Daulby had been there only once, accompanied by Langwein, to select the perfect Vehicle for Couldsen.

The Ward was set up like the others, with rooms off a central corridor. They passed along the hallway, and Rausch unlocked a door at the far end.

They entered a small room, containing a pair of glass hyperbaric oxygen tanks. The light in the room was dim, and he saw resting bodies in each. He moved closer. One was a woman, the other a child. The faces were bland, featureless, like the other developing Vehicles he had seen.

But the coloring—the hair and skin—seemed vaguely familiar despite the unformed faces.

"These are the developing Vehicles of a woman and her daughter," Rausch said, looking at Daulby. "Would you perhaps venture a guess as to their past— or future—identities?"

Daulby's flesh crawled at the display. It seemed obscene, even blasphemous, to be seeing the development of even these quasi-humans.

He was disturbed also by the blazing intensity in Rausch's eyes— was it insanity?

"I have no idea," Daulby said. "Just get to the point."

"They are the developing Vehicles of your wife and daughter, Jackie and Jenny Daulby."

At that moment, the child's body turned over and sighed, and it brought back the memory of a hundred times when he had seen Jenny move just that way at home, the same soft little sigh he had expected never to experience again. He stumbled back, his legs suddenly wobbly, and caught himself before falling.

He knew beyond any question that it really was Jenny in the chamber. The body would grow some more, the face would develop and become human, and then the little person would step out, a replica of the daughter he had lost.

He felt his body spasm then, as if it were exploding with the emotions churning through him: grief, joy, hope. He sobbed, deep, wrenching gasps that brought him back to that awful day almost 30 years ago when they came to his school to tell him that his father and sister were dead, his mother dying.

He felt Kate's arm around him, and let her lead him to a chair. He sat, his face buried in his hands, his body racking with bouts of sobbing punctuated by fits of laughter. It churned up those first terrible moments back in the University's operating room when they told him about Jackie and Jenny, and he felt the grief again as fresh and raw as if it had just happened.

Yet there was a bizarre sense of relief, even of joy.

They weren't really gone. It was all just a mistake. Jackie and Jenny were back, and life would be normal and happy again, only this time he would let them know.

But it wasn't real. These weren't really Jackie and Jenny waiting for him. These were only replicas, impostors, mockeries of the people he had known. He couldn't bear to look at them.

Yet he couldn't bear *not* to look. They weren't Jenny and Jackie, but they were the closest thing left. Maybe they would . . . would grow into . . .

He pulled himself to his feet and stumbled to a sink in the corner and splashed water on his face. He heard something that sounded like a distant gunshot, but it wasn't important.

He stole one more glance at the two figures, then walked over to stare out the window at the lights of the village across the lake.

A scream from far away tore through the air. Rausch ignored it. "The fact is that in a few short weeks, your Jenny and Jackie will be back to normal, just as you remembered them. You will have a wonderful second life with them. We hope you will choose to work with us, so you can be with them."

If only it could be true, if they did come back, then he would have a chance to tell them how much he missed them, to pick up where their lives had left off.

Jenny would have the chance to grow up and complete the life that had been taken from her.

The screams multiplied, but they were far away, and this was here.

ONE OF THE PERKS

"BUT HOW did you get cell samples from Jackie and Jenny?" Daulby asked, deliberately forcing himself to concentrate on the technical side as a way of gaining some distance from what he was feeling. He couldn't trust his emotions here.

"I told you of our CIA connection," Rausch replied. "With those contacts, it was quite easy to get everything we needed."

The screams continued, hysterical, shrill. Rausch turned to Gerda. "Go see what that hellish noise is. See that it stops."

Then he turned back to Daulby. "The fact is, we can work from the DNA of tissue even after the cells have died."

It took Daulby a moment to spot the flaw. "But the heads were charred. There was virtually nothing left— at least, so I was told. Hence no possibility of preserving brain tissue for implanting later. Maybe you can clone the bodies from dead tissue, but they'll be empty shells, mindless without the additional brain tissue, and the brains were—"

"Correction. The police apparently did not tell you the complete story. The madman who killed them removed the heads first. The heads, including the complete brains, were recovered. For various reasons, the police did not make that fact public. Not even to you, so it seems."

Daulby struggled to keep his voice steady, forcing himself to deal with it solely as a medical problem. He controlled his impulse to look again at the tissue growing in the oxygen chambers.

"In any case, too late," Daulby said. "You should know that. The brain cells would have been necrotic within five minutes. At that point, the brains were dead for all practical purposes. After those four or five minutes had passed, everything that made Jackie and Jenny the people that they were had departed."

Why am I arguing against the possibility that they really came back? Daulby asked himself, as he turned to look again at the plastic chambers. Perhaps Jackie and Jenny really are coming back to life. Maybe we really can return to a life together. It seems miraculous. Why fight it?

"You are in error, Herr Doctor," Rausch said. "We have solved all of those problems. The promise of returning Jackie and Jenny to you is a reality. Truly, within a few months, they will be living happily here with you at Hauenfelder."

RAUSCH WAITED silently while Daulby walked over to stare at the tissue developing in the glass tubes. When Daulby finally turned away, Rausch said, "I have yet more good news."

Rausch led the way to another room, further down the hall. He flicked on the light, and they saw another pair of hyperbaric chambers. A body rested in each of the clear glass tubes.

Kate's cloned body was complete, in a strange, unformed way, as if the parts were lumps of flesh held together by a plastic bag. The face was a duplicate of her own face, though it was vacant in the way the faces in a wax museum are accurate copies of the features, yet empty of any spark of life.

It was chilling to look at, worse somehow even than it would be to look at her own body in a coffin— because this empty, vacant replica was living and breathing.

She looked into the second chamber and saw the developing Vehicle of Karen.

Daulby watched Kate out of the side of his eye, ready to be there for her if she needed support, not wanting to intrude otherwise. He was amazed at how easily she accepted the sight of the two Vehicles.

Then it struck him: this was not coming as a surprise to her. But how could she not be surprised? Unless she had already known. Yet she had never hinted any of it to him.

So how open with him had she really been? Could he trust her, after all?

Rausch led the way down the hall to another small room. There was no oxygen chamber in this room, just a bed. A man lay on the bed. He didn't stir.

The light was dim, but something about that body resonated with something deep inside Daulby, and then the knowledge hit him— a jolt of fear and nausea that seemed as strong as a physical blow in the solar plexus.

He moved a step closer, then another, drawn to the body, wanting to see it, yet wishing it weren't there.

"It is growing to be another you, of course, Dr. Daulby," Rausch said, "another you, you as you were at 21 . . . and can be again."

"Dammit, I don't *want* another me, I don't want to go around again!"

The lights died. Rausch spoke in the darkness. "Perhaps you would like to have your Vehicle moved into the same room as those of Jackie and Jenny. Then they would all be together again, our first engineered family unit."

"I don't want—"

"To have a Vehicle created is one of the perquisites of the Hauenfelder staff. The opportunity for another lifetime, and then another, and then another later still."

"Perquisites, hell! I don't want to be cloned!"

"That is not your choice. It is Hauenfelder policy to prepare Vehicles for all senior staff members."

"But I don't want—" Then he recalled something that had happened months ago, even before Jackie and Jenny died. He'd been attending a medical conference in New York. For a reason he never understood, he had passed out as he left the shuttle bus, and woke up in an emergency room. He'd been treated and released. The ER physician suggested it was strain and exhaustion. That made sense, and Daulby put it out of his mind.

But there was no explanation for the odd, postage-stamp sized contusions the ER staff had found when they examined him, nor for the evidences of dried blood at the nose and rectum.

"You grabbed me in New York, didn't you? You were getting samples even then, weren't you! But that long ago! How did you know—"

The door burst open. Gerda staggered in, her face white. "The screaming was Nurse Hertl. There has been an another attack! A shooting! You must come! Quickly, before he dies!"

NOT PROMISING

THEY RACED to the recovery area. Staff-members had gathered in the hallway outside the recovery rooms, but none had ventured in. The faces were ashen with shock. They heard a woman sobbing in another room.

Daulby was the first into the room of Couldsen's Vehicle Charlie. Charlie lay in a blood-soaked bed, and heavy discharges of blood flowed from the ears, nose, and mouth. More blood seeped from the abdomen. The skin was chalk-white, covered with a thin film of sweat. The eyes had rolled back into the head, and the breathing was fast and shallow.

There were two visible concave skull fractures— indentations where the blows had struck. Soon they would fill, and swell to the size of oranges. The hair was matted with blood, but at first glance it was not clear if the skull had been opened by the blows.

He pulled back the sheet. A gaping wound below the rib-cage oozed more blood.

"That is where she shot him!" a nurse sobbed. "Then the gun jammed, and she used it as a weapon to batter his head!"

"She? Who?" Rausch asked, but now the nurse was sobbing out of control.

The weapon, a large black pistol, lay on the ground, covered with blood and bits of hair and tissue.

The perpetrator sat slumped on the floor, her back to the wall, her eyes blank. She was dressed in her working uniform, white scrubs. Her clothing, her hands, her face were drenched with blood.

"Sonja's Vehicle did this?" Rausch screamed. "Then the Vehicles are out of control!"

"No," Langwein said softly, shaking his head. "It was not Sonja's *Vehicle*, it was Sonja herself!"

The sight of Sonja drenched in blood stopped Daulby in his tracks, and he forgot about Couldsen's injured Vehicle in his astonishment. The other doctors also stood frozen in place, staring at her.

"But how could this be?" Von Schwalbenbach said. "We know her, yes? She is one of us. It is not poss—"

"Quiet!" Rausch snapped.

"Nurse Hertl is very upset," Marta, another nurse, said. "It is hard to understand her, but she seems to be saying that she heard a noise, the gunshot, and came in, and Sonja was beating Mr. Couldsen's Vehicle with the gun. When she said to stop, Sonja stopped, and slumped to the ground, as you see her now."

Sonja sat, oblivious, looking back at them with empty, incurious eyes.

DAULBY BEGAN by checking Couldsen's Vehicle Charlie. Already the eye reflexes were bad, suggesting significant brain damage.

"Prognosis?" Rausch asked.

Daulby shook his head. "There are tests we need to run to be sure, but—"

"Your impression, doctor. Your quick judgement."

"Not promising, given the blood flow from the orifices. That suggests significant intra-cranial bleeding. The pressure of that pooled blood will already be damaging brain tissue. The first priority is to relieve that pressure. Then we can see what other damage there has been.

"Then do it. But keep in mind that this is the last Vehicle of Mr. Couldsen, his last chance. It *must* survive."

"NO, NOOO, what has happened?" The low moaning startled them, and they turned to see Sonja stirring on the floor, her bloody hands now covering her face. "But what has happened?" Her words were slurred, and the scent of alcohol on her breath now mingled with the odors of blood and damaged tissue.

She tried to get to her feet, but stumbled and fell back on the ground.

"She is very—"

Gerda ran into the room. "Dr. Rausch, Dr. Rausch, you must come quickly. Now there is a security guard dead."

"Dead! Dead? How could this be?"

"He was strangled out on the grounds. Sonja's identification necklace was clutched in his hand."

"Oh God!" Hertl wailed. "Now they're coming for us all, one by one!"

"They say his gun is missing."

"His gun! Then that is where— But Sonja— You say that Sonja killed the guard? How?"

"The other guards say that he was strangled while he was . . . was fucking on the grass with Sonja!"

"Oh God, we're all going to be killed now!" Hertl moaned, then doubled over, sobbing.

Sonja screamed, a cry of anguish and terror that sent chills up Daulby's spine. "Oh God! Oh God! I don't know what came over me!" she screamed, then buried her face on the floor, her body racking with sobs. "He used me, used my body, then abandoned me!"

THE FINAL DAY

SAVED PRAYERS

THE FIRST TEST RESULTS on Vehicle Charlie confirmed Daulby's original pessimism. The blows had fractured the skull, and there was extensive bleeding within the cranial area. The trapped blood was pressing into the brain, crushing the cells.

To relieve the pressure, Daulby proposed the normal procedure for the situation: drilling into the skull to drain the blood and fluid that had built up.

But the amount of blood that had accumulated within the skull was unusual even for so serious a fracture— an indication that there was probably a secondary cause of bleeding within the brain.

Daulby reminded them of the aneurysm in Couldsen's first clone, Vehicle Alfie. "Another may have developed and burst in this second clone," he said.

They wheeled Vehicle Charlie to the operating room. Daulby drilled into the skull first at the area over the blood pool, then cut into the dura that covered the brain and resembled a filmy plastic grocery bag. As he punctured the dura, a geyser of thick dark blood burst out. That was helpful, since it immediately relieved the pressure on the brain. Fewer cells would die.

But as he removed more of the skull and examined the brain tissue, it was obvious that considerable injury had already occurred: injured brain softens like an over-ripe avocado as it deteriorates, and a two-inch square patch of cortex on the right side was already unhealthily soft.

Even more ominous was the danger raised by the aneurysm: if the vessel wall had in fact given way, the bleeding would recur. Daulby ordered another scan, hoping that now with the blood accumulation gone, the view of the vessel would be clearer.

The news was even worse when they reviewed the MRI scan: now an aneurysm was visible deep in the brain of Vehicle Charlie. It was situated on the same blood vessel, within a centimeter of the aneurysm they had found on Couldsen's Vehicle Alfie.

"If two of the clones have the identical aneurysm, then the odds are that Couldsen himself shares the defect, as well," Daulby said. "It's probably been there, latent, all his life, a congenital defect. He's lucky he didn't have a problem earlier in life. He could have had a stroke at any moment. He still could—especially— with the stress around here now."

"Is Couldsen still asleep?" Rausch asked.

Langwein phoned back to the recovery area. "He has not woken. He knows nothing of this, of what happened to his Vehicle."

"Good," Rausch nodded. "See that it stays that way."

IT WAS AFTER TWO in the morning when finally Daulby left the operating room. He had done all he could for Couldsen's Vehicle Charlie. Now there was nothing but to wait and see.

He was surprised to find Kate Remington waiting when he emerged from the OR. She walked with him down the hall. "Any change in Charlie's condition?"

"Only for the worse."

"And Couldsen himself?"

"He's doing a little better. There's a chance, a slim chance, he might make it, provided his heart doesn't quit. You may not like Couldsen, but you've got to hand it to him, he's a tough old bird, determined to hang on."

"No wonder. He's invested who knows how many years and how many millions, maybe even billions, in this place. Now, in the span of 24 hours, all three of his clones are gone, and he's left with nothing to show for it." She paused. "I mean, I *assume* you're not going to transplant any of his brain tissue to Vehicle Charlie. Or are you?"

He shook his head. "No point. Too much necrosis in Charlie."

"In plain English for a very tired semi-lay-person, what does that mean?"

"The pressure of the blood resulting from the injury had killed off a lot of brain tissue. There's no point in transplanting Couldsen's brain tissue into a fresh young body that has a skull full of dead brain cells."

"I almost feel sorry for Couldsen," she said. "Almost."

"You can pray for a miracle."

She thought a moment, then said, "I think I'll save my prayers for someone else.

THEY CAME TO THE MAIN STAIRWAY at the center of the Clinic. "I've been thinking," Kate said, "thinking about some of the things Rausch was telling us before, and things just don't add up. Do you want to talk now, or wait till . . . till whenever?"

"I'd like to get something to eat. Let's see if we can get into the cafeteria. We can talk there."

They stopped by the reception desk at the main entrance to see if there was a key to the cafeteria. The guard on duty there spoke only a little English, but once he understood what they wanted he handed them a pass-key. "But you must not tell Gerda I let you do this, yes?"

The key got them into the dining area, and they went through to the kitchen to find some food.

She poked around in one of the refrigerators. "Can I make you a sandwich? Some nice dark bread, cheese, tomato, maybe a little avocado?"

The controls broke then, and he laughed till he cried, laughed as he hadn't in years. He stumbled back, and dropped into a chair, still laughing.

"Sorry, I seem to have missed the joke."

"Damaged brain tissue is just about the consistency of an over-ripe avocado. After poking around in Vehicle Charlie's cranium for most of the evening, I think I'll pass on the avocado."

He was hungrier than he realized, and ended up having two sandwiches. I'm going to need the energy, he told himself.

KATE SIPPED herbal tea, and nibbled at bread and grapes.

"I had a lot of time to think this evening," she said, then immediately regretted it, knowing how tired he must be. This was not the time to burden him with this, not when he was already down.

But he insisted on knowing.

"I was thinking through some of the things Rausch said about Jackie and Jenny. Thinking too about what happened to Karen. Some inconsistencies kept bothering me. Once I started thinking, a lot of other things opened up."

"Tell me." Now he had to know.

"Rausch said that the police failed to tell you that the alleged killer removed the heads before burning the bodies. That doesn't make sense: why *wouldn't* the police tell you? Besides, it really would have made no difference. As you know better than I, brain tissue doesn't survive very long, only minutes, without a blood supply."

He stared at her, his flesh crawling, wondering how he could have overlooked something so obvious. But he had been distracted at the time, seeing the Vehicles growing there. Since then, he had blotted all of that out of his mind.

"The police obviously didn't catch the killer and recover the heads within those four minutes. Even if they had, it's not very likely they'd have had Rausch's tissue preservative fluid available, is it?"

She paused to see how he was reacting. Then she added, "In short, Rausch lied to you. There was no chance their brain tissue would have been usable—if things happened as he said. But things didn't happen that way."

IT WAS OBVIOUS NOW: Rausch had Jackie and Jenny killed, then grown from tissue samples taken that night as a way of luring him here. The bodies had been so badly burned that those wounds went unnoticed.

It surprised him that he didn't feel anger, just a numb acceptance. Anger would come later.

The image of the butterfly that Rausch crushed on the table that first morning came to mind. Brilliantly-colored, playful, trusting one moment, dead the next. Killed for the sake of a debating point.

"I thought then about what happened to Karen," Kate went on. "Supposedly, she was jumped by a mugger who was never caught. That, by itself, isn't remarkable these days. But the coincidences do begin to pile up. The ambulance, for some reason, transported her all the way across town to another hospital, even though she was not more than a half-dozen blocks from a perfectly good hospital when it happened. We never could understand why. We were never even able to trace the ambulance that had transported her, nor did we ever get a bill. Now I understand. It was all set up in advance. They mugged her, and had their own ambulance waiting."

She turned away for a moment, and he knew she was wiping away tears.

What she said was echoing his own experience. After he had passed out at the convention hotel in New York, an ambulance fortuitously happened to be waiting. That would have given them ten or fifteen minutes alone with his unconscious body in the back of a well-equipped ambulance, and he emerged with strange marks on his body. And that ambulance had never sent a bill for services, either.

Kate blew her nose, then continued: "By bringing Karen to a hospital on the far side of town, they gained time to take the tissue samples they needed. Then they brought the samples back here and started the process of re-growing her. The injuries from the mugging covered up what they had done, and the hospital staff never realized that samples had been taken— they just attributed it to trauma in the mugging."

She walked over to a sink, and splashed some water on her face. "There's more— another coincidence that was really no coincidence, just part of their plan. I haven't told you about—about Jeff. We were going to get married. Then Karen got hurt. One evening, as he drove home after seeing Karen and me in the hospital one evening, he was the victim of a drive-by shooting. He was killed, and the shooter never caught. It just seemed one more stroke of bad luck. But now I see it wasn't. It was part of their plan."

"But we didn't see a Vehicle cloned for Jeff."

She nodded, her eyes moist. "I wondered about that. Maybe they tried, but weren't successful with poor Jeff. Or maybe they decided not to bother. After all, Jeff was of no value to them—only to me. Maybe they just wanted him out of the way so I'd be unencumbered, and hence more likely to come here."

She looked up to the ceiling and sighed deeply. "I said 'poor Jeff.' Maybe I should say *lucky* Jeff. At least he was spared all this, spared being cloned, spared being a prisoner in this place."

Daulby was surprised at how composed Kate was as she spoke. She seemed to be beyond shock, beyond anger. He realized he was the same. He was beyond anger: this was just the way things were now. Jackie and Jenny were gone. That was the bottom line.

"THIS IS OUR LAST CHANCE," Daulby finally said.

"Chance for what?" Kate replied. She was slumped over the table, and seemed to have aged a decade.

"Chance to escape. After my attempt last night, I'm lucky they haven't locked me up. The place is still in shock over Couldsen. With luck, the security measures may have eased."

She shook her head slowly. "I'd like nothing better than to get out of this awful place. But I can't do it, I still can't leave. I can't leave Karen here in their hands. I appreciate your inviting me to go along, but it's out of the question."

Daulby forced down another slice of bread and cheese. He didn't have an appetite, but knew he'd need food energy before the night was over.

"I don't like the idea of leaving you behind. And, as I said before, there could be repercussions for you."

She thought a moment, then stood. "If you do get away, then you can bring help, rescue us."

"But—"

She shook her head. "I'll return the key to the guard at the door. That'll give you a little bit more of a head-start before they come looking for you."

PULLING THE PLUG

TONIGHT THE DOOR to Ward C was unlocked, and the only nurse on duty was asleep on one of the beds, still dressed. Things had fallen apart in the Clinic in the hours since the attack on Couldsen's Vehicle.

The hyperbaric chambers that held the developing Vehicles of Jackie and Jenny rested side by side. Now, in the dim light, they looked like miniature glass coffins.

It had seemed so simple earlier: disconnect everything. Shut off the oxygen lines. Pull the plugs on the electric power. Cut off the intravenous lines that fed nutrients. Then whatever life was in the Vehicles would slip painlessly away, and Jackie and Jenny would be free of this place.

But he couldn't do it. He couldn't take their lives— not even the lives of their artificial replicas.

HE RETURNED to the cafeteria and slipped out through the sliding door to the dining terrace.

He was climbing off the terrace onto the ground when the door to the cafeteria opened behind him and the light flicked on. He dropped to the ground, then pulled himself to the cover of some bushes to look in the window.

One of the security guards entered and headed for the kitchen.

Good timing, Daulby thought, as he slipped away into the shadows. One less patrolling the grounds.

That garage he'd come on in his walk the other day, filled with three cars and an ambulance. Maybe they'd moved the rowboat there. Maybe he'd be able to drag it down to the water.

The side door to the garage was unlocked. He eased it open, and stepped inside into total blackness. The scent of ancient wood, dust, automobile grease, and tire rubber brought him back to an aunt's farm he visited every summer before his parents were killed.

But there was something else here, and he felt sudden terror in the darkness, a creepy feeling on the back of the neck that he was not alone, that eyes were watching him, stalking his move. His instincts told him to turn and run, to get away.

He forced himself forward, blocking the memory of the Vehicle climbing out of the hyperbaric chamber to attack him the other night. Was another waiting here for him? Were there a half-dozen?

He sensed movement to the side, and felt a blow on his head. He spun away from the thrust, lost his footing, and fell backwards, landing in a wheelbarrow. He rolled to his feet, ready to lash out.

But nothing happened. He waited, his flesh crawling.

The fear overwhelmed him then, and he had to escape the garage. He bolted for the door.

The wheelbarrow tripped him, and he hit the ground, breaking the fall with his hands. His hands fastened around the handle of a rake, and he knew that it was the rake that had attacked him, moments before.

He laughed in relief. Then he heard a soft click, and saw the side door slowly open. As it opened, soft starlight cast a hint of light into the garage.

He held his breath: who would be stepping through the door? Erhart's killer? A security guard? One of the out-of-control Vehicles?

Then he saw the outline of a body in the doorway. "Kate," he whispered.

"I CHANGED MY MIND," she said, hugging tight. "I decided I can do Karen more good by going with you and bringing help. I looked for you on the grounds, and saw you come to this garage. Sorry if I scared you."

"I'm glad you're coming."

"Do you have a plan?"

"The rowboat has been moved from the shoreline. I'm hoping it's here in the garage. We could get across the lake before dawn."

"There's no way you could carry a boat down to the water all by yourself."

"And you, all 97 pounds of you, are here to do the heavy lifting?"

"Actually I'm 122, should be 118. Two heads are better than one. I mean two *hands*." She giggled, feeling giddy now that the tension of forcing herself into that dark garage was past.

They went rigid when they heard the handle turn on one of the overhead doors, and managed to slip behind a narrow pillar an instant before the door opened.

A man in a white uniform stepped in and flicked the lights on. He pulled keys out of his pocket, and settled behind the wheel of the Mercedes ambulance.

He fired it up, and let it idle a few seconds, then drove it out onto the driveway. A moment later, he returned to shut the garage door.

"They're heading out to pick up another patient," Daulby said. "That's our ticket out of here!"

They ran up the hill behind the ambulance, and saw that the driver had left it idling in front of the main building while he went inside.

Daulby's impulse was to jump behind the wheel and drive it away. Then he thought again: the guard at the gate would recognize him, and refuse to open the gate. That gate was strong enough to stop a truck.

He glanced inside the ambulance: it was a Mercedes station wagon with a raised roof. They climbed through the back door and settled under the stretcher. It was tight—strangely cozy, even erotic.

He felt her warm breath on his cheek, and he turned his head, and they kissed gently. Then both pulled away, as if triggered by the same impulse. "Not now," she breathed.

Five minutes passed, then ten. At last they heard voices. The front doors of the ambulance opened and two men climbed in, speaking German. The aroma of hot coffee drifted back.

Daulby checked his watch: it was after five. There was already faint light in the sky: soon they would be visible if the men happened to look under the stretcher.

The ambulance slowed for the gate. He picked out what sounded like airport as the driver spoke to the guard. Munich.

Munich! Could that be? It would be across the border, *whatever* border it was, and into Germany.

Fantastic! In Germany, at a big airport like Munich, they could slip away from the ambulance. Even if they were spotted, the men couldn't chase them through an airport.

Then he realized: more likely, they were not going to Munich, that was much too far. They were just picking up a patient arriving via Munich.

Still, it was a start. Maybe something would open up.

CALL HOME

DAULBY SNAPPED AWAKE, realizing that he'd been dozing. The thin blue light of early morning filtered through the frosted rear window. Kate, snuggled against him, was still asleep.

So cozy and domestic. Except they were on the floor of an ambulance, running for their lives.

Once they made it to the airport, he asked himself, What then? They had no money, and no passports.

They could go to the police. There was a chance, a slight chance, that the police might not be totally corrupt.

But what would he say to them? "They're cloning a famous billionaire at Hauenfelder."

"Jawohl, Mein Herr," the police would respond. "You must sit down. You need a rest."

"But you don't understand. I'm a distinguished neurosurgeon, a university professor. Former professor, at least."

"No, you just escaped from that ambulance. You are obviously a mental patient. Back you go to your attendants."

D.D. call home! Dr. Daulby call your office! Call the University, collect. Get Marge Hemmings on the line and explain the situation to her. She'll be able to work something out.

THE HEART STOPPED in Couldsen's Vehicle Charlie. Brain wave function had been flat for hours. Rausch, Von Schwalbenbach, and Langwein were paged, and arrived within seconds.

They looked at the flat monitors, then at each other. "There is no longer any point in continuing, I think," Von Schwalbenbach said. Langwein nodded his agreement.

Rausch shook his head. "No, we must continue. Retain Vehicle Charlie on the life-support system."

They went next door to check on Couldsen's own body. The monitor showed a relatively strong, steady heartbeat, and the nurse reported that he had slept soundly through the night.

Rausch stayed with Couldsen, reviewing the chart, looking for a sign of hope. Langwein and Von Schwalbenbach glanced at each other, then slipped out of the room.

Von Schwalbenbach waited until they were down the hall before speaking.

"Couldsen is perhaps a little better, yes. But let us be realistic. There is little chance of recovery. The cardiac damage is very severe. We must face that fact."

Langwein took his glasses off to clean them, but his hands were sweaty, and the glasses slipped out of his hands. They hit his shoe and bounced away without shattering.

He picked them up, then continued. "But how do we explain why we operated on Mr. Couldsen? He is an important man. The press will be asking questions. Why was Couldsen at Hauenfelder? Who had performed the surgery on his head? Why? What connection did he have there? What work is done at Hauenfelder?"

Langwein shook his head quickly, revealing the depth of the tension he felt. "Couldsen's own reporters will be the worst."

Von Schwalbenbach sighed. "The publicity may not matter, if we have no future here. Has Couldsen provided funds for us to continue the work of Hauenfelder?"

Langwein looked at Von Schwalbenbach, then his eyes darted away. Funding arrangements were privileged information, known only to Couldsen and Rausch. But as second-in-command, Langwein had a reasonably accurate idea of what had been arranged.

"There is not much money, not enough to last long," he whispered. "Mr. Couldsen had postponed arranging the permanent funding, until . . . until he was sure that his operation was a success."

"So the Clinic is out of money?"

"It soon will be, in a month or two. Mr. Couldsen always kept tight control."

"Where does that leave us, you and I? Nowhere at all, I think."

"So it seems," Langwein agreed. "So it seems. After all this work. After all these years. And to make it worse, the other visitors arranged by Mr. Couldsen will arrive tonight. They will expect to see him, and when . . ." he threw up his hands. "It is hopeless, I think."

"For the sake of our lives, it must not be hopeless," Von Schwalbenbach said, again feeling contempt for the weak little man before him. But he still needed him. "We must not give up, yes? We must think of something before the visitors come. Perhaps— perhaps even they will fund it even if Couldsen dies."

"Do you think that?" Langwein asked.

"Where is Dr. Daulby?" they heard Rausch saying to one of the nurses. "He should be here. Page him. Get him here now."

SECURITY FORCE

DAULBY FELT THE AMBULANCE SLOW, then pull off the roadway onto gravel. Kate's eyelids fluttered, and she snapped awake.

Both men scrambled out. Daulby held his breath, wondering if they'd been spotted. Or were they just switching drivers? Seconds passed. He slid out from under the stretcher and raised his head slowly. They seemed to be at edge of a town. The men entered a cafe.

"What do you think?" he whispered. "Take our chances in the ambulance, or get out now?"

"Let's get away, while we have the chance."

He eased the driver's door open, and they scrambled out and crouched in the shelter of the ambulance. It was parked in the open. No matter which direction they went, they'd be visible as they crossed the parking lot.

Daulby pointed a direction. She nodded. He set off at a fast pace, and she followed.

She thought of something. "Keep going, I'll just be a second," she called softly as she turned back to the ambulance.

As she guessed, there was a leather wallet in the glove compartment, filled with coins and even a few bills. Now they'd have a little cash to work with— just in case.

Then she heard running footsteps, and slid back under the stretcher.

The driver jumped in, fired the engine, and floored the accelerator. It took all of her strength to brace herself from sliding out from under the stretcher. He hit the brakes hard, and jumped out. She heard the men talking, their voices excited. She didn't understand the German, but grasped that they had spotted Doug, and that he had gotten away.

Good for him, she thought. But what do I do now?

THE CAFE DOOR banged open and the men burst out, racing back to the ambulance. "They've spotted us," Daulby called over his shoulder to Kate. "Run for it."

When she didn't reply, he glanced back. She was gone. He vaulted a fence into a back yard, and ducked behind a row of hedges on the far side. He saw one of the men pull himself up onto the fence to scan the yard. Then he dropped from sight, and the ambulance roared away.

"A CALL just came from Jochen in the village of Sturdlin," Rausch told Georg Brennerman, the head of the security detail at Hauenfelder. Brennerman's grandfather, an SS captain, had escaped Germany via the Ratline to South America after the war. At 6'2" and blond, he was a perfect Nordic specimen—apart from the brown eyes, flat nose, and lightly-colored skin he had inherited from his Paraguayan mother.

"Jochen and Hans Reichler were on their way to the airport to pick up a patient. They claim they saw Dr. Daulby leave the ambulance when they stopped for coffee. Take some of your people and find him. Daulby knows everything that we are doing. We must not let him get away. Do whatever you must. If he escapes, the whole project is finished. That must not happen."

"We'll get him," Brennerman said, a vulpine grin forming despite the hangover.

BRENNERMAN AND SIX OF HIS PEOPLE from the security force at the Clinic arrived in Sturdlin minutes after Jochen's call. They coordinated with Jochen and Reichler to hear their story, then spread out through the town.

Two of them covered the railway station, one in the waiting area, the other in the station restaurant where he had a view of the loading platform and the street.

Another pair walked through the town, stopping at each of the cafes.

The others drove around town in the two Mercedes sedans, waiting for Daulby to make a move.

They parked the ambulance near the hospital so it would be less noticeable. Jochen and Reichler stayed with it, ready to move as soon as Daulby was spotted. The ambulance would provide a perfect cover for transporting him back to the Clinic.

A little later, Dr. Hoerschner arrived in a third Mercedes, along with two more security guards. Hoerschner was wearing his doctor's whites, still spattered with some of Couldsen's blood.

ON THE WINGS OF A DREAM

HE SPOTTED Jackie and Jenny in the distance, and ran to be with them. But his legs were heavy, as if he were in deep snow, and he could barely move. Then he saw that they were on the other side of a deep chasm. They saw him and waved, but there was no way to get to them.

He heard a motorcycle, and saw a big silver cycle with no rider. He jumped aboard as it passed, and twisted the throttle, and the speed built and the ground dropped away. He soared out over the chasm, floating as on a glider. Now Jackie and Jenny smiled and held out their arms, and then he was holding them both.

He snapped awake then, and found he was still in the garden, hidden between a stone wall and a row of bushes.

THE MEN WAITED in the ambulance near the town hospital, not realizing that Kate was trapped in the back, under the stretcher. She had overheard Brennerman's orders to the security men. "We're to stop Daulby, whatever it takes. Just don't be obvious about it, understand?"

That was the bad news, she thought. The good news was that they spoke only of Doug. Apparently they didn't realize yet that she had escaped, too.

Her break finally came when one of the Hauenfelder Mercedes pulled up, and the two attendants left the ambulance for a quick conference.

She eased the back door open. Keeping low, she crossed the pathway by the side of the road and ducked into shrubbery, using it as cover. She emerged in the back lot of a garage. A mechanic looked up as she passed. She smiled and kept going, and found herself on a highway.

She cut away from the main highway as soon as she could, and headed downhill on a residential street, guessing she was heading toward the center of the town. She came on a lake, with the town arrayed along the shoreline.

But where was Doug?

If I were in his shoes, what would I do? Of course, call home for help.

But how do you make an international call from a little village in a dictatorship?

HE FORCED HIMSELF to his feet. He was stiff and cold from the damp ground, but loosened up after walking a couple of minutes. The sun had burned away the fog, and it was becoming a crystal morning. He didn't know where he was, only that he was in a lakeside village surrounded by mountains. He wasn't even sure what country this was.

He walked quickly through back streets, ready to duck out of sight if he spotted the ambulance. He emerged onto a road alongside a lake and saw the center of town a quarter-mile away along the shore.

He hurried along the wide pedestrian promenade above the water. The pavement was shaded by leafy plane trees. The shade was good cover. There were already tourists out for a morning stroll, and that gave him more cover.

The white stucco buildings of the town gleamed white in the morning sunlight, and a bell rang the hour from the church steeple.

An ornate old hotel at the edge of downtown seemed the best bet. "Do you speak English?" he asked the desk clerk, a chubby, pink-cheeked blond woman of about 20.

"Yes, a little, perhaps. But we are full, no rooms."

"I need to make a phone call, to the United States."

"Then you must go to the post office. There you will phone." She opened a color brochure to a map of the town and quickly traced the route.

Half a dozen glass phone booths lined the back wall of the post office. The clerk spoke some English, and understood at once that he wanted to phone collect to the United States. Daulby was surprised that after all these months, and all that happened, he still remembered the phone number of the University Hospital.

The clerk directed him to wait in booth two. "I must first dial the international operator. You will wait until you hear it ring, then pick up the phone and speak."

The phone rang in a minute or so, and he picked it up in time to hear the operator in Chicago answer: "University Hospital."

"A collect call for Dr. Douglas Daulby," the local operator said.

"Dr. Daulby is no longer with the University Hospital."

"Sorry," Daulby interrupted, "there was a misunderstanding. The call is for Dr. Daulby's secretary. Her name is Marge Hemmings."

"Dr. Daulby is no longer with the University Hospital. Dr. Daulby is deceased."

"Dead? No, Daulby is not dead. I'm Dr. Daulby."

"Dr. Daulby is no longer with the University. He died recently, someplace overseas, I think it was."

"You're wrong, I tell you, I'm alive."

The operator cut in. "You must not talk without paying for the call."

"Then make it collect for Marge Hemmings, and forget the part about Dr. Daulby."

"Ms. Hemmings will not be in until nine o'clock."

"But it's already after nine."

"You must not talk," the local operator said harshly. "In our country it is almost nine, yes, but in Chicago it is seven hours earlier, two o'clock in the morning."

SICK JOKE

MONTHS EARLIER, Rausch's people had arranged to have Kate's purse and luggage stolen at the airport the morning she arrived. They planted the bags in a car that she supposedly rented, the car that was found a couple of days later in the Danube.

But they missed the single credit card and $100 American she had tucked into her shoe for the trip, as she always did when traveling, just in case. There was also the money she had found when she went back to the ambulance.

She settled at the back of one of the cafes along the small main street of the village. There would be a public phone there, and with luck someone in the café would speak enough English to help her place the call. The call would have to be collect.

But who to call? Who could help from nine time zones away?

Debbie Whalen, back in San Diego. But Debbie isn't very practical. I'll have to spell out all the details of what she needs to do.

Good question: what should Debbie do? Have the American police notify the local police? But what would be the point? This was a dictatorship, a police state, and without doubt the local police were on the take from the Hauenfelder group..

Option two: Ask Debbie to notify the State Department in Washington and have them pass the word to the American consul here? But tell the State Department what? That Parsons Couldsen was being cloned in some undisclosed location in a dictatorship in middle Europe?

THE WAITRESS, blond, maybe 20, placed the collect call to Debbie Whalen. It was almost midnight in San Diego. Pray God that Debbie is home.

She heard Debbie's sleepy voice answer, and a wave of relief washed over her. It was going to be all right. The local operator told Debbie there was a collect call for her from overseas.

"From whom?" Debbie asked, her mouth sounding still fuzzy with sleep.

"It is from a Kate Remington."

"It is *not* Kate Remington! Kate is dead! Who *are* you?" Debbie said, her voice suddenly awake and angry. "This is a sick joke —*very* sick. Leave me alone!"

"Debbie, it's *me*. I'm not dead," Kate said, but too late: Debbie had already broken the connection

The blond waitress stared at her, her eyes wide. Dead! I'm not dead!

"The international telephone lines are not for to make jokes," the operator scolded.

"But this isn't a joke. I don't know what— what's with Debbie, but I'm alive. Please, just get her back on the line and let me explain. If she just hears my voice—"

"That is not permitted. And I am making a note of this, so if you try this again the police will be notified."

At that moment, Kate saw one of the Hauenfelder security guards walk past the café.

DAULBY, IN THE POST OFFICE IN THE VILLAGE, slowly replaced the receiver on the hook, wondering what to do. There must be a police station in the town.

But go to the police now and lose the chance to talk to Marge later. Without corroboration for his story, and without a passport, the police might just hand him back to the people from the Clinic.

Actually, almost certainly that's what they'd do: almost certainly, the whole country was on Couldsen's payroll.

"Not a sign of him," Daulby overheard. He turned his head slowly, sure he knew that voice, and saw Brennerman, the head of Hauenfelder's security force, out on the street. Brennerman's back was turned, and he gestured as he spoke.

Daulby felt his heart-rate jump. Now it was not just the two from the ambulance after him, now it was the whole team. Plus the police.

He saw the black Mercedes idling outside as he stepped onto the street. The driver glanced at him. Mutual recognition flashed: he was one of the Clinic's security men.

Daulby sprinted down the side street. He heard tires squealing. The Mercedes slid past like a long black shark, then jumped the curb to cut him off. His shoes slipped on the pavement, and he skidded into the front fender. He was boxed between the car and the wall of a building. The driver popped open his door, closing the trap.

Daulby scrambled over the car's hood and darted across the narrow street, just missing a car going too fast down the narrow roadway.

He ran into a shop, brushing past a mother with a little boy in tow, and raced through to the back entrance. That put him in a narrow alleyway. He sprinted down the alley, then ducked into an open door. The burly driver ran past, muscle-bound and sluggish.

Daulby reversed course to get back to the Mercedes. Maybe the driver had left the motor running. Steal it and get out of town. He ran back the way he had come, again cutting through the same shop.

But the car was gone.

He jogged along the little street, guessing the search now would be centered downtown. What he needed was a place to hole up for a few hours—seven long hours—until he could call Chicago again.

Either that or find a way out of town.

CANCELLED

KATE STOOD at the phone in the back of the café, fighting panic. If Debbie Whalen wouldn't take her call, who would?

The lawyer who drafted her will? But it was midnight in California, and she couldn't remember his name now, let alone the phone number.

The chairman of the psychology department back at the college where she'd been teaching? A nice man, but a wimp. He'd convene a committee to cover himself before phoning for help.

In any case, would the local operator follow through on her threat to notify the police if she tried another collect call?

She was feeling too exposed now in the café. It seemed that the whole Hauenfelder security force was out looking for them. That made very bad odds.

Maybe they still don't realize I got away, she thought. Maybe they're still only looking for Doug. Maybe if I can change my appearance a little they won't even recognize me, since I'm not on their minds.

She paid for her tea, using up too much of the money she had taken from the ambulance, then slipped out onto the street after looking both ways for familiar faces.

She had gone only a few steps when she spotted one of the Hauenfelder security men turning a corner ahead. She ducked into a shop: it turned out to be a women's clothing store, featuring pricy versions of traditional clothing. The shop took Visa and MasterCard. That was good news: she still had the one Visa card that she'd kept in her shoe.

At least she could hide out in the shop for a while, trying things on. She tried a Geiger skirt and jacket combination, a hat with a broad brim, and new sunglasses. Perfect camouflage, she thought as she admired herself in the mirror.

A shadow passed across the room, and she caught a glimpse of a face in the shop window. It was the Hauenfelder security guard. She ducked back into the changing booth.

She called the clerk over and handed her Visa card over the door. "I'll wear these clothes now, a surprise for my husband. Go ahead and write up the sales slip. I'll be out in a moment."

She changed quickly, then peered through a crack in the door. The street outside looked clear. Maybe the guard had just been looking into every shop, and now he was gone.

"Madam?" the clerk called in to her. "There seems to be a small problem, yes? Your Visa card has not been approved. It has been cancelled."

"Cancelled? Why?"

"They did not say."

"Maybe if you put it through again?"

She settled in a corner of the shop, out of sight of the window. But again her card was rejected.

Kate asked the clerk to find the reason. The store manager, a stocky woman in her fifties, made the call, spoke in rapid German, then hung up the phone, and immediately dialed another number.

When she hung up, she came over to Kate. "I spoke with the credit card company. They do not approve your purchase."

"I don't understand how that can be. Did they give a reason?"

"Do you have the cash to pay for these clothings?"

Kate shook her head.

"Then you will take them off now, and then we will talk, yes?"

"The card should be perfectly fine. What reason did they give for not honoring it?"

The manager looked over Kate's shoulder. "They said the card had been cancelled."

"But what reason did they give? I know I'm current on the payments."

"It seems the person to whom this card belonged is dead."

"*Dead!* It's my card. Do I look dead?"

"You have perhaps a passport with your photo to prove who you are?"

Kate hesitated. "I don't have my passport. It was stolen— along with my purse and luggage."

"You are required to have a passport and the proper papers."

"Look. I don't know what's behind this, but—"

"You must talk with the police."

"I've done nothing wrong. It's an administrative error."

Two men in suits walked into the shop. They had the look of police.

Now through the shop window she saw Dr. Hoerschner talking with one of the security guards. A moment later, the Hauenfelder ambulance pulled up in front.

She bolted for the back door, slipping past the younger policeman, and found herself on the street.

Then she saw Doug Daulby half a block away.

CHANGING PLANES

DAULBY WAS IN A SOUVENIR SHOP, pretending to look at the racks of postcards, when a motorcyclist pulled his big silver BMW onto the sidewalk in front. He left it idling, and strutted to a tobacco shop across the way, still wearing a silver helmet and black faceplate.

Daulby vaulted onto the cycle and hit the power. Too much power: the rear wheel slid on the pavement, burning rubber. The cycle slewed from side to side. He caught it before it rammed the curb.

He'd owned a cycle for a couple of years in college— a little Kawasaki, but that was a toy compared to this big BMW with a hairy engine.

He twisted the throttle again, gentler now, and the cycle shot forward, again almost sliding out from under him with its unexpected surge of power.

Another Hauenfelder Mercedes, this one maroon, pulled across the intersection ahead, blocking it. Men jumped out, ready to grab him.

Daulby braked, and pulled the cycle in a U-turn in the narrow street. The rear wheel slid out from under. He threw out his foot and caught it before falling. He hit the gas again, and headed back toward the center of town.

A black Mercedes pulled across the intersection ahead. Two men jumped out. Daulby feinted to pass on one side, then twisted the handlebars and slipped past on the opposite side before they could react.

"DOUG! IT'S ME, KATE!" she called, waving her arms, but he shot past on the cycle, and swerved around the big Mercedes that blocked the street. She recognized the men as they jumped out of the Mercedes: more Hauenfelder security.

She tried to bolt across the street, then drew back to the safety of a parked car as another Mercedes roared past. Then she felt the cop's heavy hands grab her arm.

HE'D SEEN MOVEMENT, but things were happening too fast for him to recognize Kate. The cycle was too powerful, a monster. He should spend hours driving around a parking lot in a helmet and leathers to get the feel of it. But there was no time for that— he'd learn by doing.

Or die trying. Anything was better than going back to the Hauenfelder Clinic.

An image from the dream flashed through his mind: wandering in a desert, spotting Jackie and Jenny, trying to run to catch up with them, realizing they were on the other side of a deep chasm. Then the silver motorcycle without a rider.

He headed out along the road that ran by the lake, trying to hold the power down while he got a sense of the thing. The morning air whipped through his hair, and brought tears to his eyes.

He checked the rear-view mirror. The maroon Mercedes was a hundred yards behind, its headlights blazing, cutting around the morning traffic.

Direction signs flashed past too quickly to read. It didn't matter: the names meant nothing to him. All he knew was that he was somewhere in central Europe, and anyplace else was better than here.

Another intersection loomed ahead. A car cut across his path. He braked—too hard. The cycle began to slide out from under him. He caught it in time, and found himself on a road that headed up a hill. Maybe that would lead back into the town. The cycle was agile: he could lose the tail in the streets. Or find the main road out of town. He roared up the hill, exulting in the surge of power.

By now the police would be looking for the stolen cycle. In police hands he would at least be safe from Rausch's people— unless they convinced the cops he was an escaped mental patient from the Clinic.

He found himself at an intersection with the main road, and turned left to head out of town. This road was busier than he expected. But that also was good news. On a busy road, a cycle had the advantage: it was faster and more mobile.

All he had to do was keep the cycle on the road, and stay out of the way of the oncoming traffic.

He glanced down at the speedometer, and eased off on the gas: 100 kilometers, 60 miles per hour. Too fast for a tight road like this. The object of the exercise was to escape from Hauenfelder *and* stay alive.

A bus pulled out of an intersection close ahead, and a logging truck blocked the on-coming lane. He hit the brakes.

He checked the mirror again: an ambulance, lights flashing, had joined the maroon Mercedes. Both were closing fast. Still there was no way past the bus. Now the Mercedes was on his tail, a half-car-length behind.

The ambulance pulled out into the passing lane, its blue emergency lights clearing the oncoming traffic.

The ambulance pulled alongside him, and the maroon Mercedes moved up closer, boxing him in. A nudge from the car would push him off the road into the trees.

He hit the gas and shot for the gap between the front of the ambulance and the rear fender of the bus. He slipped through the gap with inches to spare, then soared away.

This was his last chance: if he didn't lose them now, they'd be on his tail until the gas tank ran dry. He gave the cycle more throttle, exhilarated by the surge of power. With it, he felt omnipotent.

The trees and cars flashed past as he wove his way through the traffic, slipping through gaps between cars, dodging around on the shoulder when he needed an opening.

The cycle was part of him. It moved at his thought more than touch, surging forward with unlimited power, flicking right-left-right to wind around obstacles, braking with gut-wrenching strength.

He glanced at the mirror: the ambulance was far back. Its flashing lights cleared the traffic, but the heavy vehicle was no match for a fast cycle.

A piece of grit flew into his eye as he rounded a bend. He caught a glimpse of a tractor pulling out of a driveway ahead, and hit the brakes. Too late, he saw a film of water across the road, leaking down from a stone cliff.

The tires lost grip in the sudden wet, and the cycle slewed across the road. He fought to keep his balance.

The dirty pockmarked grill of a grey logging truck filled his vision. So this is how it ends, he thought, squashed like an insect on a truck grill.

In a blink, he was safely past the truck and onto the gravel shoulder. The shoulder dropped off below, and he and the cycle floated through the air. The cycle rolled away beneath him, as if in slow motion, and it reminded him of watching the booster rockets falling slowly away from the space shuttle.

Time slowed, and another snippet from the dream came to him: Floating across the chasm, Jackie and Jenny holding out their arms, and then the three of them hugging, crying with joy at being together again.

He saw the tree coming at him, and had all the time in the world to study it, to see the pattern of the bark, and the way one side of the tree had been scarred by a car years ago.

The scent of balsam filled the air, and he was struck by the ethereal beauty of the sun glistening off the silvery-green needles. The forest stretched behind, rows of stately pines sloping down the mountainside like soldiers in columns.

What a beautiful morning, he thought. How exquisite the world is, the clear sunshine, the fragrant air, the variety of colors. How wonderful it is to be alive on a morning like this.

There was no avoiding the tree. When he hit, it felt no worse than a belly-flop into a pool. He felt his wind knocked out, and his body stung for an instant. *Then it was as if he had passed through the hard, flat surface, and was slowly tumbling through soft, warm water.*

POOR GIRL

ONE OF THE POLICEMEN held Kate while the other handcuffed her. They led her back to the shop. "If you will come quietly with us now," Dr. Hoerschner said, "no charges will be placed."

"No!" she said to the women in the shop. "I've done nothing wrong. I don't want to go with these men. They're trying to kidnap me."

"I do not understand what you say," the woman shrugged, turning away. She had spoken nearly-perfect English earlier.

Hoerschner spoke in German to the police and the manager from the shop, and pulled out his wallet to display his license.

Then he turned to Kate. "You may not realize it now, Mrs. Evans, but you are a very sick young woman without your medication. We will—"

"He's lying. My name is not Evans, and I'm not his patient."

"Yes. Well," the older policeman said, slipping his notebook into his pocket. "You may proceed, Herr Doctor."

Kate spun out of their grip. She threw herself against a table, knocking a lamp to the floor. Then she kicked, catching the second cop solidly in the shins. But another blocked the door.

"Now arrest me. I've caused property damage and I've assaulted an officer. Arrest me. Let's clear this up."

Dr. Hoerschner took out his wallet again. This time he put some bills on the counter.

The shop manager slipped them into a pocket of her jacket. "But there is also the matter of the clothing she bought."

Hoerschner handed her more money, and she smiled and said, "Yes, I will press no charges." She glanced at Kate. "Poor girl." She turned away.

Hoerschner and one of the guards took her by the arms.

"Please! Someone! Help me! Don't let them—"

She felt the pin-prick on her arm. "I want to talk to the American consul," she tried to call out as her consciousness faded.

THE OTHER SIDE

DAULBY FINDS HIMSELF on the other side of the tree. He checks himself for injuries: no pain, no blood. Lucky, he thinks, incredibly lucky. Must have only brushed the tree in passing.

He hides in shrubbery when he sees the ambulance stop at the top of the embankment, its emergency lights flashing to block the traffic in both directions. Two men in white jump out, then stand at the side of the road looking across the gully at the tree. He wonders if they see him in the bushes.

People from the other cars and trucks get out to look. No one seems to be saying anything. One of the drivers turns away and vomits. A couple of the others cross themselves. Others walk back to their cars, silent, heads bowed, subdued.

The ambulance attendants drag the stretcher down the slope, assisted by security men he recognizes from the Clinic. Daulby's initial impulse is to run; then he decides it's best to stay where he is, not draw their attention.

The men approach the tree. Daulby shifts position a little. Now he sees the motorcycle off to the side of the tree. The frame is twisted. The seat and fuel tank lie in bushes a dozen yards away.

The men stop at the tree. They set the stretcher on the ground, then bend over as if pretending to load a body.

Another Hauenfelder Mercedes pulls up behind the ambulance, and Dr. Hoerschner jumps out and scrambles down the bank to join the others. He makes a show of pulling a blanket over the stretcher. Then they carry it back up the slope.

What's their game? Daulby wonders. A charade to fool the other drivers. But what's the point?

A white police Volkswagen arrives as they are sliding the stretcher into the back of the ambulance. A pair of officers in gray uniforms step out. Dr. Hoerschner cut them off before they get to the stretcher. One of the police steps around him and reaches out to pull the blanket back from the stretcher. For the first time, Daulby notices that Hoerschner had pulled the blanket over the whole stretcher, as if covering the face of a corpse.

Hoerschner, shaking his head, puts his hand on the blanket, holding it down over the face. One of the officers points at him, apparently ordering him to step back. He does, his arms moving in hard, angry movements. He flips his wallet open, and shows something to the officers. His medical license, Daulby guesses.

The police examine it, then nod, and the men carry the stretcher up the slope and load it into the ambulance.

Daulby thinks again about turning himself in to the police for protection, but decides against it. Hoerschner speaks the language, and he has a doctor's credentials. The police would take his word over that of a ragged tourist on a stolen motorcycle.

Call Marge in Chicago first, have her prepare the way with the police.

The police hold traffic while the ambulance turns around in the road to head back toward the village. Daulby watches Hoerschner climb into the Mercedes and pick up the phone.

IT SEEMS VERY LONELY after the police leave. But peaceful. He still feels no pain, and his body seems oddly light: probably the aftershock. The world seems unnaturally quiet, as if the background hum of a motor has suddenly shut off.

He notices a cloud of silvery mist swirling through the trees toward him. A hole forms in the center, as if it were a giant smoke ring. The ring floats over him, and he looks up through the center, and it feels as if he is standing in the funnel of a slow, gentle tornado. He feels a gentle force from the tunnel pulling him into it.

This has to be an hallucination, but why? Concussion? Shock? Exhaustion? Oxygen deprivation? And the pull. It's like . . . like I'm being sucked into a vacuum cleaner. I can't let go, can't give in to it. Got to get help, got to get back to Hauenfelder for Jackie and Jenny, for Kate, for Karen. Can't leave them with Rausch. Got to shut that evil place down.

"Let go," a voice seems to say. He looks around. He sees no one. "Let go, Douglas. Pass over. Relax and pass over."

He knows that voice. But it can't be! It can't possibly be Mom!

He looks up into the tunnel, extended now, seeming to stretch up through the sky into infinity. He sees them in the tunnel, Mom and Dad, holding out their hands to him. They seem shadowy, surrounded by a bright, warm, white light, coming from back at the end of the tunnel. What is going on?

Mom is crying and laughing, reaching out to hug him. Dad smiles and holds out his hand.

A small girl is standing with them, Connie, his sister. But Connie died in the car crash with them.

The images—so vivid. Why? Result of a concussion? Not likely: he'd felt hardly any impact.

"Let go, Douglas," he hears his mother's voice say. "Let go, and come with us. We've come to help you over."

He touches his head, feeling for a bump. Something was wrong: could a hallucination be this vivid?

"It's true, son. You're over. You're with us now. Accept it and let us guide you across." Dad's voice.

Daulby blinks away the tears, suddenly filled with the love for them that he had repressed through the years. Get your mind on the present, he tells himself. Forget about them. Get on with what needs to be done in the here-and-now.

But the love comes surging back, and it's as if the energy of the love is pulling him upward into the tunnel, the vortex that would lift him through the evanescent sky.

He pushes away from the tunnel, from the energy, refusing to give in to the impulse. There's no time for regretting the past. He has things to do. Stop the Hauenfelder work. Rescue Kate. Help Jackie and Jenny.

"Don't you understand, son? You've changed planes. You've crossed over. You're with us now. You're not on the earth plane any longer."

"I've got to help Jackie and Jenny," Daulby says out loud to blot out the voices. "I've got to destroy Hauenfelder."

He feels the force pulling him upward again, almost like the feeling of nodding off in front of the TV. It would be so easy to just let go and let sleep come. Stop fighting, just float away.

He fights it as he fought off sleep. He has to help Jackie and Jenny. He has to stop Hauenfelder so Jackie and Jenny will be safe. And Kate and Karen.

PERVASIVE CHILL

WHEN THEY BROUGHT KATE back to Hauenfelder, Rausch ordered her locked in with Karen. That way, she could tend to her twin's needs, freeing up the ward nurses' time. Couldsen's VIP visitors were due to return soon from Vienna, and things would be very busy. Later, when things settled down, they could decide what to do about the two of them.

Karen even seemed to smile when Kate bent over to kiss her forehead.

Kate pulled up a chair and took Karen's hand in hers. The wrist was braced to keep the hand from twisting over, and she released the brace for a better grip.

"What a place, little sister, what a place."

DAULBY MAKES HIS WAY back to the village, confused, as if in some weird kind of jet-lag. He scans the area around the village post office as he enters: no sign now of any big Mercedes or muscle-bound security guards. The people inside are all locals, and they pay him no attention.

Strangely, the telephone clerk who had been so pleasant earlier now ignores him. He clears his throat, but still the clerk refuses to look up.

He feels himself shoved out of the way by a woman pushing past to get to the window. A strange anger flares. If you want to be that way, he says to himself, fine. I can be just as rude. He pushes back into her.

That works. She shivers and pulls back, an odd, vaguely frightened expression on her face.

The clerk points to one of the glass phone booths. The woman walks to the booth, and the clerk dials the number. Again he ignores Daulby, and goes back to his papers.

"I want to call Chicago again, as I did this morning," Daulby says. "Can you arrange that for me, please? I'll need to make the call collect."

The man squirms in his seat, and glances up. Though he looks at Daulby, his eyes seem not to focus on him.

TIME PASSED, and Kate wondered who would come back, and how they would punish her for escaping. But it didn't matter what they did to her, so long as they didn't harm Karen. And as long as she and Karen were together till the end.

A key tinkled in the lock, and she braced herself. It was Marta, one of the nurses. "I would have come sooner to help," she said, "but things are very crazy. More of Mr. Couldsen's VIP guests are on their way."

"What happened to Dr. Daulby? Did he get away?"

Marta blinked several times, her eyes darting away to avoid contact with Kate's. "I must go."

Karen drifted off to sleep after Marta left.

Kate stood in the window looking out across the lake. Dusk was settling now, the end of a day that had begun with sunshine and hope, and now was ending in melancholy. It seemed almost certain that Doug hadn't made it. If he had, then by now he'd have sent help.

She saw no way out: life, her life and Karen's life, had effectively ended.

They can never take the risk that we might escape. We won't even have the freedom of this place. We'll be locked up around the clock. We'll become laboratory animals for their weird experiments. They'll use us, then dispose of us. Better for us to die now and be free of it all.

There's no point in going on, no point in living.

Immediately she was annoyed at herself. If people could survive Auschwitz, could survive the thousands of disasters that happened all over the world every year, then I can endure this! They may win in the end; they hold most of the cards right now. But I will not make it easy for them! I'll fight every step of the way!

Karen's eyes snapped awake, and she turned her head to stare at the wall. The eyes moved, as if following something. Kate felt the hairs stand up on the back of her neck as a deep pervasive chill passed by

INFLUENTIAL PEOPLE

LANGWEIN AND VON SCHWALBENBACH came on the run, responding to Rausch's page. Gerda arrived a moment later.

"This moment I received a telephone call from our contact with the local police," Rausch said. "He told me that two investigators will be coming here soon, following up on Dr. Daulby's accident. We must make preparations quickly."

"What preparations?" Gerda asked. "What can we do?"

"We must make it easy for them. They will want to see Daulby's passport, so we must have that ready for them so they will have no reason to explore beyond the main floor. You, Langwein and Von Schwalbenbach, you will meet with them in the conference room on that floor."

"We? But what of you? If they see you like this . . ."

"Tell them I am ill. If they see me with bruises on my face and broken teeth and a broken nose, their curiosity will be aroused, and curiosity is something we do not want. Let us make this easy for them, a routine matter, so they will do their work quickly, then go."

"Yes, yes, exactly," Langwein nodded.

"There is another precaution we must take," Rausch said. "See that the donor patients—the AIDS patients, all of them—are moved onto the sun-room on the main level. Place them so the police will have to walk past them when they arrive. When they see them, and the condition they are in, I think they will not stay long. They will have no desire to explore the Clinic, I think."

"But some of the patients— some have a very fragile hold on life," Langwein said. "Because of the events today, not all have been fed. It is late. It will soon be dark."

Rausch shrugged. "What difference does it make now? They were research subjects. If they die now it saves us the trouble of terminating them later, yes?"

"And Couldsen's important guests? Are they still coming?"

Rausch nodded. "It seems so, yes. I tried to postpone their visit, to give us time to . . . to get things under control. But they insisted."

"And of Couldsen's health? What do we tell them? He is still in coma."

"We must first deal with the problem of the police."

RAUSCH TELEPHONED the VIP guests, and they agreed to arrive at Hauenfelder by car rather than helicopter. For the sake of "a lower profile," he put it, without telling them that the local police would also be arriving shortly.

When they arrived, the American Senator seemed to lead the group. Rausch confided in him that Couldsen was not merely "ill," as they had been told, but had in fact slipped into what was almost certainly a terminal coma.

The Senator shrugged when he heard the news. "I suspected something like that was the case when Couldsen didn't come to Vienna with us. I've been thinking about what that might mean for the rest of us."

On television, he was the epitome of senatorial presence: a tall, elegant man, with flowing white hair, a deep, sonorous voice, and an often-voiced concern for "the typical, hard-working, God-fearing American." Seen in the flesh, he was shorter and thicker than he appeared on the tube, and his face was a mass of red blotches and broken veins.

Lobbyists and fixers around the world knew that his interest in his constituents and country ended when the cameras stopped running. Then he showed a shark-like self-interest.

"Ask not what I can do for you until you've shown what you will do for me," he'd once parodied after an evening of drinking. The comment had been overheard by a journalist, but it never made it to print because of the Senator's connections.

"We are of course sorry indeed to hear about Mr. Couldsen, an esteemed friend, and a gentleman of the first rank," he continued. "But we are all realists. The fact is, you folks are doing some very interesting and important research here, and none of us would want to see Couldsen's misfortune slow it down any. He was a wonderful, wonderful man, and I know he'd want the work to continue."

"It would be a tragedy if he doesn't live to reap the benefits of his investment," Rausch intoned, "but such is fate."

"I can make some introductions to other folks who'd be very interested in your work," the Senator said. "Influential people who could help out financially, now that Couldsen is out of the picture. Men who can quietly invest millions, men whose discretion we can count on. Men who'd be willing to do anything at all to get another bite at the apple."

GERDA TAPPED LIGHTLY on the door, then entered and handed Rausch a message slip: "The police detectives have just arrived at the front gate, and are being escorted to the second floor conference room."

Rausch forced a smile, and told the visitors that he and his staff had a medical emergency to deal with, then instructed Gerda's assistant to arrange "refreshments." From Couldsen, she had learned that the visitors favored stiff drinks served by a friendly female staff. The Senator had informed Rausch that they would be spending the night, so this was a night out, away from reporters and the prying eyes of the public.

"Dr. Hoerschner will remain with you in my absence," Rausch said.

AWAKENING

DAULBY WOKE, and tried to piece together the jumbled images of the dream: something about a motorcycle, about his parents, about almost drowning, about Jenny talking to him. Even an image of putting his arm around Kate and saying he was there to help. None of it made sense, yet it seemed so real, not like a dream.

It was dark in the room. There didn't seem to be a window, just a little light seeping under the door.

He raised his hands to rub the sleep out of his eyes, but one of the hands missed and slammed into his nose.

Wow! he thought, I really must have been out of it to be that uncoordinated. Must have really needed the sleep.

He looked around, but the place didn't seem familiar. It was as small as a monk's cell. Or a jail cell.

Then he remembered more of the dream. A motorcycle. Something about stealing a motorcycle. Weird.

He pulled up, and sat on the edge of the bed, but felt clumsy, as if his body were stiff or weak or . . . He groped for a word to describe the feeling, but words were slow to come. Even his brain didn't seem to be working quite right.

The gleam of a small white sink drew his eye. He stood, but his uncoordinated legs gave way, and he fell back onto the bed.

He tried again. This time he made it across to the sink, bracing himself first on the bed, then on the sink. His legs felt oddly disjointed: strong, but not quite under control.

It was hard to move his hands to accomplish the simple task of splashing water onto his face. It was as if the arms were asleep, almost out of his control.

The face, as he touched it, felt odd: somehow tighter, smaller than normal.

Maybe I've been sick, he thought. Maybe I've had a fever. That would explain the bizarre dream.

The cool water was refreshing, and he flushed some of it through his mouth. He fumbled along the wall, looking for a light switch. Then he found a chain over the mirror and gave it a tug.

"Oh!" He exclaimed, stumbling back. He grabbed the sink to steady himself.

The face in the mirror was not his face. Rather, not the face he had become accustomed to. This was a face he hadn't seen in years. The skin was tight and unwrinkled, and the bags that had grown under his eyes from too many nights without sleep were gone. Even a couple of teen-age acne scars had disappeared.

"I look like . . . like I did in college . . . when I was 20, 21," he said aloud, but his words came out slurred. Even his lips and tongue seemed clumsy, as if a dentist had pumped the mouth full of anesthetic.

That triggered a dim memory: something about being 21. Words echoed in his mind: "They emerge from our process at their physical primes, roughly equivalent to 21 years of age."

Who said that? Someone with glasses, I can see the glasses, someone who was constantly cleaning his glasses. A room full of athletes. Something like a health club.

He looked again at the face in the mirror. There was something else different about it, too. It took a moment, and then he had it. It was the hair, his hair was wrong, too dark.

White! His hair had been white for years, he was sure of that. So what the hell was going on? Dark hair? How could that be?

He tried to recall his age. Why was it so hard to remember things? 39? But this face in the mirror, *my* face, is half that, maybe 20, 22—something like that. Is this a dream— *another* bizarre dream? Or an hallucination?

He fumbled his way into the small shower-stall and ran water until he felt better, gradually getting more control over this strange body.

He dried off, looking at himself in the mirror. The body, at least, was in good shape. *Great* shape. Lean, good muscle tone. So that rules out the idea that I've been sick.

He found a new toothbrush and smeared toothpaste on it. Then he froze in place: his mouth was full of tiny teeth. Baby teeth!

He brushed the teeth. They're in my mouth, obviously they're mine. But how did I get baby teeth? I'm 39 years old, 39 going on 21. With baby teeth?

He pulled on clothes he found in the room, and walked out into the hall.

But his body still felt odd. He felt lighter on his feet, and he sensed a bounce in his movements that he'd forgotten. It was becoming easier to control his legs now.

It was the same with the arms: he tried to scratch his nose, and his hand bounced off the chin. He tried again, now focusing on the movement. This time it was easier. He tried again, and it was easier still.

It just takes a little concentration, and some practice, he told himself. But why should I need to practice using my own body?

He had no idea of where he was, though the place did seem vaguely familiar. Then it came to him that it was a kind of hospital, and that he was a doctor, a neurosurgeon.

He looked out a window. The sky overhead was still light, but down where he was it was nearly dark. A ring of tall grey mountains blocked the light. When he saw the mountains, he knew he was in Europe. But what am I doing in here?

He had an image—a memory?—of riding a motorcycle fast along a lake, with mountains like these rising up from the far shore, and then pine trees on that same beautiful morning. Why was that significant?

He mouth felt odd, and he ran his tongue over the small teeth, and he had image of a dull young face with empty eyes. He also had . . . baby teeth . . . in a face that was 21 or so.

Vehicle 27—a person they called Vehicle 27. But why? Someone saying "Vehicle 27 is nothing more than a moving vegetable."

Images and memories came tumbling through his mind now, a moving montage of events and snatches of conversation. The pieces began falling into patterns, and it was coming back to him now. The place was a hospital no, a clinic. But where were the doctors, the nurses, the patients?

Then he understood what had happened, and why he had been drawn back to the Hauenfelder Clinic.

FEAR

GERDA HURRIED down to meet the police when they arrived at the front door, and escorted them past the assembled patients to the conference room. It was hard to tell whether the sight of the wasted bodies had any effect on the men.

Von Schwalbenbach and Langwein let them wait a couple of minutes to establish dominance, then entered the room.

As they expected, the police wanted Daulby's passport. "Yes, that does seem to be the man as he was described to us," the senior police investigator said when he saw the photo in Daulby's passport. His name was Rudi Schenck. He was grey and balding, though his large moustache was still black. He was a big man, over six feet, and his stomach pushed at his rumpled grey suit.

He passed it to his junior, Hergl, for confirmation. Hergl was 20 years younger, and still thin. His straight, light brown hair fell shapelessly over his head. He also wore a lumpy grey suit. He nodded, "It's him, all right."

"Your Dr. Hoerschner told the officer at the scene that the deceased, a Dr. Daulby, was on the staff here. Is that true?"

Langwein licked his lips, then said, "He was an eminent American surgeon, here for a few days only, as a consultant, nothing more."

"A surgeon? Surgery is performed here?"

Langwein realized he had blundered, and tried desperately to recall the story they had fed to the local authorities about the purposes of the Clinic. Was surgery part of it? "Dr. Daulby was a consultant on our research."

"What research is that?"

"It is confidential. Surely you can understand that."

"Police are trained to keep secrets, doctor," Schenck said, then leaned back in the chair and stared at Langwein. "Your accent, Dr. Langwein— what is it? Not Austrian, not German exactly. Seems to have a trace of an undercurrent— can it be Spanish?"

"I was born overseas, of a German father."

Schenck nodded. "Ah, I see, of a German father. In South America?"

"That is so."

Schenck turned to Von Schwalbenbach. "And you—were you also born in South America?"

Von Schwalbenbach's hand went to the dueling scar on his face, his habit when he was feeling stress. "Yes, in South America. But of what concern is that? You are here investigating a highway accident. I do not see what these questions about me have to do with that."

Schenck stared at him until Von Schwalbenbach was forced to look away. Then he said, "You will produce your papers for us. And you, Dr. Langwein, you are also a foreigner working in my country. Your papers, please."

"That will—"

Schenck cut him off. "Also the director of the Clinic, Dr. Rausch, he should be here with us now. Where is he?"

"As I told you, Dr. Rausch is ill today. He cannot see anyone," Langwein said.

Schenck pulled himself to his feet. Hergl took the cue and stood also. "Then we will have to content ourselves with a thorough examination of the Clinic at this time, and we will come back tomorrow to meet Dr. Rausch. At that time, we will need to see his passport and other documents."

"No, no, it is not possible to tour the facility. Because of health considerations. You have seen our patients, they are very ill."

"They can hardly be so very sick if you can let them sit around like this."

"You have no authority to search," Von Schwalbenbach said.

Schenck's mouth smiled, but his eyes remained hard. "I thought you would be proud of your Clinic, eager to show it to us."

"Langwein told you: some of what we do is confidential research."

Langwein stood. "I must consult with Dr. Rausch before I allow any of this."

"What you say you will allow has no bearing on my investigation," Schenck said. "In any case, while you're out, bring back the documents for all of the staff and all of the patients."

Langwein hurried out of the room.

Schenck turned to Von Schwalbenbach, and was surprised to see the fear on his face. Professionals, like doctors, were usually skilled at hiding their emotions. If this one was cracking so soon, then there must be something very interesting here. The trick was to find it before they could get to their friends in the capitol and have the search stopped.

"Your Dr. Hoerschner insisted on taking Daulby's body back here, claiming there was some kind of emergency procedure to be performed. Can you tell us about that?"

"You must ask Hoerschner himself."

"An excellent idea. Bring him—"

The door burst open. A nurse ran in, out of breath from running. "Dr. Von Schwalbenbach, you didn't answer your page, you must come quickly, it is an emergency, Mr. Couldsen is having another cardiac incident!"

Von Schwalbenbach ran after her. The two policemen followed.

$500 MILLION RIDE

DAULBY FOUND his way out of the Ward to the central staircase. He was beginning to feel at ease in this body.

He saw a man running up the stairs. *Von Schwalbenbach!*— the name came to him. And he remembered that the man was a neurosurgeon and a pain in the ass.

But who were the two men in grey suits following Von Schwalbenbach? Then he saw the guns and handcuffs beneath their lumpy jackets: police. Why were police here?

He tagged along behind them.

Von Schwalbenbach ducked into one of the rooms along the corridor. The police stopped at the door. Daulby, a plan forming in his mind, positioned himself in the doorway beside the police.

He saw Von Schwalbenbach and another man working over a patient in a bed. *Langwein*, that was the other doctor's name, the one with the glasses.

Another man stood off to the side. He seemed to have been in a fight: both eyes were black, his lips were swollen, his nose was taped as if it had been broken. *Rausch*— yes, that was the name, also a doctor.

He saw the paddles, and recalled the drill: they were defibrillating because the patient's heart had stopped. But they were clumsy, not pulling together as a team. The monitor kept its steady shrill warning: nothing was happening. They were losing the patient, and Daulby wanted to push forward and save him.

But it's not my patient, he told himself. I don't know who he is. Keep out of it. That's not the reason I've come back.

The younger policeman turned to Daulby and asked, "Who is that man with the broken nose?"

"That is Dr. Rausch." His pronunciation was still fuzzy. Operating the lips and tongue involved a complex of fine-motor skills: it would take some practice to coordinate those skills again.

The policeman stared at him. You look like you're seeing a ghost, Daulby chuckled to himself. He saw the policeman nudge his boss, then whisper in his ear.

The senior policeman stared at Daulby, then reached into his pocket and took out a blue booklet. Daulby recognized it: it was his

American passport. The cop looked at the photo on the passport, then at Daulby, then back at the photo again.

"He's back!" Langwein screamed. "We've brought him back! I have heart-beat!"

The police turned back to the room. The old man's hand twitched.

"Yes, good, good, he's holding," one of the nurses said. Daulby recognized her: Elizabet.

"Jesus, but that was close," the man on the bed muttered, pulling the plastic airway out of his mouth. "You got me back just in time, I could feel it."

"You must take it easy, Mr. Couldsen," Elizabet said. "You are back, now you must rest."

Couldsen rotated his head to look at the men in the door. "Who're those guys? I know Daulby, but the others, what're they doing here?"

The doctors turned. Daulby laughed at their double-takes when they saw him.

"I know this man," the younger policeman said. "His face was on the television. Couldsen, yes, Couldsen, the American billionaire."

"Shit!" the older cop said. "We've hit gold!" He turned to Daulby. "And you— your name?"

"Dr. Douglas Daulby," he said, but the words again came out mushy, unformed. It was hard to get the tongue and lips positioned quite right.

"I thought so," Schenck said. "I thought you were Daulby. That's your picture on the passport. But Daulby's supposed to be dead. And he's a hell of a lot older than you. What the hell's going on?"

"You tell me, what the hell *is* going on?" Couldsen said. Daulby looked back at him. His color already seemed a little better. Maybe he was going to make it, after all.

"Mr. Couldsen, you must rest," Nurse Elizabet said. She turned to the others. "Now you must all leave and let him get some rest."

"I don't *want* to rest, goddam it!" Couldsen croaked. "I want to know what's going on."

"You must relax for the sake of your heart."

"Better take it easy, Mr. Couldsen," Daulby said from the doorway, conscious of how Couldsen's face was suddenly darkening. His blood pressure was skyrocketing, dangerous enough in an unhealthy man of his age, but lethal if he shared the tendency to aneurysms that his clones had developed. If that weakened blood vessel blew in his brain, that would add a stroke to a body already borderline with heart problems.

"Take it *easy?* Take it easy when I almost died? Take it easy when these goddam con-artists took me for a $500 million-dollar ride?"

He turned to Rausch. "That's what you've done, you've wasted $500 million of my money, and I'm *still* going to die."

"What is he saying?" the older cop asked the younger one.

The younger officer translated, "Couldsen says also that he has spent $500 million, and despite it, Couldsen is going to die."

"Too bad, we all die."

"You must relax, Mr. Couldsen," Rausch said. "You are hallucinating. We have already isolated the problem and have a solution. Now you must rest. Everything will be fine."

"I'm *not* damned hallucinating. I found you people, gave you everything you asked for, and . . . Oh God! It's my head that hurts now Oh God it hurts somebody is up inside my head sticking needles into my brain and he's drilling in like a dentist and I can hear my brain vibrate Oh God! Oh! Oh!"

The rhythmic beeps of Couldsen's cardiac monitor slipped into a steady whine. Daulby checked the screen: the wave was flat. Couldsen's heart had stopped again.

Daulby was the first to react: he ran down the corridor, headed for Ward C.

SEND IN THE CLONES

"STAY WITH COULDSEN," Rausch ordered Langwein when the police ran off in pursuit of Daulby. He didn't see Von Schwalbenbach.

Rausch knew it was time to slip away. The cover here was blown, along with Couldsen's funding.

Where to go, even how to escape the grounds was not clear yet. But he had learned one thing for certain: When trouble comes, move fast, think later.

He turned to Gerda. "Walk with me to my office. I am not feeling well. I need to rest." Gerda did exactly as she was told, and never asked questions.

Once away from the others, he sent her back downstairs: "Go quickly and get my Vehicle and your own, then bring them to the rear side entrance. We must leave here immediately."

Then he hurried to his office to prepare for his escape.

DAULBY DUCKED into a utility closet on Ward C and stayed there for a couple of minutes, catching his breath. He had run, thinking that would draw the police deeper into the Clinic so they would see the Vehicles. That seemed the best way to get the work stopped.

Another minute passed, and he was thinking that maybe he had been too quick for his own good. Either he had lost the police, or they had drawn back to wait for reinforcements.

Time to play rabbit again.

He eased the closet door open. There was no one around. It was dark in the ward. He stepped out.

THE VISITORS had been drinking since the end-of-conference luncheon in Vienna at noon. They drank more in the pair of helicopters that brought them here, and still more while they waited for Rausch and the other doctors.

They were important people—American Senators, German, British and American bankers, a key British politician, a London media baron, four American venture capitalists—and were not used to being kept waiting. "What the hell is keeping Rausch?" the Senator finally asked Dr. Hoerschner.

"An emergency situation came up," Hoerschner said. He was distracted, terrified at the thought of the police coming here, and what they might see.

"What kind of damned emergency? He didn't tell us a damned thing!"

"Oh, it's nothing, nothing really, just a minor crisis with one of the patients. A patient who had surgery ... surgery earlier today."

"We've come all this way to see these goddam clones, and I for one and damned tired of waiting. Take us there now."

"I'd need clearance from—"

"Don't you know who I am? Forget clearance, I'm telling you to take us there now!" the Senator bellowed. "You hear me? Take us to them, *now!*"

An hour earlier, when the "distinguished visitors" arrived at the Clinic, Langwein had ordered the physical therapy staff to rouse eight of the best-developed Vehicles, four male and four female, and hold them on stand-by in the exercise room, ready to put on a show.

The plan was to show off the Vehicles' capabilities after the police had finished their work and left the area, but Hoerschner felt the pressure to act now. "Very well," he said.

He paged Langwein, then brought the visitors to Ward E on the top floor.

THE VISITORS, by now exuberantly drunk, laughed when they saw eight fit young people jogging and biking in place. It was the faces that they found especially funny: so earnest yet so impassive— like hyperactive wax dolls.

Funniest of all was Langwein's Vehicle, pedaling furiously in place, thick glasses strapped in place. It paused once to clear steam and sweat off the glasses, using the front of the T-shirt.

"Send in the clones," the British publisher sang off-key, the words slurring.

"They look so damned weird. They're so intent, yet their faces are as stiff as statues," the American industrialist said. "Can they hear us? Do they think?"

"The Vehicles you see here," Hoerschner replied, "presently operate only as automatons, living in what might be termed a mobile vegetative state."

"Interesting," the British publisher said, "but of what practical use are mindless automatons? Perhaps as slaves? As mindless soldiers and servants?"

"Perhaps it is not so bad that they are mindless," the German banker said, looking at the shapely young Vehicle of Gerda as it bicycled in place oblivious to the visitors. With long flaxen blond hair framing a classically angular Nordic face, she bore an uncanny resemblance to the old Nazi posters depicting the Aryan ideal.

A light film of sweat coated her body. She wore shorts, a light cotton sleeveless top, and no bra. The top, damp with perspiration, clung to her body, revealing full breasts that rippled with her movements.

The German laughed harshly, set his empty glass on the floor, looked for a place to set his cigar, then crushed it out on the floor.

He stood behind Gerda's Vehicle and reached around from behind to grip the Vehicle's breasts. "I like nothing better," he laughed, "than blondes with big boobs and tiny brains."

As his hands closed around the Vehicle's breasts, she slowly stopped pedaling, and stepped off the bike.

She smiled at the chubby little banker, and put her arms around him, pressing her body into his. Her hands roamed his back, then his groin. She was a head taller.

The Hauenfelder people watched, speechless. This was not in the script. No Vehicle had ever shown any spontaneous sexual interest. Langwein hoped the hidden video cameras were catching this. Hoerschner had a sense that this was going to end badly, but didn't know how to intervene.

The visitors watched also as Gerda's Vehicle eased the little German over to a bench by the wall, pushed him gently onto it, then climbed on top. His head hung over the end of the bench, but he didn't seem to notice the discomfort.

Despite his fears, Dr. Hoerschner found himself becoming aroused at the scene, and pushed forward to get a better view, regretting that Langwein was not here with his video camera to capture this for later.

Gerda's Vehicle now had the chubby little German pinned to the bench. She lay atop him, grinding her body into his. He grunted with pleasure, his face flushed with excitement

She laughed, a sultry deep chuckle, and her hands snaked up to caress his bald scalp.

The other visitors laughed at the spectacle, cheering them on.

At that moment, Hoerschner realized what was wrong about Gerda's Vehicle: it was the smile. The Vehicles, before the arrival of the Conscious Essence, were expressionless.

But the insight came too late.

The Vehicle's body rocked backward, then down with the full weight of her body, and she pushed the little German's head back with both hands, using the hard edge of the bench as a pivot against his neck. He screamed. As the neck snapped, the other Vehicles sprang off bicycles and treadmills and plunged into the group of visitors.

The Vehicle of Dr. Von Schwalbenbach pushed through the crowd to find Hoerschner, frozen in shock. It grabbed his arm, twisted it behind him, and ran him the few steps to the window, catapulting him through the glass to fall three stories to the ground.

Gerda's Vehicle grabbed a small lead barbell and killed the Senator with a single blow.

SMOKING GUN

DAULBY HEARD SCREAMS from somewhere above, followed by the sound of shattering glass, then heavy thumps that reverberated through the old building. People running? Or fighting?

A door opened. He ducked under a table. It was Gerda, finding her way with a flashlight. She hurried past him and down the hall.

He watched her take a ring of keys from her belt and unlock one of the doors and step inside. Then he settled back to wait. He would follow her when she left.

Then he heard the door to the Ward open quietly again, and Dr. Von Schwalbenbach stepped through. He carried a flashlight in one hand, a large automatic in the other. He tiptoed down the hall, stalking Gerda.

Now Daulby remembered what was special about Ward C. It was the ward he had snuck onto the other night, the night Von Schwalbenbach caught him as he discovered the Vehicles resting in their hyperbaric oxygen chambers. That was the first time he got a sense of just how many of the Vehicles they had growing here.

He eased himself to his feet, and followed Von Schwalbenbach. Neither Gerda nor Von Schwalbenbach had turned on the lights. That made it easier.

He heard a door open ahead, and pushed back against the corridor wall.

Von Schwalbenbach, walking ahead, did the same.

Gerda emerged into the corridor, still holding the flashlight. Now she was pushing someone in a wheelchair.

The ward lights flashed on as Von Schwalbenbach hit the light switch. Now he blocked the corridor, holding his gun on Gerda. It was Dr. Rausch in the wheelchair. No! Not Rausch, it was Rausch's Vehicle, its expression blank, oblivious.

"Where are you going?" Von Schwalbenbach demanded.

"Get out of my way. I am acting on Dr. Rausch's orders."

"I said, where are you going with that Vehicle?"

"Get out of my way."

"Rausch—that bastard!" Von Schwalbenbach screamed. "He is running, yes? And leaving us behind. Well, no, not this time!"

"Get out of my way, I warn you!" Gerda said.

"I have given my career, my life, to this work. If Rausch is running, then I run with him. I escape with him, or no one escapes."

Glass shattered back at the entrance to the ward. It startled Daulby, and he turned. Then two sharp cracks stung his ears. He looked back. Von Schwalbenbach staggered.

Gerda held a smoking pistol in her hand. She fired again. A ceiling light exploded down the hall.

Von Schwalbenbach braced himself against the door frame and fired twice. Rausch's Vehicle tumbled backward out of the wheelchair, then lay still on the floor.

Gerda fired again and again but the shots were wild. Von Schwalbenbach, still leaning back against the wall, aimed and fired. Gerda slammed back against the wall, her limbs as loose as a rag doll, then dropped to the ground and was still.

Von Schwalbenbach sank into a chair. Then he spotted Daulby for the first time.

Their eyes locked. "You!" Von Schwalbenbach muttered, his voice a rasp, "You did this to us, you ruined it all." He raised the gun and fired.

The bullet caught Daulby, and the world went black.

DOCTORS' ORDERS

THE NURSES WORKED on Couldsen, trying to keep life in him. But they had been trained to wait for the doctors' orders, and all four doctors—Rausch, Langwein, Von Schwalbenbach, and Hoerschner— had run away. Now they were at a loss.

They had heard the screams from the top floor where the VIP's were being entertained, but that was nothing to be concerned about – often the parties here got out of control.

What mattered was that Couldsen had suffered a stroke—that accounted for the bizarre final monologue as the brain circuits misfired. Cardiac arrest followed.

The nurses, unaccustomed to handling the defibrillation unit normally controlled by the doctors, were slow to respond. They worked on him for three minutes, then five. Couldsen still showed no response. There was no doctor present to declare death, so they carried on.

Then the electrical power cut off, plunging the room into darkness. Marta ducked her head into the hall. "It's dark out here, too. I think the whole building is dark."

"Where is the emergency generator? It should come on automatically."

"I think it is too late for Mr. Couldsen, yes?" one of the nurses said. In the dark, no one knew who said it. They pulled back from the body, and walked into the corridor.

Hertl ran up to them. She was holding a flashlight. "Did you hear? Up in Ward C. I think those were gunshots!"

"No, we were busy in there . . . with him, with Couldsen. He didn't make it. Where are the police now?"

"They went outside. They are waiting for reinforcements. I must go," Hertl said.

"I think it is all over here at Hauenfelder now, that is clear enough," Elizabet said.

"What happens to us?"

"Who knows? Was this a crime, cloning Vehicles? I think not. We're not part of any of the rest of it, are we? That had nothing to do with us. We only worked here, that's all. We were only following the doctors' orders, yes?"

FIERY PATHS

THE IMPACT OF THE BULLET knocked Daulby off his feet. The area was totally dark.

He tried to stand, but flopped back from the pain in his right shoulder where Von Schwalbenbach's bullet had struck. That arm was useless. He felt it with the other hand, and touched jagged flesh, broken bone, slippery fluid he knew was his own blood.

Twenty feet away, Von Schwalbenbach switched on a flashlight, and pulled himself to his feet. Gerda's shots had hit an artery, and blood gushed from beneath his jacket. He staggered, pushing on, cursing in German as he moved.

The lights died again. Daulby was having trouble getting enough air. He tasted blood, and sensed that bubbles were forming on his lips— bloody bubbles, the sign of a punctured lung.

He pulled himself to his feet, knowing he should just lie still, wait for help.

But would help be coming? The shots should have drawn the police. Why aren't they here by now?

The lights came on again, and he saw Von Schwalbenbach braced against the wall, nearly doubled over.

Then he looked beyond, and saw Dr. Rausch at the end of the corridor, running toward Von Schwalbenbach, carrying a lighted candle, the other hand cupping the flame against the wind.

Von Schwalbenbach raised his pistol and fired. The shot went wild, slamming into the wall.

Rausch ducked into one of the rooms, and Daulby understood that this was not Dr. Rausch, not the *real* Rausch. This was another of Rausch's Vehicles, apparently operating independently. But why was it using a candle? Daulby wondered. Why not a flashlight?

The electricity died still again, and now the only light was the dim flickering of the candle as it played on the ceiling.

Von Schwalbenbach, cursing, pulled himself another dozen steps to the door the Vehicle had entered, raised his gun, and fired.

Daulby heard glass shatter, then a hissing sound, then a soft Whoomph! The hallway flashed as if lightning had struck. Daulby knew it was worse than lightning. Far worse.

THE BULLET fired by Von Schwalbenbach hit one of the hyperbaric chambers. When the glass shattered, the high-pressure oxygen escaped into the room, the hiss of the open valve audible even over the blast of the gunshots.

The room flashed as the oxygen found the flame of the candle carried by Rausch's Vehicle.

The first explosion scorched the tubes carrying the oxygen between the high-pressure tanks and the six glass bubbles filled with pressurized oxygen.

The flexible lines split in the sudden heat, and the flames raced along them in both directions: forward to the other glass bubbles, backward to the big oxygen storage tanks, the size and shape of bombs.

As the heat touched them, the glass bubbles of the remaining hyperbaric chambers exploded, and oxygen-rich flames gushed through the door and into the hallway.

The pressure-flow gauges at the tops of the storage tanks burst in the flash-fire that followed the explosion.

The oxygen, compressed to 2,000 pounds per square inch, spurted out undiminished from the tops of the heavy bomb-shaped oxygen tanks.

The flame ignited the oxygen hissing out of the tanks. Propelled by the escaping gas, the big tanks became rockets, slithering along the floors, spewing flames behind.

One tank slid down the hall toward Daulby, bouncing from wall to wall. He jumped out of the way, and thought he was clear, but another tank coming just behind caught him and slammed him against the wall.

The two tanks skidded the length of the ward and crashed through the heavy wooden door. They ricocheted down the main staircase, found an opening on the next floor and careened along the corridor the length of the Clinic before losing force. As it moved, it sprayed flame, and the flames ignited the wooden floors of the old building.

The other tanks followed, each taking a different route through the corridors and staircases of the old building, each spreading its own fiery path.

TUNNEL

DAULBY WATCHED the oxygen bottle skitter at him along the floor. It reminded him of old movies of torpedoes slicing through the water. It seemed to move in slow motion, and he was fascinated by the tail of flame that pushed it along.

He tried to get out of the way, but the tank ricocheted from wall to wall as it slithered down the hallway. He fell, and his head hurt for an instant, then *he feels a sudden burst of energy. His body seems light, so light that he bounces softly off the ceiling.*

He looks back down at the body on the floor. The back of the skull is open, smashed by the heavy oxygen tank as it passed. Most of the cortex at the back of the head is gone, giving a clear view through to the cerebellum and the brain stem at the top of the spinal cord. It's his body, he realizes, his new *body. But it doesn't matter, he doesn't need it any longer.*

He feels himself pulled up into the darkness, and then he is moving fast through a black void, though he hears no sound, feels no movement. He sees a speck of light far away, a speck that grows as he flies toward it, and now the speck is round, like the end of a tunnel, and then he is through the tunnel into the light, and he sees Mom and Dad and little Connie smiling and coming toward him with open arms, and they join with him as he moves on toward the source of the light, and he sees Jackie and Jenny. Jackie is waving and Jenny is jumping for joy.

"You're here, Daddy, you're finally here. We've been waiting for you."

ETERNAL FIRE

DR. RAUSCH was descending the dark central stairway in the darkness when he heard the first gunshots. He didn't know where the police were now, but they would go toward the shots. That was good: it would draw them out of his way.

He carried the briefcase that he had always kept locked in his office safe. It contained $100,000 in cash in Euros, Swiss, and American bills, and there was plenty more stashed in accounts in Switzerland and the Bahamas.

The briefcase also contained four disks. One was a video documenting the growth of the Vehicles. That would be the proof he would use to win more financing when the time came.

The other disks contained back-ups from the hard-drive on his computer: the complete record of the research was there, daily logs going back as far as the beginning of the research, carrying on up to yesterday, the details of the methods that had worked, and those that had not. It was all here, everything needed to pick up from here.

If Gerda was ready with the Vehicle, then they could slip away and start the work again. If not, he would go alone.

More gunshots. That troubled him. Police? Or someone else? It would not be Langwein or Hoerschner: they were too passive to do anything. But Von Schwalbenbach might: he had always been a problem waiting to explode.

Then he heard the first explosions, and felt the building shake. More explosions, followed by strange thumping sounds that shook the building, as if giant bowling balls were bouncing down the corridors. A chill passed over him. He was on the third floor, and it normally took a couple of minutes to make it down the stairs and outside. There might not be time.

He saw orange flames flickering somewhere on the lower levels. He smelled smoke now, coming fast.

It looked like the central part of the building was already aflame. The central staircase could be a death-trap.

But there were other staircases, and, if all else was blocked, open fire escapes on each end of the building. Smoke billowed up the central area now, and he could already feel the heat from the flames below. There was no time to lose.

THE CLINIC BUILDING was over a century old, built mainly of wood. The beams and floors had long since dried, and were as flammable as tinder, and the floors had been waxed hundreds of times, dried fuel waiting for a spark to ignite.

The flames flashed through the floors, then raced along the dead-space between floor and ceiling. In that confined area, the temperatures soared instantly, pre-warming the wooden beams so they erupted into flame as soon as the first tongues of fire touched them.

RAUSCH WAS CHOKING in the smoke as he scurried down the central stairs, still clutching the briefcase. It held everything that he had dedicated his life to gathering. To let that go would be to renounce the work. He could never do that.

How ironic! he thought as he struggled through the smoke and fumes. To have discovered the secret of renewing life, yet to be caught with no Vehicle ready!

Flames licked at his feet as he raced down the stairs, the briefcase clutched to his chest like a baby.

At the landing on the second floor, he felt the floor lurch at the same moment that he saw a carpet of orange flames erupt below. The old beams gave way with a soft crunch, and he felt himself floating out into the flames.

The flames seared his skin and lungs, and his body exploded in pain, *and he realizes that these are no ordinary flames. These are flames of infinite depth, and he understands that he will tumble forever through them without reaching bottom. Even now, he senses, if he would throw away the briefcase, renounce the work, he would have a chance of escaping the flames. He grips it even more tightly as he falls.*

As he watches, his fingers blacken and twist into charred claws. The skin on his arms flashes away like a sheet of newspaper in a campfire, and he sees the bones blacken in the heat.

He is dead, he knows that. He has to be dead, yet he still feels searing pain from the flames, like no pain he had ever known, and it doesn't ease.

If I am dead, then why the pain, why not the release of final darkness?

Were the priests right about the eternal fire?

AWAKENED

KATE HEARD THE SCREAMS, then the gunshots. The shots awakened Karen, who had been dozing in her wheelchair. Then they heard the first explosion. It seemed to come from the far end of the building, a floor or two higher.

The lights had gone out moments before. Kate found a flashlight in a drawer and turned it on. The batteries were weak, and it cast only a dim yellow beam.

More explosions followed, shaking the building like earthquakes. Karen's eyes tracked the sound. That surprised Kate: for months, Karen had been almost completely oblivious to her surroundings. Had the events today stimulated her to begin arousing from the coma?

They heard heavy things rolling and thumping along the corridors above, shaking the walls. Kate smelled smoke within seconds. Karen's nose wrinkled as she sniffed the air. "...iire, ...moke," she seemed to say. Her face, normally blank, now showed fear.

They were trapped. There was a window, but no fire escape from it, and it was two stories up. She grabbed a chair and beat against the door, but the chair broke before the door gave way.

Then she heard a key in the lock. It was Marta, the nurse. "Get out, get out! Everything's on fire. You help your sister, I must help the others in their beds!" Then she disappeared down the smoky hallway.

"What floor are we on? Is there a clear way out?" Kate called, but her words were lost in the roar of the flames.

It was hot in the corridor, and the dense smoke burned her eyes and seared her throat and lungs, choking off oxygen. The more she gasped for breath, the more smoke and fumes she took in.

She realized then that she had left the flashlight behind, and was disoriented in the darkness and dense smoke. She ran, pushing Karen's wheelchair down the hallway toward what she thought was the center of the building, but then she spotted the glow of orange flames through the smoke ahead.

She turned the wheelchair around and raced back the other way, her lungs burning from the thick smoke. She looked behind and saw orange flames shooting toward them down the hallway as water through a funnel.

"...aster, Kate, ...aster," Karen grunted.

Kate was disoriented in the inky darkness and dense smoke. Where was a door? Where was at least a window?

Lost, she kept moving, trying to go where it was cooler, to get farther from the flames, pushing Karen's chair forward with fierce determination, though she could barely breathe in the smoke. But the flames were outracing them, flashing along the ceiling and upper walls of the hallway.

They came to a staircase, and Kate felt a cool breeze blowing fresh air down to them. She lifted Karen out of the wheelchair, slung her over her shoulder, and staggered up the staircase. *The staircase seems to go on forever. After a while, the smoke no longer burns her eyes and lungs, and it takes no effort to climb, now it seems as if they are floating up the staircase.*

The staircase becomes a tunnel, a soft, safe round tunnel, and they can see light at the end of it, a pure white light. It is the brightest, warmest, happiest light she has ever known.

Now she sees people in the light at the end of the tunnel, and knows that everything is going to be all right. The people are holding out their arms to welcome them. The welcoming arms grip her and Karen, and they pass through the end of the tunnel and emerge into the light. Now the air is clear and cool.

She looks back and sees the firemen at the top of the ladder pass two limp bodies down to the ground, and others, working in the glare of spotlights, clamp oxygen masks onto the bodies. Just before the masks go on, she recognizes the faces: herself and Karen.

Then she was coughing, and she reached up to pull the oxygen mask away from her face, but the fireman held it in place, soothing her gently with words she couldn't understand.

She turned her head and looked across at Karen, and Karen was looking back at her, her eyes aware now. The eyes smiled above the mask, and Karen's hand reach across to take hers and squeeze.

"Thank God!" she managed.

Then she heard a crackling, ripping sound as loud as a freight train, and turned to see what it was. Flames shot up like geysers through the roof of the Hauenfelder Clinic. As she watched, a wave moved along the old building, and the roof collapsed into the flames like a row of falling dominoes.

"Thank God for that! Thank God it's ended!" Kate managed.

"Tha' God," Karen echoed.

NOTES / ABOUT THE AUTHOR

OTHER BOOKS

Thank you for reading *A Remedy for Death* and exploring some of the what-ifs that may be lurking in the not-so-distant future.

Acknowledgements

Many thanks to all of who have contributed to this book, including beta readers, editors, idea and information contributors, and to the inn-keepers who provided lodging, input, and, not to forget, food.

Special thanks to Jerome A. Davis, M.D., for his friendship, and his counsel based on his years as a neurosurgeon.

Special thanks also to Laurel Scharf for the photo of the distinctive butterfly that fluttered onto the cover.

And very special thanks to my wife, Susan, for advice and input along the way, for the interest she shares with me in the unusual topics addressed here, and by no means least, for her tolerance of the piles of notes and discarded drafts . . drafts that I hang onto just in case there might be something useful tucked away!

About the author

Michael McGaulley, author of *A Remedy for Death, The Grail Conspiracies*, and the related book, *Joining Miracles*, is a lawyer and management consultant.

You will find a sample of The *Grail Conspiracies* a couple of pages ahead.

These books bring together his interest in the intersection of the spiritual and metaphysical with the possibilities raised by the new physics' discoveries that the world is very different than we assume.

www.MichaelMcGaulley.net

Other books by Michael McGaulley

Science technothrillers

The Grail Conspiracies. Tapping the mind and beyond. The legends of the Grail as a cup are centuries-old "disinformation". The deeper Grail is dormant within the human mind, and is the most powerful force—or, potentially, most powerful weapon—ever. It was sought by the Nazi Occult Bureau, now by the scruffy, brutal "army" of Twisted Messiah –an international super-star rock group with neo-Nazi political ambitions and occult dimensions.

<u>To order via Amazon</u>

<u>To order via other retailers</u>

<u>View sample</u>

A Remedy for Death. It's said we only go around once in life . . .but what if? What if there is a "Jurassic Park" for rich old guys? What if today's emerging bio-science offers a select, secretive elite the chance to come back into "healthy, horny 21-year old bodies complete with all the accumulated savvy from this lifetime? What if the project is almost successful, but opens dangerous doors that cannot be closed?

<u>To order via Amazon</u>

<u>To order via other retailers</u>

International mystery and crime

Infinite Doublecross. The French Riviera. Art theft. Art forgery. Artful duplicity. A "perfect guy." And a vacationing techie who finds herself caught up in a tangle of duplicity and deception and doublecross. If she can't trust herself, who *can* she trust?

To order via Amazon

To order via other retailers

To read a sample

The Man Who Created Gho$t$. Dirty money. Dutch chocolate. Swiss banks. Stealing from the "worst people in the world" And "ghosts" who are not pleased.

To order via Amazon

To order via other retailers

To read a sample

Career-savvy people skills

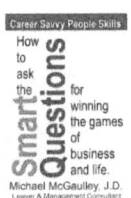

How to Ask the SMART QUESTIONS for Winning the Games of Career and Life—provides the tools for looking through to what's really going on in situations at work and in life, on spotting the "real rules" of the game, on focusing what matters, avoiding unnecessary confrontations, and selecting and defending the best options under the circumstances.

To order e-book or print version from Amazon

To order via other retailers

To read a sample chapter

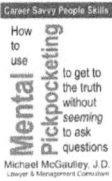

How to Use MENTAL PICKPOCKETING to get to the Truth Without Seeming to Ask Questions. Most of the time, most people will do their best to tell the straight truth. But not always. And sometimes even to ask a question is to give the game away, raising flags on what they may want to fudge, avoid, or distort.

To order e-book or print version from Amazon

To order via other retailers

To read a sample

SAMPLE: THE GRAIL CONSPIRACIES

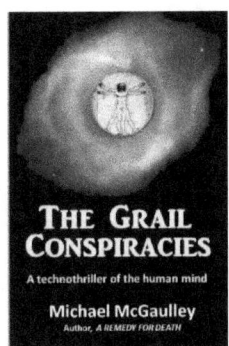

**THE GRAIL
CONSPIRACIES**

A technothriller of the human mind

Michael McGaulley
Author, *A REMEDY FOR DEATH*

In Washington, a message arrives unexpectedly, inviting Greg Tapscott to a meeting in La Rochelle, France, with the promise that he will finally learn the "truth" about his uncle, an OSS agent, "alleged to have been killed in action in France in 1944, along with the secrets that he uncovered at that time." The family has long been convinced there was a government cover-up.

Intriguingly, Paul was last seen in La Rochelle, the main Atlantic port of the Knights Templar, legendary guardians of the Holy Grail.

At a concert in Berlin, simulcast around the world, Twisted Messiah, a nihilistic, destructive international rock group, calls on the world's angry and alienated to regroup in a kind of world-wide quasi-political cult, under its leadership. Some journalists describe that concert as "a Nuremberg rally on steroids, updated to today's mindset and technology."

A Washington journalist, a friend of Greg's, claims the two strands— Twisted Messiah and its political ambitions, and what was turned up by Greg's uncle in 1944—are intimately linked. He is murdered before he can explain.

What did Paul Tapscott find? No one shows for the promised meeting in France, but Greg pushes on to England, Germany, and back to Washington in his own personal quest.

He encounters one source who claims that Paul uncovered "the truth behind the Grail legends, the reality behind the centuries of deliberate disinformation."

Another source echoes that Paul's discovery "may have been the truth behind the legends of the Holy Grail, or perhaps the most powerful force—or weapon—ever known, a technology for tapping the highest human potential. Or perhaps that force, and what we think of as the Holy Grail, may be one and the same."

Why is the private army of Twisted Messiah desperate to find that, whatever it is? (It is known that in the middle of World War II, the Nazi

"Occult Bureau" sent a team to search around the last Cathar fortress, at Montsegur, France. The Cathars, along with the Templars or Knights Templar, were rumored to be guardians of the Grail.)

Why has the CIA found recurring mentions of the name Paul Tapscott and what he discovered in the intercepted "chatter" of a certain terrorist group? Or is that deliberate disinformation, used to distract Greg?

Why the 70-year cover-up . . . by Americans? How does it relate to today's Inside-the-Beltway Washington political battles?

And does that cover-up also extend to a treasure-trove of Nazi gold, nearly forgotten about for all these years?

THE GRAIL CONSPIRACIES

A Technothriller Exploring Deeper Human Possibilities

ISBN: 978-0976840602

"So I decided to summarize the conclusions I had drawn from all these experiences, over all these years. . . .

1. Consciousness has legitimate dimensions not yet guessed at.

2. At least some psychic phenomena are real.

3. There are energies associated with the human body that are not yet understood."

--Michael Crichton, M.D.
Travels

"We will first understand how simple the universe is when we recognize how strange it is."

— John Archibald Wheeler

"I learned aikido from a teacher who operates from the premise that the perfect move, the perfect throw, already exists. Our mission was simply to join it."

— George Leonard
The Silent Pulse

DAY ONE

Twisted Messiah

A SHOT TAKEN from a helicopter hours earlier, just before sunset, caught the size of the crowd massed at the abandoned air base outside Berlin for the live performance.

It seemed an eerie reminder of the old photos of the 1963 Civil Rights march on Washington, when the sea of faces listening to Martin Luther King filled the Mall from the Lincoln Memorial back through the Reflecting Pond toward the Capitol, bodies packed together as densely as blades of grass.

That was no coincidence; that was one more carefully planned part of the Twisted Messiah message.

Nor, of course, was the name Twisted Messiah a coincidence.

THE DIRECTOR CUT FROM BERLIN to shots of the other audiences in Munich, Paris, Sydney, Miami, all sitting as quietly as church-goers; it was as if the same young faces had been cloned in cities around the world, a rag-tag army in dirty clothes, unkempt hair, rings in noses, lips, cheeks, ears, and assorted tattoos. Skinheads co-existed alongside kids whose long hair was streaked day-glo purple and chartreuse.

Some of the faces were tattooed beyond recognition, several with death-head skulls like the performer in the Toilet Video.

All in all, they were the kind of lost kids seen on the streets of any city, messy kids with angry, unhappy faces, hanging out together to pass empty days.

Yet there were also very ordinary-looking kids among them, kids no different in looks than ones you see walking home from school, or wandering the malls.

It was those "ordinary" kids, I'd find out later, that the intelligence agencies and police considered the real threat.

They were, in the term first used by Cal Katz, "the world's worst nightmare" *because* they looked so ordinary. They looked as normal and harmless as the kids down the block, yet were indoctrinated in the Twisted Messiah outlook. They were the sleepers who could do the real harm if they were awakened.

The cameras zoomed in on individuals here and there, and I began to realize what was different about these faces. These kids weren't here just for music. There was a quiet intensity tonight: these had come with a deeper agenda than just partying. Had they come here, as one of the news articles suggested, in search of "a way to put some kind of meaning into their chaotic, aimless lives?"

The silence in the stadiums was chilling: tens of thousands sat immobile, as if waiting for the Rapture.

These were not just *fans*, I realized, these were *cultists*.

IT WAS NIGHT IN BERLIN. The lights dimmed, and the crowd stood in a wave that rolled a half-mile along the runways.

A single spotlight found Jesse Cripes. He raised both hands, as if giving a blessing, then walked slowly up the aisle to the stage.

The other members of the group followed a dozen paces behind. A drum beat a march rhythm. The spectators stood in reverent silence.

Jesse wore his trademark beard and shoulder-length blond hair. Coupled with his usual ankle-length loose robe and sandals, he was a look-alike for the Jesus of the holy pictures—though the image was jarred by his fluorescent orange and hot purple robes.

He arrived at center stage and turned to the audience. The hush continued as he reached into his robe, pulled out a pack of cigarettes and lit one. The brand happened to be one of the corporate underwriters of the world-wide telecast.

He held the pack up to the cameras and waved as if to say, Join me, and the kids in the crowd did, and held up their cigarettes as if to say to the world, We do what we want, We do what Jesse wants.

Hundreds of thousands of hands, held into the air, waving like a vast field of grain in the breeze.

And uncannily like those old newsreels of the crowds at Nuremberg , right arms raised in tribute to Hitler. The Hitler Salute had been banned in Germany after the war, but who could object that this was anything political, this was just some kids flaunting their right to smoke.

"THE BEST SEX," The opener, the group's early hit, began as a soft ballad, as sweet as the bubble-gum music of the early '60's. But the tone shifted in the second piece, a harsher, harder beat building, concluding with Jesse screaming, the massed voices of the audience joining in:

> *The best sex*
> *Isn't what turns you on.*
> *The best sex*
> *Is what turns your stomach!*

I caught a shadow passing across the screen behind the stage, then another. Part of the show was an array of lightning-fast visuals flashing across the sub-conscious, synchronized with the beat of the music.

Each lasted only an instant, not long enough for the eye to focus, just long enough for the image to register somewhere back in the mind, triggering intriguing dark impulses.

Scary, horrifying images balancing arousal and disgust. Yet magnetizing. That scene from their old video of the couple copulating in the grungy public toilet.

A pair of naked girls, wispy blonds with pre-pubescent breasts, straddling a black—no, not a man, it was a decaying corpse.

"Do it! Taste it! Screw it!" the audiences around the world roared along with Jesse to wrap up the piece.

THE VRIL SONG came next, controversial from the group's second album, *"VRIL!"*

The sound built until it seemed to reverberate in my chest, drawing my heart-beat into its pounding rhythm. The audiences around the world rose, as if hypnotized, to sway with the rising beat, their fists pounding out the music: *"The Vril is high! The Vril is high!"*

The camera drew back from Twisted Messiah on the stage in Berlin to cut to arenas in Paris, Amsterdam, Moscow, London, Atlanta, Tokyo, Los Angeles. Audiences around the world joined in the mantra: *"The Vril is high! The Vril is high!"*

Something I noticed only then: the kids in the audiences were all wearing sunglasses—or something more like the plastic glasses for 3-D movies. Were they seeing something that the rest of us did not?

JESSE LED THE CHANT; as his tempo and volume built, the music rose to match it, a peculiar mix of rock in a march tempo. His gestures were jerky, almost mechanical, so he seemed like a strange puppet dancing in synch with the music and words.

The camera moved in for a close-up as he finished. His eyes were blank, rolled back in his head, and the words shrieked out of lips covered with a fine foam. His face gleamed with a weird intensity, the sweat casting a sheen across his porcelain-white skin.

When he came to his climax, the music abruptly stopped, and there was only the sound of his voice, shrieking across the Berlin airdrome and echoing around the world:

The Vril is high!
We move with a Different Power!
We follow a New Cross!

Jesse raised both arms and crossed his hands over his head, forming the asymmetrical X of the New Cross—the proportions of the Christian cross, twisted onto its side as if broken off at the base.

The camera cut to the audience, and tens of thousands duplicated the gesture, chanting, "We follow a New Cross!"

Now the director shifted to another camera, and the flaming red X—the New Cross—appeared in the night sky over Berlin, a holographic image beamed up, a gyrating apparition in the dark night.

We move with a Different Power!
We follow a New Cross!

The red New Cross in the sky began to turn. The music built, a rough, crashing heavy-metal rock-march, and the New Cross in the night sky turned faster and faster, spinning until it was like a flaming red wheel. Jesse resumed his chant, and the crowd chanted with him, a single massed voice, the low rumble of an earthquake:

We move with a Different Power!
We follow a New Cross,
We follow the Twisted Messiah!
We are the world's worst nightmare!
We are the bringers of destruction!

THE LIGHTS CUT OFF, *leaving the arena and the screens around the world black. Total silence for a long moment before the lights flashed on again.*

The crowd joined Jesse in one deafening roar:

We are the world's worst nightmare!
We are the bringers of destruction!

DAY TWO

"Celebrations"

Washington, D.C. 7:15 A.M.

I DIDN'T GET MUCH SLEEP AFTER THAT SHOW. I don't think anyone did, not with police and fire sirens racing past through the night, and not with those nightmare images imbedded from the spectacle.

I finally got up around five. I flicked on the TV and stood transfixed, morbidly fascinated by the scenes of the overnight riots: Flash-mobs of Twisted Messiah fans in cities around the world burning, looting, and destroying as a way of celebrating last night's concert.

That concert, and all that followed, was being billed as "Jesse Cripes' 33rd Birthday Gift to the World."

The hype had been building for weeks. An estimated 500.000 fans from all over the world had been gathering at the concert site, an abandoned air base in the former East Germany, not far from Berlin. Most had been camping out there despite the October chill, and more were on the way.

The live concert had been beamed by satellite to audiences around the world.

Over the previous week, "pre-celebrations" had sprung up in London, Paris, Tokyo, and dozens of other cities world-wide. The kids were destructive "for the hell of it, just to show what we can do," as one of them put it. A British kid put it, "Got nothing else to do, so let's just go break stuff."

The earlier mobs had been relatively small-scale, and politicians and police had mostly opted to hold back, not wanting to risk provoking bigger riots.

Others weren't so sure that was prudent. As one pundit put it: "There's a potential undercover army of dead-end losers spread out across the world. They're looking for a leader, and I fear that Twisted Messiah, and Jesse Cripes may attempt to fill precisely the role that their name suggests. And if that happens, what's the core: Neo-Nazi, or destructive nihilism?"

Butterfly

ON THAT HAPPY THOUGHT, I moved on to check the fax before hitting the shower. This had come in overnight from Cal Katz:

WARNING!
You are the butterfly!
You're about to set off a storm that spreads around the world!
Have crucial new info regarding our recent conversation.
We need to talk, ASAP!
Meanwhile, watch your back!
You're involved, like it or not.
Don't call me, I'll call you when/if it's safe
THIS IS <u>NOT</u> A DRILL!

It sounded like just another bubble in that vast ocean of jokes floating around cyberspace. But this was hand-printed in the distinctive scrawl of Cal Katz, as thick and stubby and intense as the man himself, and Cal was definitely not into jokes.

He was a strange little guy, one day hush-mouthed and conspiratorial, the next day ready to tell you more than you ever wanted to know about what was *really* going on behind the scenes in Washington.

A conspiracy nut, but an intelligent one who did his homework . . . obsessively.

Have important info regarding our recent conversation: Typical Cal, at the same time both paranoid and forgetful: Which part of which recent conversation? Why am I the butterfly? Why watch my back?

To Cal, everything was of life-and-death importance. That conversation, a week or so ago, hadn't been so much a conversation as Cal talking *at* me about his latest project, an upcoming expose of

284

Twisted Messiah.

Then, in one of his characteristic mind-jumps, he'd asked whether, by any chance, any relative of mine had served in the OSS during World War II.

To which the answer was yes: my uncle, Paul Tapscott, who had died at the time of D-Day invasion of France, in 1944. But before I could follow up, Cal had moved on, saying we needed to talk, "mucho and pronto."

In Cal's eyes, Twisted Messiah wasn't just a rock group. It was, as he'd put it in an op-ed piece in the *Washington Post*, "media superstardom consciously morphing into a world-wide political force."

Strong words, typical Cal Katzian exaggeration, I'd figured. At that time, the possibility seemed bizarre. But that was before the "celebrations" had begun. The feedback to the *Post* reflected that: *Rock stars as a world-wide political force? Get real!*

Alas, as events turned out, Cal wouldn't live quite long enough to see his prophecy coming to life.

HIS MESSAGE was on my mind as I showered. *You are the butterfly about to set off a storm that spreads around the world!*

"Butterfly"—I understood that much of it. The term came from Chaos Theory, suggesting that small, unanticipated events, like the tiny puff of wind set off by the wings of a butterfly, can trigger a chain of events that bring about major, unpredictable change.

But me as a butterfly? Not likely. I was just another faceless soldier in that army of Beltway Bandits living off government contracts. I had no politically embarrassing documents to leak, no secrets the media or anyone else would find the least titillating.

So I thought then.

But a storm *was* brewing, and I—the 180-pound butterfly— was indeed about to set it off.

That storm would spread, and merge with another storm, and before it all ended, less than a week later—on Election Day, no coincidence— things would be changed forever, not just in my life, but in Washington, in the Establishment running it, in politics, in the whole country.

Changed even in how we human beings view the world and what is possible within the reality we experience.

---

*End of this sample of **THE GRAIL CONSPIRACIES**.*

To order via Amazon

To order via other retailers

www.ingramcontent.com/pod-product-compliance
Lightning Source LLC
Chambersburg PA
CBHW071259170626
46809CB00001B/279